Brummie,

If you ~~~~ ~~~
you'll like this.

Trevor

27, 01, 2016

Murder on the Train to Skaville

Trevor Clark

© Trevor Clark 2013

First published by Pirate Radio Skankdown Publishing

Order from www.pirateradioskankdown.co.uk

ISBN 978-0-9568971-0-7

A CIP catalogue record for this book is available from the British Library.

Prepared and printed by:

York Publishing Services Ltd
64 Hallfield Road
Layerthorpe
York YO31 7ZQ
Tel: 01904 431213

Website: www.yps-publishing.co.uk

Special thanks to
Leuny, Iris, Pearl, Victor, Angoly,
Wally, Ann, Baz, Neil, Sam, Rik and Siobahn
for their support

Contents

Glossary

Abbreviation in book	Translation
A	
a round of fucks	a good telling off
aaye	yes
aboot	about
affa	after
an'	and
anuddah	another
areddy	all ready
B	
'bout	about
bab	shit
babber stabber	homosexual
Babylon	authority being the police
baddah	worse
bairns	children
bakome	back home
baldhead	usually politician in this case detective
bambaclaat	see bloodclaat
bedsit dub	bedsit lived in by a Dub Reggae fan
bes'	best
bettah	better
blagging	bartering

bloodclaat,	there's no real translation, it's the equivalent of calling someone toilet paper
blurk	bloke (man)
boneheads	the name given to Nazi skinheads by skinheads who believe they stole their culture
boun'	bound
bruddah	brother

C

canna	can not
canny	great
cas'	cast
covah	cover
com'	come
coz	because
cyaan	can't

D

dat	that
de	the
deh	there
dem	them
dey	day
dis	this
divvent	don't
do what John	am I hearing correctly
Doc's	Dr Martens
don'	don't
doon	down
droonin	drowning
dunna	don't
duppy	ghost

E

eas'	east
emptee	empty
evah	ever
everyting	everything

F

'fore	before
fe	for
filth	the police
fin'	find
fuckin	(I think we all know what this means)

G

gander	look
geezer	a man
gender bender	homosexual
get away out of it	would you believe this
gettifu	get the fuck (out of here)
gi	give
goffer	go fetch this/that
gud fer yer	good for you
guttersnipe	a snitch/a grass/an informer
guv	govener
gwaan	going

H

had away and shite	get lost, go shit yourself
haffe	have to
hatting	Holding your hat out to collect tips
heez	he's
Hingland	England
hog	motorbike
hoh	how

hoos	house

I

innitt	isn't it
irie	(can be question or answer) is everything Ok? everything is Ok
iyl	I will

J

jig	Irish folk dance
jus'	just

K

knaas	knows

L

latah	later
leave it out	you can't be serious
lef'	left
Lemmy	lead singer – Motorhead
likkle	little
lurds	loads (lots)
lurking	playing

M

mek	make
mi	me
mon	man
murdah	murder
mus'	must

N

ne	no
neet	night
nevah	never
nise	noise
no'	not

noh	now
noo	now
nor	know
nuttin	nothing

O

o'white mate	alright friend?
och	Oh yeah (realisation)
oot	out
orf	off
overstand	understand
overway	underway (Rastas feel the word under is demeaning)

P

pley	play
puff	homosexual

R

raasclaat	see bloodclaat
ramble	a walk in the country
reet	right
reight	alright
remembah	remember
res'	rest
righ'	right
roond	round

S

screw face	looking with an expression of scorn
see the cut of his jib	look at the state of him
seh	say
sen'	send
sistah's	sisters

slack twat	literally dumb pregnant goldfish/in this case, stupid cunt
Slash	guitarist Guns 'n' Roses
snitches	informers
snivelling	whining/moaning
soun'	sound
stitching	convicting

T

t'eory	theory
tallewah	taller
tat	bits and pieces/odds and sods
tedeh	today
teggedah	together
tek	take
tha nors	you know
tha'll	you will
tha's	you are
thee and thee	you and you
tings	things
tink	think
toe rag	meaning lower than low
tohn	town
toon	town
tought	thought
trewsers	trousers
tru'	true
tuther	the other

W

waan	want
Walt Jabsco	a logo stood aside 2Tone record label
wasne	was not

watah	water
weh	where
wehn	when
wes'	west
wey	way
wha'	what
whaagh	(in this case) Oh great
whallo	hello
whappen	what happend
wi	we
wid	with
wihl	while
widout	without
wind your neck in	keep calm
wiv	with
wobbler	got angry
wuz	was

Y

ya	you
yam	a sort of potato vegetable
yarns	stories
yeez	you
yer	you
yo bro'	hello brother

Chapter One

TRAIN TO SKAVILLE

05.00am Leeds, Chapeltown, England.

A cassette tape was playing:

Sitting here hands propping up my chin
I tell you man the four walls closing in
Gets so boring looking at cold ash in my grate
The clock's ticking like it just can't wait
Think I'll get up and switch on my TV set
Aint got a licence but they aint caught me yet
Tells me all about the diet of a movie star
Where to go scuba diving and who shot JR
Advertising all the things that I can't afford
For all this knowledge I must thank you lord
'Cause for a while I can forget i'm lonely and
sad
Pretend I'm just a happy go lucky lad

In this your bedsit dub, your bedsit dub yeah
Your bedsit dub yeah...your bedsit ruba dub

DJ Dread was sitting in his bed in his own bedsit dub, hands propping up his chin. He wasn't watching his TV set or looking at the cold ash in his grate. He was staring above the mantle piece at the flag pinned to his wall portraying Bob Marley, fist held above his head declaring freedom. This was the first thing he saw every morning, which gave him his first thought every morning: freedom. Four walls and the Babylon had been closing in on DJ for too long, today was the day he was going to get his freedom. Nobody was going to give it to him – he was going to create it, he was going to grab it with both hands and run off with it.

Suddenly there comes a knocking on my door
In steps me landlord, all he comes here for
Is to hassle me for me money, he hassles me
for me rent
He threatens to evict me if I'm short of two
pence
When I tell him about the leaks and about the
rising damp
The slugs and the mould, the wet and the cold,
and the door goes slam
He disappears like a snake slithers under a
stone
It aint no use trying to telephone
This clever bastard is ex directory
It'd be easier to have a chat with her majesty
In this your bedsit dub, your bedsit dub yeah
dub dub dub
your bedsit dub yeah...

DJ had always faced reality; his youth had been spent in a tenement yard in Kingston, Jamaica. Here, he didn't have much time for education; he had been too busy surviving from one day to the next, taking the bus out in to the country with his parents from the age of six to work in the fields pulling up yam. When he was thirteen, he had worked on the beach during the summer in Ocho Rios, Saint Ann's Bay, taking tourists out on a boat scuba diving, breathing and living that natural mystic, until the age of fourteen when he emigrated with his parents and baby brother to live with his uncle in Leeds, England.

Five minutes later my meter runs out
Need fifty p but he's left me with nowt
Just sitting in the darkness twiddling me
thumbs
When what d'you know I said an idea comes eh
Reach deep into me pocket and I pull out my
stash
Stick three skins together mix me baccy with
me hash
Then I riff it, spliff it, I roll it up
I lick it, stick it, I light it up
And what d'you know I'm lying laughing with
my legs in the air
A huffing and a puffing my favourite armchair

Your bedsit dub, your bedsit dub yeah
Your bedsit dub yeah...what you know
Your bedsit rub dub dub dub dub
Dubwise dub dub dub dub dub dub dub dub

DJ climbed out of bed. Rude boy Winston, his now nineteen-year-old brother's bed across the one room they shared, was empty. DJ dressed in his black tracksuit with official Tuff Gong trademark with the Rastafarian colours of red, gold and green stripes running down the sides of his sleeves and legs. He put on socks and white Adidas trainers.

Breakfast was cornmeal porridge. This was just like his mother used to make for him back in trench town. This was DJ's ritual breakfast when he had a busy day ahead of him and today he had a busy day ahead of him.

05.00am York

It was a foggy morning at Leeham Road York Train Museum where engineers had been working all night to get The Hawkwind, a black prestige 1892 six-wheeled steam train out on the line. It was mechanically preserved and still in full working order. The furnace had been fired up and the steam brought up to pressure. A coal car and eight carriages had been coupled to it.

The Hawkwind was being prepared for the two Irish engineers – Seamus, the driver, in his sixties, wearing blue overalls, red neckerchief and a blue cap, and his son Michael – the fireman, broad-shouldered, in his early forties, dressed like his father.

They were big Rock and Roll fans, both sporting the DA hairstyle. Hanging up in the engine were their Teddy Boy suits which they would be changing into at the end of the day when they were going to see Jerry Lee Lewis.

This morning they were to drive The Hawkwind to York Central Station, where at 11.00am they would pick up 100 lottery winners from the UK trainspotters club to take them on a 100 year anniversary historic journey from York to London.

05.00am Selby

Rude boy Winston was already up. He'd spent the night at the house of two of his friends, two nutters he'd met at various Ska gigs around England, whose claim to fame was being the star players in the England skinhead football squad against the rest of the world across the road in Finsbury park during the 2nd International Ska Festival, London, George Robey, 1989.

They'd spent the whole night up watching Madness and Young Ones videos, drinking Thunderbirds and skanking on down in a room that was a shrine to Ska. The ceiling, skirting boards and door frame were painted in black and white squares with a life size Walt Jabsco painted on the door.

Rude boy Winston, wearing highly polished eight-hole cherry red 1460 Dr Marten boots, Levi jeans, a Ben Sherman shirt, black and white chequered braces, and a 2mm skinhead, left his friends sleeping off a hangover and walked the ten minutes to Portholme Road, Selby train station.

05.20am Leeds

Tell you my friend if you should ever get stuck
Inside a bedsit then you're out of luck
You'll never get to nibbling somebody's ear lobe
When your living in a room the size of a
wardrobe
You sit tight, you sit down and see, mister
You could do worse than take a tip from me
Now you get up to the Hayfield, you get up
Chapeltown
You get a bit of whatever's going around
Then you wrap it in your rizla, you bung it in
your bong
Smoke it how you like but don't you take too
long
And what d'you know you're lying laughing,
your legs in the air
your huffing your puffing you don't have a care
Your bedsit rub dub dub dub dub,

Your bedsit rub dub dub dub dub dub
Watcha

DJ sang along, thinking that when he was back on air he'd promised his friends Little Chief he would play a couple of tracks from this demo they had given him. Breakfast was washed down with a cup of tea followed by a coffee. He read through his plans for the umpteenth time, and took a last look at his maps, meticulously studying the routes he would be taking. He tore them up and threw them in the oven which was set to gas mark four. They instantly burst into flame, curling up and transforming into black carbon leaves.

Taking the cassette, with a stopwatch in the palm of his hand, *"Bleep"*, 05.30 am, DJ opened his front door on Harehills Avenue seeing the Three Hierachs Greek Orthodox Church across the road as he took the two steps down, leaving his bedsit dub for what would be the last time. With a sprightly step, the kind of step only someone from Caribbean descent can take – a sort of effortless rhythm, almost like a dance – he turned left and walked up Harehills Avenue. He was proud of who he was, he was going out to get his freedom and he was taking the whole cast of Pirate Radio Skankdown with him. Together they were going to form an exodus out of England.

05.30am York

Seamus and Michael were making their first test run, checking that all the valves and gauges were functioning and if necessary making any final adjustments. It was still dark and the fog had not yet lifted. They had not gone more than 100 metres when Seamus saw a single light coming out of the fog straight at them. With his hand he crossed himself, saying, "Holy mother of God." He pulled on levers and turned wheels, closing off valves he'd just opened and opening valves he'd just closed, reversing the charging up sequence into an emergency stop.

The Hawkwind came to a halt, hissing and spewing out steam not three metres from the light which now appeared to be a motorbike. It was, in fact, a Harley Davidson Soft Tail R Cross Bones TM in dark custom black with shotgun exhaust, from which dismounted a black, leather-clad wannabe Hells Angel.

Wannabe, as he didn't pass the initiation test of pulling a wheelie the full length of the high street. Wannabe, because when the police flagged him down, instead of showing his arse, burning rubber and riding off in to the sunset, he pulled over, and was duly arrested.

He is known as Mad Axe Man, so-called for the axe he carries in a workman's holster on his belt used for axe throwing competitions in the now disbanded motorcycle club house, The Devil's Arms. This was a club which, after failing the Hells Angels, he'd set up with his redundancy money from the closure of the Selby pit. Mad Axe Man, being the only member, fell behind with the rent which forced him to give it up. The club, situated on the outskirts of Leeds, has now changed to a pub – keeping its name and housing the local drop-outs of society.

Still sitting all bunched up on the Harley were another three drop-outs.of society A misfit bunch of two scruffy looking Hippies and a rocker.

05.30am Selby

A Weatheralls furniture delivery van parked in the unloading area of Selby train station.

Parking it, in his mid fifties, was Mr Zoot Sharp, a Laurel Aitken look-alike complete with two gold front teeth. He wore loafer shoes, a black suit, white shirt, black cravat, wraparounds and a pork pie hat.

Zoot, a native Jamaican, talks in rhyme because he was one of the original MCs and Toasters (toasting is chatting over a rhythm track). This originated from his friend Osbourne Ruddock, better known as King Tubby, who had a TV repair shop, and like Winston was an electrical genius. He built and ran a pirate radio station in his back yard during '61/'62 which after a tip off he closed down before the Babylon could find it.

King Tubby was hired by Duke Reid to take the vocals off singles, producing instrumentals. Tubby started to play around and learnt that he could make a new track by removing sounds, moving the emphasis and adding special effects and echoes. This created a whole new record which the original Toasters, Ewart Beckford a.k.a. U-Roy and Dennis Alcapone, would talk over.

Zoot has spent most of the last 30 years travelling around the world using his Jamaican childhood survival talents of wheeling, dealing, ducking and diving. Zoot could sell oil to an Arab. It was rumoured, but never proved, that he was the one who once sold Nelson's Column to an American business man. Because of his contacts around the world he has the reputation of being able to supply anything, absolutely anything, within 24 hours.

Zoot climbed out of the van and produced a key which he'd wrangled from the station master the night before. It cost him a couple of pints and a box of Cuban cigars. With a forklift he began unloading the truck onto platform 1A.

Winston, being DJ's brother, was delegated to see that all the cast made it on time. He was waiting on the platform.

Zoot, speaking in American rhyming slang, said, "Yo bro how's it go. Do you think, the dudes will show?"

"Dem a show," answered Winston confidently.

Just then two Heads (travellers) – one male, one female – entered. You could smell their body odour a mile away. The male was carrying a huge rainbow coloured woven bag on his shoulder which on first appearance appeared to be alive. Winston quickly disregarded this thought and greeted them with, "Nice one, if ya can jus' wait deh," while pointing to the end of the platform. "Dat will be great."

The male struggled with his bag, trying to look casual as they both made their way to the end of the platform.

Next in was a figure you just couldn't help but think was in disguise, wearing black and white baseball boots, blue overalls and a blue cap.

Winston and he eyed each other. They didn't speak but gave an auction bidder's sign. This was not a wink of the eye, a nod, a wave or any other body language. In fact it wasn't a movement at all – more a look of recognition.

The figure in blue's trained eye scanned the station without looking, noting the kitchen equipment, foods, drinks, cooking utensils, broadcasting equipment, boxes of records, CDs, trays of Red Stripe beer and Mc Ewen's lager, crates of Holsten Pils, Special Brew, Newcastle Brown, bottles of Jack Daniels and Thunderbird wine. How Zoot had come to acquire all this was nobody's business but the figure in blue made a mental note of it as he walked to the end of the platform.

05.31am York

The misfit bunch stiff and cold from a half hour ride up the track from Selby climbed off the Harley and hobbled up to the Hawkwind, the biggest one of them pulling his underpants out of his arse as he hobbled.

"See the cut of his jib," said Michael to his father.

Seamus called down, "Jesus son of Mary, you could have got yourselves killed."

The biggest one, a Hippy called 7 Bellies in his mid-forties, was wearing jeans, T-shirt, a knee length Afghan coat, and yellow John Lennon sunglasses. He had a ZZ

Top beard, shoulder length curly hair and a Benny hat. In a voice like gravel, and oblivious to Seamus's rage, he replied "Whallo," as he struggled to climb up. He requested his party to give him a bunk up, and after some pushing, shoving, grunting, groaning, huffing and puffing, he climbed on board.

He was followed by Coke, the other Hippy, who wore flares, a flowered shirt, an orange jacket, white silk scarf, red John Lennon sunglasses and a Slash top hat. Seamus protested, "Oh you can't be coming up here."

With his Yorkshire accent, Mad Axe Man – who looked like Animal from The Muppet Show – replied, "Well that's where tha's wrong tha nors," as he pulled himself up.

Coke who began every sentence with a *sniff* added, *sniff*, "Yeah 'cause like we're already here maan."

The Rocker Pot belly, 7 Bellies' brother, looked like a pregnant 16-year-old. He was dressed in jeans and a denim jacket covered in sewn on patches of heavy metal bands including AC/DC, Black Sabbath, Rainbow, Deep Purple, Jimi Hendrix and Led Zeppelin. He had the IQ of a five-year-old and, while still standing on the line, whined, "I don't fink we should be doing this. I want to go home." Nobody reacted.

Mad Axe Man said in an intimidating voice to the driver, "Tha's been a change a plan, thee and this train'll be coming with us."

Seamus replied, "Wind your neck in," then tried to protest by adding, "I don't tink dat'll be a good idea."

7 Bellies, always blunt and to the point, butted in: "It's a bloody great idea if yer know what's gud fer yer".

"Bleep" 05.31am Leeds

With trees lining both sides of the road, DJ walked up Harehills Avenue crossing Ellers Road and Shepherds Place. Further up, across the road on the corner of

Avenue Hill, stood the Trinity United Reformed Church. Across the road from that was Potter Newton Park which DJ jogged around daily and on most days played football.

DJ had many fond memories of the park. One was the '81 Leeds carnival which The Specials played, supporting the Rock Against Racism campaign. DJ crossed Spencer Place, thinking of all that he was leaving behind. He walked the full length of Harehills Avenue, crossing the road at the end and stopping at the PARADISE RESTARAUNT with EAT IN OR TAKE OUT printed underneath the title. DJ smiled to himself, turned left and walked up Chapletown Road.

DJ zig-zagged, crossing the road every 100 yards or so, looking as if he was lost or wasn't sure of which way to go. He stopped at Dutch Pot, another restaurant which served West Indian food, smiled to himself again and walked on.

Still crossing the road backwards and forwards, he stopped again at the Continental supermarket, or the Multicultural Supermarket or the Halal Meat Centre – which ever title fitted your cultural background. It advertised that it catered for Asian, African, Afro Caribbean, Mediterranean and the Middle East.

Although DJ was a Rastafarian he wasn't a vegetarian. There were different sectors in the Rastafarian communities one of which praises the smoking of marijuana but does not permit the drinking of alcohol. There are many Rastafarians across the world that don't smoke but do drink or do eat meat. A Rastafarian's body is his temple and he can choose what he wants or does not want to put in it.

05.31am Selby

Two cockney Mods walked in as if they owned the place. One of them said, "Owhite mate" to Winston who replied, "No mi all black mate, *he he he.*"

The Mods smiled and sauntered onto the platform.

Five minutes later, two Scottish Punks, dragging their feet and looking worse for wear, hobbled in.

And so it was that they all arrived in dribs and drabs. Later came a gay juggler in bright spotty clothes, followed by a chef cook and his assistant arguing persistently.

Winston counted the heads and thought the way the subcultures fitted together seemed a bit odd, but in reality not too hard to understand. As with all music cultures they come and go in waves. They come, everybody jumps on, they go, and some jump off onto the next wave. Over a time more drop by the wayside, outgrowing the fad, fashion, the dance craze, or because of work, mixing with other people, moving away, getting married, having kids or whatever else.

The die hards stay, hanging on to that time that changed their lives, changed the way they dressed, how they wore their hair, the way they thought, the way they lived. It gave them an identity or something they could identify themselves with – and whole groups of friends to share it with. As cultures get smaller and smaller so too do the scenes, the venues, pubs and hangouts, because their venues, hangouts get taken over by the next wave. From being the majority, they become the minority.

This is how they all became to hang out in the Devil's Arms, opening its doors to the hangers-on of Punks, Teds, Natty Dreads, Mods, Rockers, Hippies, Skinheads, and other minority groups. It gave them a place of their own, to hang out with others who understood, because they themselves were still living their lives in a fashion from a wave that was 20 or more years old.

05.32am York

Michael the fireman by now had begun to understand what was going down and spoke for the first time."You don't mean te say you'll be hijacking this train do you?"

"*Sniff.* Yeah," smiled Coke.

"Aye and thee and thee's goin' te drive it" added Mad Axe Man.

"We're not really going to hijack a train are we 7 Bellies bruvver man?" whined Pot Belly who was still standing on the line.

Seamus was looking down at him thinking, "If brains were chocolate, this one doesn't have enough to fill a Smartie."

Mad Axe Man, irritated, sighed. "Oh whose idea was it te bring him along?"

7 Bellies answered, "You was at the meeting, DJ said everyone."

Coke *sniffed*. "Yeah that's our instructions maan, follow them to the letter."

"Have we got a letter? Who's got a letter, I haven't seen a letter," whined Pot Belly.

"Right Pot Belly get tha's snivelling arse up here," commanded Mad Axe Man, and pointing at Michael and Seamus, said, "Thee, shovel coal, thee, get tha's foot down and follow thee."

As Pot Belly climbed up Mad Axe Man jumped down. Michael shovelled and Seamus pulled some levers. The Hawkwind let off some steam and slowly shunted forwards. Mad Axe Man mounted his hog, kicked it into life and spun it around in one motion. Then he shot off back down the track like a bat out of hell.

"Bleep" 05.45am Leeds

DJ wasn't stopping to look in these restaurants or this supermarket for food or meats, he was using the windows as a mirror to see if he was being followed. Having grown up in Trenchtown he'd learnt to live on his wits, to develop his senses and trust his feelings. Constantly on the look-out for danger, for a meal, for an opportunity, any opportunity.

For a Jamaican, life was difficult. For a Jamaican living in a high unemployment area, you couldn't afford to miss a chance. It maybe only came once in a lifetime.

It was not that DJ wanted to work for anyone else but himself. He was on a mission. His mission was to put Pirate Radio Skankdown back on the air and carry on Bob Marley's work of One Love, and nothing or no one was going to stop him. "Definitely not," he thought to himself, "de baldhead following 20 metre behind."

05.45 am York

As Mad Axe Man disappeared into the fog with the Hawkwind following, Seamus enquired, "Just where might we be goin'?"

"None of your bloody business" answered 7 Bellies.

Being the driver Seamus thought it was every bit of his business, and feeling pissed off by 7 Bellies bluntness he retaliated with, "Say, when you fell out the ugly tree, did you hit every branch goin' down?"

"Just follow that bike," answered 7 Bellies.

"Oh it be a Mystery Train is it?" said Seamus, and then he began to sing:

"Train I ride sixteen coaches long
Train I ride sixteen coaches long
Well that long black train, got my baby and gone
-"

"Hey is that 'Mystery Train' by Bon Jovi or is it The Band?" said Pot Belly who may not be too bright in day to day life but has watched so many rock documentaries he can reel statistics off parrot fashion.

Seamus explained that it was "Mystery Train" but Elvis Presley's version from the B-side of "I Forgot to Remember to Forget", released August 20th 1955. Then

14

he went on to say the original was released in 1953 by Junior Parker, also known as Mr Blues, whose band was Little Junior's Blue Flames.

"Oh so you know a thing or two about Rock and Roll do you?" said 7 Bellies.

"Well actually he does, he's written a book on it, haven't you Father?" said Michael.

Sniff "Yeah 'cause like Rock and Roll was the beginning of all music maan," said Coke.

"Well actually you're wrong there" Said Seamus who then went on to tell them how Rock 'n' Roll didn't just evolve from thin air you know – you'd have to go back to 1619 when African music was brought to America, played and sung in the plantation fields. Songs that went something like "Waiting for the Sun to Go Down" because when the sun went down they could stop working and sleep. This song and music style was followed by European colonists bringing music over like church hymns and Gospel.

By the 1920s a music called Blues had evolved. This developed into a popular music style called the Boogie Woogie. By the 50s there was Jazz, Gospel, Country, Blues, Rhythm and Blues... It was out of these music styles during the early 50s that a new music was fused – the music of course was Rock and Roll. It was Alan Freed, a disc jockey in Cleveland, that gave the music its first name in 1951 as Rak n Roll'n, named after the song, "My Baby Rocks Me with a Steady Roll".

Rocking and rolling was a Blues innuendo for sexual intercourse and was used in Blues lyrics and song titles such as Roy Brown's 1947 "Good Rocking Tonight", Bill Wymore's 1948 "We're Gonna Rock We're Gonna Roll" and Scatman Crother's 1949 "I want To Rock and Roll".

Before the war, children listened to what their parents listened to: white music such as Gospel, Country, Jazz and Swing. In the early 50s, children had free time after school and pocket money to spend with which they could influence the record market. Rock and Roll took America by storm and became big business; the new music was being played on television and radio shows. Teenagers were having fun and learning to make decisions for themselves. They grew out of parental influences and rebelled, later becoming known as the generation gap.

Parents themselves had never experienced this rebellion, so didn't know how to handle it, or know that they would grow out of it in their twenties. What they did know was Rock and Roll was everywhere, influencing the youth, singing about school, dating, drive-in movies and bringing with it new fashions, dances, hairstyles, hot rods and slang.

Rock and Roll also gave the youth an opportunity to show off their athletic skills on the dance floor. It was fast and they could release their energy. The parents blamed everything on the music but the more it was attacked, the more popular it became. The kids liked it because their parents didn't.

"How far is it to Selby?" interrupted Pot Belly.

"Selby is it? said Seamus. "Well there's going to be a whole lot of disappointed spotters when this train doesn't pull in at York station at 11.00am this morning. They're mostly fathers and sons, but it's the kids my heart goes out to."

7 Bellies interrupted, "Hey we're just following instructions same as you."

Seamus was concerned and said, "Well I hope when you're sliding down the banister of life the splinters are pointing the right way, because by ten past eleven there's going to be a national alert. The whole of England will be looking for this train."

Sniff. "We'll be through the channel tunnel before eleven o' clock," said Coke and then added, "It will be like the train just, disappeared maan."

"You mean we be going to France?" smiled Seamus.

Sniff. "I mean we're going right across Europe maan and then further," bragged Coke.

"Joseph husband of Mary," jigged Seamus. "This is the best thing since two candy apples on the one stick, I tought I was only going to drive to London for the day".

Sniff. "Naa, where we're going, it's going to take about six days man" said Coke, who was now dancing with Seamus.

7 Bellies, Pot Belly and Michael joined in and they all danced a merry jig and laughed together. Seamus said, "Jez were having a lot of fun here," and he pulled on a rope letting the whistle blow. The Hawkwind sped through Brabant, a small village at 5.45am, waking local residents who believed they had just dreamt something from the wild west.

05.45am Leeds

DJ had been aware of the Babylon behind since the Paradise Restaurant at the end of his road. It was a lone private detective hired to keep him under surveillance. He'd been watching him around the clock the last few months, just trying to catch him putting out another show, probably hired by other radio stations because when Pirate Radio Skankdown was on the air, their ratings plummeted.

So the last few months, DJ had not been putting out his show. Instead he'd been planning his way out, which is why when he saw the Babylon he calmly smiled to himself. He had been expected and accounted for, which is why DJ was playing this cat and mouse game with him – leading him to Leeds city centre.

DJ felt a tingling from his toes through his whole body. He was excited. He walked the length of Claypit Lane on the opposite side to Oakland Flats passing the

Eagle Tavern, walking along the grass verge of Little London Lovell Park and under the bridge with the road signs notifying drivers which route to take to Headingly, City Centre, Halifax or the M62.

As he walked, DJ was breathing in slowly and deeply through his nostrils and slowly out of his mouth. DJ was meditating; he was preparing his body and mind to take him through the last stages of his plan. In his mind he was going through the motions he was going to make. He could picture himself taking the route that was coming up; he knew what he had to do and he was mentally prepared and totally focused on doing it.

05.50am Selby

All the cast were there, except one: Sir Johnny O.B.E. Flannell – the 1970s alcoholic disc jockey, ex-Top of the Pops presenter, and still good for a top ten run down. DJ wouldn't be happy; Johnny had been there since the first show.

As Winston pondered over this, Mad Axe Man raced up the line followed by The Hawkwind. He rode his Harley up the ramp, roared along the platform and skidded to a stop at Winston's feet.

The Hawkwind steamed in and hissed to a stop, filling the small station with clouds of steam. 7 Bellies, Coke, Pot Belly, Seamus and Michael all climbed down from the engine.

"Whaagh this guy knows a shitload about Rock and Roll," said 7 Bellies with his hand on Seamus's shoulder. Winston quickly made his acquaintance and then above the noise of the steam engine shouted everybody together and gave out instructions. The cooks were to load the kitchen equipment and foods. Everyone else was to load their own drinks on. Special brew for the Mods, Newcastle Brown and Thunderbirds were for Coke, 7

Bellies, Pot Belly and Mad Axe Man, Guinness for Seamus and Michael, cola and wine for the travellers, pina colada, cherries and umbrellas for the juggler, Budweiser for the man in blue, trays of McEwen's lager for the Punks, boxes of Jack Daniels for the missing Sir Johnny O.B.E. Flannel and Red Stripe for DJ, Zoot and himself.

Winston then asked Zoot to load the broadcasting equipment, records and CDs in the first carriage and the barrels, bar, more crates and the –

It was then that he noticed lots of cardboard boxes not on the itinerary list. He queried, "Wat dem fer?"

To which Zoot replied, "Yo bro don't you know, I make money wherever I go, a Yen a Deutschmark a Pound a Buck, all these things will bring me luck."

Winston, looking surprised and shocked, was annoyed. "Ya mean te seh all dem boxes full a lucky charms? DJ seh te bring nuttin extra or of personal value."

As Winston was saying this Mad Axe Man was struggling to ride his Harley into one of the carriages, Winston ran up the platform, waving his arms about and shouting, "NO MON, NO MON!"

Mad Axe Man argued,"There's no way thee's leaving thee's hog behind tha nors."

Winston was just about to argue this when he saw that down the platform, Coke and 7 Bellies who had a reputation for liking a drink now and again (more now, and more again), going for what must have been a world record. They were finishing off a crate of Newcastle Brown, licking their lips and each opening a bottle of Thunderbird.

Winston ran back down the platform past the Punks who were doing the pogo and chanting,

"We're all off to Wembley stadium, we're all off to Wembley."

When he saw Zoot, who as quickly as he could was loading his boxes on, the travellers were smoking some strange smelling tobacco while the juggler was riding his uni-cycle and juggling five clubs.

Winston couldn't pull his hair out, so he stopped to look up into the heavens to ask some invisible God to help him. That was when he saw the platform clock. It was 05.58. "BLURDCLATS", he thought – the station would be open in two minutes.

DJ's plan and instructions rang in his head. They were supposed to go unnoticed till Leeds by which time everybody would be on board and they would be on their way. Winston screamed, "GE' EVERYTING ON DE TRAIN NOH. SEAMUS, LEEDS FULL STEAM AHEAD."

Everybody loaded the train in ten seconds flat. Michael shovelled coal, working like a demon firing up the furnaces of hell. Seamus put the engine into gear and The Hawkwind slowly began to roll out of the station....

When Sir Johnny O.B.E. Flannel made his appearance and staggered on to the platform, half a bottle of Jack Daniels in one hand, fish and chips in the other – where he'd got them this time of the morning was anybody's guess – he saw The Hawkwind and slurred, "Who'sroundisit."

Winston jumped off grabbed him and tried pulling him towards the train, but because Johnny was so lubricated, his mind was looking forwards but his body was leaning backwards at 45 degrees, and his legs were in reverse. 7 Bellies jumped off, went over, grabbed the fish and chips and said, "Whaagh thanks, I'm starving!" then jumped back on the train. "So much for comradeship," thought Winston, who struggled on. Zoot came to his aid and together they dragged Johnny on board as The Hawkwind slowly picked up speed and left Selby behind.

"Bleep" 06.55am Leeds.

DJ had spent the last hour walking up and down the same roads, walking around blocks and looking in windows.

Now he stopped and stood on the corner of Cookbridge Street. The lone detective some thirty metres back also stopped, hanging back and pretending to read some sign at the Leeds College of Technology.

DJ was still focused and breathing deeply through his nostrils. The time was 06.55 and 56 seconds. DJ was early. He idly walked around the corner, reflecting on his youth and seeing flashbacks of his past. Trenchtown Jamaica, Ska, Reggae, 57 poverty, sun, laughter, 58 yam, cornmeal porridge, guava jelly, 59 Jamaican Air Lines, England, cold grey, 15th birthday, school.

"Bleep" 06.56.

DJ set off like a primed Olympic athlete – head up, chest out – his hands and fingers were rigid like knives cutting through the air. His aim was to run the four minute mile. He filled his lungs with air, his heart pumped this vital oxygen and fed it to the muscles in his thighs, calves, shoulders and arms, his legs taking enormous strides, his Adidas trainers bouncing along the pavement. He ran past Bourbon off licence, across Great George Street, passing Leeds Cathedral on the corner, ran across Headrow and up into Park Row. The Babylon rounded the corner with DJ nowhere to be seen; it appeared he'd disappeared in to thin air.

Could he still do it? There was no doubt in his mind. He'd ran this course every day, Monday to Friday, when he left his home for school. Standing at Cookbridge Street corner, stopwatch in hand, he would wait till 8.26 am before he ran, ran, ran. In them days it was how he released his anger and frustration. He didn't run to school – they couldn't teach him the facts of life there or anything about street culture. Having grown up in Trench Town he knew and had seen by the age of 14 more than any of his teachers would in a lifetime.

Instead of running to school he ran straight to Platform 12 of Leeds central train station in four minutes flat and caught the 08.30 to London, Kings Cross, where he would jump on the underground which would take him to Camden Town station.

It was 1979, the time Two Tone were bubbling over and flooding the nation with their brand of British Ska. It was almost right next door to Camden Station at Holts shoe shop, 5 Kentish Town Road, with the Two Tone office above, where he would meet up with the London rude boys and hang around Camden market.

"Bleep" 06.57 am.

DJ ran that same course, he was 18 years older but he'd kept himself in shape by playing football three or four times a week – the only passion he had next to his music and putting out Pirate Radio Skankdown. He ran up Park Row, passing Bekkets Bank on the right and TSB on the left. Although he was somewhat heavier than when he was 15, his legs were longer, his mind and determination stronger. He ran past a man out walking his dog who probably thought he was just a regular guy out running for his health and fitness but DJ was running for his freedom, for his show, for his friends who would be waiting and counting on him to make it happen. DJ always made it happen.

"Bleep" 06.58am.

He reached the corner where a statue of The Duke of Wellington sitting on his horse had been placed across the road from The Queens Hotel on Wellington road. DJ realised he was a couple of seconds behind schedule. His legs had got heavier, his breathing harder, but in his mind he knew he would make it. So he pushed on, there was no medal, rosette, trophy or ribbon at the end of this race: this was the race of his life, this was the race for the rest of his life. In 60 seconds he would know if the last months of planning would come off. He had worked it all down to the last minute, this minute, the most important exciting minute of his life. In 60 seconds he would know if his friends who to him were brothers had been successful. If they like him, had made it this far unchallenged.

Leeds 06.59am, Leeds central station, Platform 12.

It was a Saturday morning. For some, Saturday was another work day. Early business men and women, and industrial workers who worked outside the city were waiting for the 07.05 to take them to London's Kings Cross. A father with his three-year-old son was waiting for the train to take them into London city. It was Grandma's birthday.

Alongside were students from Leeds university (those who had got themselves up) waiting to go home for the weekend. They stood idling, some still half asleep, some reminiscing about the night before, some planning the day that lay before them, when from in the distance they heard and felt a strange rumbling coming through the station.

As they looked down the track they saw one light instead of the normal two. Something was odd, something was not right – the clock said 06.59; the 07.05 was six minutes early. But instead of a 20th century electric/diesel blue Intercity, a black 1892 steam engine pulling eight carriages in a cloud of smoke and steam hissed to a stop on Platform 12.

In the engine Seamus and Michael had changed into their Teddy Boy suits and in the doorway of each carriage stood either a Skinhead, a Hippy, a Rocker, a wannabe Hells Angel, a Punk, a Mod and two Heads. All stood with their feet apart and arms folded as if they were bouncers on a Nite klub doorway, refusing to allow any of the commuters on board.

The Hawkwind stood there a full minute. There was silence, nobody spoke, the bouncers stood their ground, menacingly. The commuters looked bewildered at the train, at the bouncers, at each other.

"Bleep" 06.59am

DJ crossed Boarlane running down Bishopgate down towards the dark arches where, there at the Neville street entrance, was his friend's local Reggae outfit Little Chief who had gotten up early to see him off. They were dressed in lumberjack shirts, jeans, and work boots, looking more like contractors than musicians. They jammed out:

> *"Train's waiting at the station*
> *Rock it to your destination"*

which couldn't have been more appropriate. DJ smiled and gave a nod of acknowledgement as he ran past and up the steps to Platform 12. And there it was, just as he had planned and dreamed, gleaming in all its glory... The Hawkwind.

"Bleep" 07.00am.

Seamus pulled on a rope and let off two shrieks on the whistle. Everyone's heart on Platform 12 skipped a beat; the three year old screamed and hugged his father. The memory of that fright would stay with him for the rest of his life. Others looked at The Hawkwind angrily, while some, frightened, some just froze in shock. The Hawkwind let off another cloud of steam and slowly chugged forward. DJ's heart almost burst through his chest as he ran in between the flabbergasted commuters like a man possessed.

Further up the platform, three racists stepped out to block DJ's path. Word on the street had obviously reached ears quicker than all the local establishment's efforts. The three racists were quickly intervened and marched off by the London rude boys that had stayed over from The Toasters gig at The Duchess of York the night before.

DJ thanked Jah Rastafari as he ran on, passing, one by one, the eight carriages. Standing in the doorways were the Heads, Mods, Punks, Mad Axe Man, Pot Belly, Coke, 7 Bellies, up to the first carriage where his blood brother Rude Boy Winston with a big smile on his face stood to one side and allowed DJ to jump on.

It was then with the Rock 'n' Roll circus complete that Winston pressed a button on a remote control and over all the speakers in the station you heard The Selecter's Charley H Bembridge's rim shot which was followed by Arthur Gappa Henderson's announcement, **"THIS TRAIN IS BOUND FOR SKAVILLE... ALL ABOARD."**

Chapter Two

SKAVILLE UK

"Bloodclaat of a bruddah," scolded DJ.

"Wha' wi on time an' all de cas' on board," said Winston.

"Ya jus' pley announce dis train boun' fe Skaville noh everyone nor weh wi ago," complained DJ.

"It seven o' clock, dem a jus' go te work or out fe de dey," protested Winston. "No one nor de train a gwaan missin' till eleven o' clock an' dem a no see de news till tonight, an' it only de likes of anyone wid any music credibility dat evah heard fe Skaville nevah mind nor weh it is."

"Ookaay Winston mi suppose ya right an' by dis afternoon wi' be hidin' in a disused tunnel in France during de dey an' only travellin' by night which is how wi' goin' te get right across Europe an' de continent widout being seen."

DJ, feeling relieved that it was all coming together, started to sound like his normal self again. He said, "Yu seh everyone on board."

"Yeah mon," Said Winston, who then explained that everything had gone just as DJ had planned. All the supplies were on board and he'd fitted state of the art bugs and on air lights supplied by Zoot in all the cabins and the engine. Everything was working so they could tune in at any time, and the mobile broadcasting unit was digitally tuned to a satellite, ready to hit the air waves.

DJ, lost with all these technicalities, asked, "Wha' ya talk 'bout?"

"De soun' system DJ, it up an' runnin'."

DJ, overwhelmingly happy, started to laugh. *"He he he he.* Oookay shall wi' start de show Winston." Winston pressed a button, a red light came on and they were on the air.

"He he he Rastaman Vibration gonna covah de earth like watah covah de sea. Hello deh listeners, rude boys, rude girls, rastas, bruddah's an' sistah's, dis is ya host DJ Dread."

"An' Rude Boy Winston," interrupted Winston.

"An' I bruddah, Rude Boy Winston, de selector. Yu listen te Pirate Radio Skankdown, de hottest show in tohn, de show dat bring yu Ska, Reggae, roots an' culture wid comedy sketches fe all yu favourite characters, tell dem Winston."

"Fe bettah reception tune inte frequency oh oh seven, ocean eleven, wi on long wave, wi on short wave, medium wave an' a permanent Ska wave. Wi on FM, AM an' PM, skanking tru de air waves all tru de dey, an' de night."

"Irie Winston an' wi takin' all de cas' an' equipment wid us," interrupted DJ, who then went on to say they were on their way to do a live on stage Pirate Radio Skankdown show in Skaville which was a bit like the old Radio One Road Show. DJ finished by saying, "Dis is de Pirate Radio Skankdown train te Skaville show an' wi puttin' it out live on ar wey. Seh Winston, wha' wi goin' te open de show wid?"

Winston excitedly fingered his way through his record collection of which he knew every one from the top of his head. They were all categorised in band order from date of release so he was able to directly pull out the single he wanted, saying, "Cause wi a go Dover te Calais mi waan pley dis why wi still in de UK."

With the record on the turntable, Winston lovingly lowered the record arm onto the disc and Buster Bloodvessel's voice boomed out.

THIS AIN'T DOWNTOWN JA,

THIS IS SKAVILLE UK,

BAD MANNERS TO SKAVILLE, which was followed by a ska stomping instrumental, with

ALL ABOARD THE BLUE BEAT TRAIN being announced halfway through, and finishing with,

THIS AIN'T DOWNTOWN JA,

THIS IS SKAVILLE UK.

"Yeah mon I an' I hope dat track get yu listener' on ya feet an' a skankin' on down like I an' I here in de studio at Pirate Radio Skankdown, *he he he*. Winston, tell de brethren who a sing dat."

Winston told the listeners that it was Bad Manners led by Douglas Trendle alias Buster Bloodvessel who, before fame, and being an avid Arsenal fan, got his first booking in court for singing *"Who the fuck is Stanley Bowles?"* on the terraces at Loftus Road.

The band started out as six schoolmates at Woodbury Down, North London in '76, playing along with teachers in the assembly hall under the name Snacks at the Bar. Their next gig was at Stonehenge under the name Standback. From there they progressed on to Stoop Solo and the Sheet Starchers, after which they switched to Buster Bloodvessel and His Bad Manners and then shortened it to Bad Manners.

Somewhere along the line they were joined by three outsiders, swelling their ranks to nine. Bad Manners have made the headlines countless times with their front man Buster, a figure literally larger than life. Buster started out in the music business weighing in at 17 and a half stones and just kept on getting bigger.

He is famous for having a 13-inch tongue and a bald head (which he first shaved for a five pound bet) and according to the papers, attempting to eat 30 beef burgers in one sitting, reaching 27 before the band ran out of money (truth be known he has never eaten more than two).

Another story is when they played San Remo with everyone and supposedly the Pope watching live on TV when Buster bent over and dropped his shorts. A stunt he was to repeat in Ireland which earned Manners a lifetime ban. Maybe not the done thing... but all good publicity.

They turned down an offer of a debut single on Two Tone, signed to Magnet and went on to have four top tens.

Winston finished by saying, "Dat was 'Skaville UK' deh on de Blue Beat label, dat track is taken from de 'Return Of The Ugly' album released in July '89, de single jus' mek de top 100."

DJ took the mike, saying, "Fe all yu listener' a jus' tune in dis not downtown JA, dis Pirate Radio Skankdown OK ... *he he he,* seh Winston, who wi gonna tune in te?"

Winston replied, "Mi haffe a surprise fe ye, it turn out Seamus noh a shitload a stuff 'bout Rock an' Roll, mi tune inte de engine an' let him tell som' fe de story."

"Wha' Rock an' Roll haffe do wid Ska an' Reggae?" asked DJ.

"It all connected DJ, listen wha' him haffe seh."

DJ announced, "Oookaay den listoner' here' Seamus an' Michael te tell ye a shitload 'bout Rock an' Roll."

Winston tuned in to the engine, allowing them to listen in and at the same time send it out live through the airwaves. The Hawkwind was steaming towards London when Michael saw the red light come on and pointed it out to his father, asking, "So who was the first to play

Rock and Roll?"

Seamus began to explain that there were early records with elements of Rock and Roll in them such as blues singer Big Joe Turner's "Roll 'Em Pete" in 1939, Gospel singer Sister Rosetta Tharpe's "Rock Me" and "This Train" in 1938 and Roy Brown's "Good Rocking Tonight" in 1947.

The first whole R&R record would be "Rocket 88" by Jackie Brensten and his Delta Cats who were Ike Turner and the Kings Of Rhythm playing under another name in 1951.

Some argue that Elvis Presley's "That's Alright Mama", recorded in 1954, was the first R&R record but that's "probably prejudice to colour", said Seamus.

"What about that Haley fellow, wasn't he first?" asked Michael.

Seamus smiled and told of William John Clifton Haley – Bill Haley – who made a guitar out of cardboard when he was a child; his father was so impressed he bought him a real guitar. At 13 he was earning $1.00 a night playing at an auction. At 15, he set out on the road with his guitar and, living on one meal a day, gained experience travelling place to place.

After playing in several bands, in '46 he formed his own: Bill Haley and The Saddlemen, who played country swing. In '52 that changed to Bill Haley with Haley's Comets. In '53 they recorded a song that was the first R&R record to enter the charts – "Crazy Man Crazy" – reaching number 15 on the billboard in '54.

Name changed again to Bill Haley and His Comets, they made another impact with "Shake Rattle and Roll", originally a blues song with innuendos from Big Joe Turner. Haley rewrote it, and it sold a million copies. It was also the first R&R record to enter British charts in Dec '54.

"Rock Around The Clock" was originally a b-side but when first released as an A-side only entered the chart for one week in April '54. However it went on to spread R&R around the world when it re-entered the charts again in '55 and went to number one. This came from the song being used three times in the teenage film "Blackboard Jungle" which is considered to be the first R&R film. It was the first record to sell over a million in Britain and Germany. When they screened the film at a cinema in south London's Elephant and Castle in '56, teenagers went wild, ripping out cinema seats.

The '56 film "Rock Around The Clock" told the story of how R&R came to be. It also featured his third million selling single "See you Later Alligator", originally recorded in'55 by Bobby Charles in a New Orleans blues style.

In '56, The Comets starred in the film "Don't knock The Rock", while in January '57 they played Australia, and February the UK, where they were mobbed by thousands at Waterloo station – being described by the press as the second battle of Waterloo. That same year in October they had five songs in the UK's top 20.

Winston cut back to the studio saying, "Dat Michael an Seamus deh, up in de engine room, wi tune in deh anuddah time, an' if yu jus' tune in here, yu listen te Pirate Radio Skankdown."

"De show dat steamin' down de track a hundread miles an hour," added DJ. "Seh Winston I an' I hear nuttin 'bout Ska an' Reggae in all dat Rock an' Roll chat."

"It like a big puzzle DJ, an' dat only de firs' piece."

"Tcha mon Winston, well it a lot a talkin', seh why don' wi tune in te som' fe de udder cas'."

Winston answered, "Mi waan check out Coke an' 7 Bellies' compartment, dem aready a steamin' in Selby an' wid Mad Axe Man an' Pot Belly on board, dem always good fe a laugh."

"Ookaay listener' check dis out. Seh Winston hoh dis work?"

Winston pointed out a button on his desk which DJ pressed and tuned into the misfits compartment.

Mad Axe Man felt settled, his Harley out in the corridor. He stretched out with his biker boots up on the table and commented, "Aye well this is right up thee's street, champion, bloody champion."

To which Pot Belly whined, "But this is not your street, Axey – this is a train line and you live on..."

"Thee bloody nors where thee lives, and thee nors this is not thee's street, thee means te say like, that this is just the ticket tha nors, this'll do for thee."

To which Pot Belly asked, "Have you got a ticket? 7 Bellies he's got a ticket, why haven't I got one, where's our tickets?"

"Whoa dunno," answered 7 Bellies who asked Coke, "Hey Coke where's our tickets?"

Who replied with a *sniff*, "Like we haven't got any maan."

Pot Belly cried out, "But we'll get thrown off or fined by the ticket inspector."

Sniff. "Leave it out Pot Belly there isn't a ticket inspector maan, we've hijacked this train," said Coke who added, "to take us down to Skaville, to do a big show down there, live on stage maan, it's going to be really big, bigger than 7 Bellies here."

"Hey cool it Coke, no personal stuff maan or I'll get personal, a personal punch in the mouth right."

Coke, knowing when to quit, sensibly changed the subject.

Sniff "Hey like it's a long way to Skaville so why don't we like, play a game of Monopoly?"

Mad Axe Man complained, "Monopoly, that's a bloody bairns' game."

"Yeah Monopoly's for kids, in't it Axey?" agreed Pot Belly, trying to sound grown up.

To which 7 Bellies blurted, "Now just hold on a minute, this isn't the Monopoly as you know it."

"Na," *sniffed* Coke, "Cause like me and 7 Bellies."

"And DJ Dread and Winston," reminded 7 Bellies.

Sniff. "And DJ Dread and Winston," said Coke, "have completely rewritten the game."

"And changed the name," said 7 Bellies enthusiastically.

Sniff "Yeah like we thought Monopoly sounded like a negative single track recording of a parrot maan, so like we positively Stereophonic'd it up a bit and called it..."

"Oh Yeah Alcoholy," blurted out 7 Bellies, adding, "It's bloody good maan you can drink beer and get pissed."

Coke added, with a *sniff*, "Yeah we often play – me, 7 Bellies, DJ Dread, Winston and Johnny Flannel, like sometimes we start Friday night..."

"And play through to Sunday or Monday," said 7 Bellies, finishing the sentence off for him.

Sniff. "Well, till the beer runs out usually," added Coke.

Mad Axe Man, sounding enthusiastic, responded with, "That sounds like thees sort a game, aye get it out then and let's have a gander."

Coke took the board out the box and laid it on the table saying, "Here it is, me and 7 Bellies will talk you round the board shall we?" Pointing to the corner of the board he said, *sniff,* "Here we go then, like all games right, have gotta have a start yeah, and Monopoly starts with go, so me and 7 Bellies came up with our start for Oh Yeah Alcoholy."

"OFF LICENCE," blurted 7 Bellies, "'Cause that's where we usually go, hey Coke."

Sniff "Yeah, we always go to the off licence, even if we're going to the pub, we call in at the off licence first, it's like good for a starter. We usually call in and pick up a few bottles of Newcy Brown, and that gets us to the pub. So that's our start to the game, and you collect two pints every time you go past, nice one hey. And the next one on the board funnily enough is a pub, The George Roby, Finsbury park, London."

"Yeah," butted in 7 Bellies, "that's one of DJ Dread and Winston's – they used to go down to the International Ska Festivals there."

Coke continued. *Sniff* "Next is our version of community chest or chance where on the original version you have to pay income tax or shit like that..."

Only to be interrupted by Pot Belly, "It's got a picture of a bottle and some arrows, what's that mean, what's that mean Coke?"

Sniff. "Well like its Spin the Bottle right, and like who ever lands on it yeah, they got a spin the bottle. And like it goes round and round and round, and like when it stops, whoever it points to, they gotta read the card out."

"Whoa and like every card's a winner maan," added 7 Bellies who continued with, "The next one's another venue. The London Astoria where DJ and Winston went to see a Ska Explosion."

Sniff "WOW," said Coke. "Dangerous stuff that ska"

7 Bellies told of the next one being The Roxy on Neal Street, Covent Garden, which opened its doors to the first Punk bands in their infancy. Next on the board was Camden Station, and next door to that was the Rock On record shop. Another spin the bottle and you've got the Holts shoe shop. Then if you go back round the corner and up Camden road you've got Camden Market, a good place for hanging out, meeting up with the locals and picking up some tat.

And so they rabbitted on and on around the board, naming Glastonbury festival in the corner instead of the jail, followed by Islington's Hope & Anchor. In keeping with the game, they replaced Electric Company with Drax power station where some of the cast have friends who still regularly tune in to Pirate Radio Skankdown.

Next to that, London's Rainbow Theatre that housed Bob Marley's famous concerts of June '77, then a jump up north to another venue, Leeds city hall with Leeds station next door followed by two more venues, The Duchess of York, spin the bottle, Leeds Astoria. Free Parking was replaced by Free Beer where you could pick up another beer to get you to the off licence. Next door to that is Bradford St Georges Hall. Another spin the bottle, Bradford Queens Hall.

Over to Jamaica at the Studio One recording studio followed by Kingston Station and Orange Street, Waterworks were replaced with Toilet, take a piss, where you were allowed to leave the game to relieve yourself. Coventry was replaced by Tiffany's, next door being Coventry Poly University. In the corner the policeman was replaced by John Peel pointing Go to Glastonbury festival go directly to Glastonbury festival but you could call in at the off licence on the way and pick up a crate of Newcastle Brown if you wanted to.

Winston cut back to the studio. "Hello deh, Rude Boy Winston here an' yu listen te Pirate Radio Skankdown, de show wid all ye favourite characters, music and sketches, dat was de misfit bunch deh."

"Dat right an' dit is DJ Dread, reddy te mash it up fe ye one time, seh Winston yu tell I dat Rock an' Roll chat herlier like a puzzle, an' dat only de firs' piece"

"Dat right DJ, yu tell I it always important te nor ya roots", answered Winston.

"Roots," said DJ, surprised. "Wi com' fe Jamaica, wha' Rock an' Roll haffe do wid Ska an' Reggae?"

"It all connected DJ, in one wey or anuddah, ye see as de show ago on," answered Winston.

"Dan connect it up mon, an pley I some Ska," said DJ.

"OK but firs' mi tell hoh ska com' te be."

Winston went on to say there are many factors contributing to the development of Ska and that he would try to tell it chronically.

In 1494 Columbus discovered a West Indian Island called Jamaica.

Two other islands in the West Indies, Trinidad and Tobago, had a local folk music called Calypso which was used to tell news over the islands.

During the early 1900s the Islands were populated by African slaves, some of who were transported to Jamaica – taking Calypso with them. Jamaica's version of this music was called Mento and was played with an upward stroke called the skank on the banjo or acoustic guitar.

Just like Calypso, the songs were about how they were living in poverty, poor housing and, like the Blues, a tongue in cheek – spicing it up with sexual innuendos.

After the Second World War, Jamaicans began to purchase radios. The Jamaican radio stations were similar to the BBC way of broadcasting, playing light Jazz and small talk. The radios could also pick up from the 500 miles away, including US southern coast transmissions from New Orleans, Miami and Memphis. These stations were playing Blues, Jump Jazz and R&B such as Fats Domino, Ray Charles and Count Bassie. It was these stations that the Jamaicans tuned in to.

There became a demand for this music and it was the Jazz Show bands that played these songs on the big lawns and in clubs such as The Glass Slipper and Silver Bucket. This was where the middle class were entertained and danced the night away.

Not everybody could afford radios or go to the clubs. The lower class went to the sound systems. These were mobile turntables with enormous speakers so big they were transported in furniture removal size trucks bringing the music Jump Jazz, R&B and Jamaican Boogie to the people.

In the '50s the two biggest sound system operators were Clement Seymour Dodd, better known as Sir Coxsone (named after his favourite Yorkshire cricketer) Dodd, whose system was called The Sir Coxsone downbeat, and Arthur "Duke" Reid, a former policeman known as the Trojan because he transported his sound system on a Trojan flat bed truck. Reid had opened an off licence called Treasure Isle where above, he would later run his studio and record label of the same name.

With these systems they influenced the Jamaican youth and controlled what they listened to. It was during these early days a musical war was played out between Dodd and Reid competing for the biggest crowd and selling the most alcohol. They themselves didn't physically fight, but instead they employed rebellious youths known as rude boys to go trash each other's equipment and fight with the crowds.

The rude boys took their look from American gangsters who wore black suits, thin ties and pork pie hats. They were unemployed youths who couldn't find work so found identity in forming gangs and working in the marijuana trade. Because they lived outside the law, scoffing at the law and crashing dances, they were also known as Scofflaws and Dance Crashers. Not only did they frighten public citizens, they were also feared by the police. Today the term rude boy /girl is used to describe a dedicated Ska fan.

Mad Axe Man interrupted, saying, "Thee thought tha' said tha' an tha' had helped rewrite this like, up te now it's all DJ and Winston's nostalgic clubs pubs and Ska venues."

"Hold your horses we're just getting to ours now," said 7 Bellies. "The home run, back to the off licence, next is The Devil's Arms."

"Well about bloody time," said Mad Axe Man, as he gulped from his bottle of Newcastle Brown.

Sniff "Yeah right," said Coke who was drinking heavily himself, "and next door we've got the Reading festival, three days of drinking maan, and next door to that is Donnington's Monsters of Rock."

"Aye that's more like it." said Mad Axe Man as he sunk his bottle down and opened another.

"Then we've got another station, Skaville, where we'll be pulling in at the end of this journey."

"Yeah and that's followed by Stonehenge," said 7 Bellies, "where you can get well chilled out, then it's another spin the bottle."

"What's that one?" said Pot Belly. "It says C/nueva de San Anton, 251/4A 3005 Murcia Espana. What's that mean? What's there, what's Murcia Espana?"

"Well I think you better say that Coke 'cause like I don't wanna spill the beans," said 7 Bellies.

Sniff. "Naa you'd wanna eat em wouldn't yer, yer fat bastard." and then started singing:

"You fat bastard, you fat bastard
You fat bastard, you fat bastard
You... Fat... Bastard!"

"*Ow.*" said Coke.

"I warned yer, no personal stuff maan," said 7 Bellies.

Coke, with a hand over his mouth and a thick lip, continued. *Sniff* "Seriously now, don't tell anyone right." He leaned forward and whispered, "That's where Speed's been hiding out the last five years."

"SPEED, SPEED." shouted Pot Belly "IS HE THERE, IS SPEED HIDING THERE?"

"*Shhh shhh,*" whispered Coke and 7 Bellies together.

Coke told the story of how they'd all got a bit out of it one night and they held up a petrol station with water pistols. It was all fun and games, they were just having a laugh but the coppers didn't see it that way and he and 7 Bellies at Her Majesty's pleasure served 12 months each.

Speed was having a piss around the back when the police came, saw all the blue lights flashing and legged it. He's been hiding out there in Spain since, playing a bit of guitar on the terraces entertaining the tourists and hatting them for tips to keep him in tequila and a rented room.

"Thee thought thee hadn't seen him for a while," said Mad Axe Man.

Sniff. "Well moving on, the last one just before you get to the off licence again is the Woodstock revival."

7 Bellies interrupted, "Where you get out your head and miss a few goes."

Winston told by the end of the '50s, travelling Mento bands that were playing local dances and weddings were influenced by American pop and began to get adventurous. Jamaican musicians were fusing Calypso and Mento with American Jazz and R&B, creating music called Shuffle. At this same time Rock and Roll was taking America and the world by storm, leaving Jazz and R&B in its shadows.

Jamaicans couldn't get to grips with this latest sound or dance to it, and because radios and record sales were now only playing Rock and Roll it was becoming harder and harder to find new Jazz or R&B records which had now become the old sounds.

Jamaica's Federal studios had opened in 1954 and because of the American music industry which now made it possible for music to reach all over the world, the next step for Jamaica was to start putting out their own material.

They began to record their own Mento records which were then played in bars reaching the middle class who had up to then only listened to Jazz. It soon went national and swept across the country, becoming the new big rage.

There was no copyright so musicians were free to record anyone's music. They began to record their own versions of what they had been listening to on the radio – Soul hits from Atlantis and Motown.

So as not to rely on what they had no control over, sound system operators began paying artists to record tracks. Often only a small number of these tracks were produced, which were known as specials (which is where the Two Tone band in 1979 took their name from) that were solely for the sound systems. Often the label would be scratched off so other sound systems wouldn't know what they were playing. This made each sound system unique, giving their crowd something the others didn't have.

The sound men would keep the track for several months exclusively for his crowd, they believing it was their tune. Later they would be printed and sold in larger numbers earning the producers a profit, especially if the record went high up in the charts. Musicians though were only paid the one recording fee.

Coke finished with, "Good hey, and we play it the same with dice but instead of using a hat, dog, ship, car, or an iron we just use..."

"BOTTLE TOPS," interrupted 7 Bellies. "Newcastle Brown, Thunderbirds, Holsten Pills, Special Brew, Red Stripe."

Sniff. "Anything that's close at hand really," said Coke.

Mad Axe Man, now eager to get started, said, "Come on then, thee'll be Holsten Pils."

To which Pot Belly argued, "Or I wanted to be Holsten Pils, I wanted to be that one; it's green, green's my favourite colour, tell him he can't have that one, I want that one."

7 Bellies, irritated by Pot Belly's continuous whining, told him, "Whoa stop moaning Pot Belly and take something else. 'Ere have a Black Jack."

"Oh thanks 7 Bellies, I like Black Jacks."

"Good. I'll be Newcastle brown," said 7 Bellies.

S*niff.* "And I'll be Thunderbirds."

Pot Belly excitedly asked, "Can I go first, can I, can I?"

"Mad Axe Man responded with, "Aye go on then, just stop whinging will tha?"

Pot Belly, picking up the dice, said "Oh thanks Axey." He shook and threw a five and a three, then counted out, "One, two three, four, five, six, seven."

Sniff "It's eight maan, five and three is eight."

"Is it? Is it Axey? Is five and three eight?" asked Pot Belly.

"Aye," answered Mad Axe Man. "Now get tha's Black Jack moving."

Pot Belly counted out, moving along the board one, two, three, four, five, six, seven, eight. "Holts shoe shop, Dr Marten retailers," he said.

Mad Axe Man picked up, shook the dice and threw a four and a three and moved his Holsten Pils bottle top, landing on spin the bottle. He spun the bottle. It stopped, pointing to 7 Bellies.

Coke told him, *Sniff* "You gotta pick up a card and read it out maan."

7 Bellies, slightly annoyed, replied with, "Whoa I know how to play the game. I helped bloody write it didn't I?"

7 Bellies picked up a card and read out, "You have won a Lemmy look-a-like competition, collect two pints from the bank and one pint from each player."

"I know him he's the lead singer of Motorhead," said Pot Belly, feeling clever.

Sniff. "Yeah he's all covered in warts, *ha ha* Axe Man Wart Face," mocked Coke.

Mad Axe Man, looking smug, said, "That'll be a pint each lads, so just pay up like."

Coke picked up the dice and shook a one and a four. He moved his bottle top along, saying "Thunderbirds are go", which put him on Camden Station. 7 Bellies threw a double five, stopping at festival where he sunk a quick half a crate, belched, and shook again. This time he rolled a one and a six which put him on spin the bottle. He spun the bottle, felt dizzy, shook his head with shoe laces of saliva swinging out the corners of his mouth, farted, belched again and with a boy grin on his face said, "Whao, that's better."

The bottle stopped spinning on Coke, who was feeling quite drunk himself. He picked up the card and had to focus before he read out, "Oh you sexy 7 Bellies you've won a wet T-shirt competition. Collect two pints from the bank and one pint from each player."

"Ha ha ha ha ha," laughed 7 Bellies who happily received his pints and duly drunk them one after another, licking his lips, rubbing his seven bellies. Speaking in belch language, he said, "I love my fatty fa."

Pot Belly shook and threw a double six.

Mad Axe Man said "Twelve, that'll put tha' on free beer then."

To which Pot Belly protested, "Oh I don't want free beer, I don't like beer, I like Tizer or Dandelion and Burdock."

Mad Axe Man's patience ran out and he swore, "Why don't tha go make tha self a cuppa tea," then added, "and tha can fuck tha' self an all, whilst tha's at it."

Pot Belly, not recognising sarcasm, said, "Oh shall I go put kettle on."

Coke, who was feeling more drunk by the minute, *sniffed*. "Naa, you're on a double, you've got to shake again, hurry up maan."

Pot Belly shook again, a double four, putting him on Toilet take a piss. "Oh hang on while I just go to toilet."

7 Bellies interrupted, "Hey you're on a double, you've gotta shake again."

Coke *sniffed*. "Yeah and when you've been to toilet, don't forget to shake when you're finished."

"Aye," said Mad Axe Man, "only twice though, else tha say tha's playing with thaself."

Pot Belly, not understanding any of the last comments, asked, "What do you mean playing with thaself."

7 Bellies threw an empty bottle of beer at him saying "Whao just shake will yer."

Pot belly picked up the dice for the third time and this time threw a two and a one which put his Black Jack on John Peel pointing across the other side of the board saying go to Glastonbury festival go directly to Glastonbury festival but you can call in at the off licence first and pick up a crate of Newcy Brown if you want to. Pot Belly complained, "But I don't want to go to Glastonbury festival with a crate of Newcastle brown. I don't like Newcastle Brown, I like Tizer or Dandelion and Burdock."

Mad Axe Man exploded. Jumping out of his seat he grabbed Pot Belly by the scruff of his neck and gave him a round of fucks, telling him he was a little moaning shite and to bloody grow up or he would throw him off the train. He then took the dice off him and said, "Now where's thee? Oh look thees on spin bottle, hey 7 Bellies tha still hasn't paid thee, thee's pint fer Lemmy look-a-like competition."

7 Bellies replied, "Naa maan, err, it looks like we're outta beer."

"What!" protested Mad Axe Man, "we can't be outta beer yet, we've only had a couple dozen, like when we were at station we had crates of the stuff, and a box a Thunderbird."

7 Bellies began to explain, "Whao, well like when you was busy loading your hog on the train maan, like all that beer was just like looking at us, like what was we supposed to do."

Coke now officially drunk, slurred, *ffsni* "Yeahitwasthereforthetakingmaan."

Mad Axe Man, his blood boiling over, threatened, "If tha's drunk all beer, thee'll kill tha."

7 Bellies reasoned, "Whao, I haven't drunk it all I've got some beer and Thunderbirds stashed in a real cool place maan, I'll go and get them."

"Aye an thee's coming with tha, in case tha drinks them before tha comes back like."

"*Ha ha ha*. Whao there's no catching you out Axe Man."

They both left the cabin staggering in high spirits, leaving Coke grinning to himself in a stupor and Pot Belly eating his Black Jack.

Winston told Coxanne Dodd was looking for a new sound and with the big Jazz musicians being the backbone of the Jamaican music industry he had the tools to do it with. Jamaica's independence was coming up on August 6th 1962, the economy was good and there was a feeling in the air of celebration and more time for creativity. Dodd told Cluet Johnson, the bass player from Clue J and the Blues Blasters – who used to greet his fans with skavoovie (some say the name ska comes from skavoovie) – that he wanted to fuse together Mento, Jazz and Jamaican R&B, Boogie.

Up until then all music structures were built up from the drum playing first, giving the rhythm. Ska changed the order to drum playing 2nd and 4th beat with guitar playing mentos up skank 2nd 3rd and 4th, joined by the piano playing 2nd and 4th. This was nearly all the right ingredients, they had something new, but something was still missing.

Living on top of each other in Kingston with mostly the same musicians (who would later become The Skatalites) playing on almost everyone else's productions, nothing could be kept secret for long. Soon Duke Reid, Byron Lee, King Edwards, Leslie Kong and Prince Buster were all competing for this new sound.

It was the latter Cecil Bustamente Campbell, better known as Prince Buster, who finely tuned it when he told Jah Jerry (Jerry Hines) on guitar to speed up. He said, "Change gear man, change gear". That up-tempo skank was the missing ingredient and as Byron Lee once said, "This is Ska."

Early Ska was almost all instrumental with a vocal percussion of "Hup hup hup chu ka chu ka" added in some tracks (A good example being Prince Busters "One Step Beyond") which comes from Pukamine, an African religion which was revived in 1834 – the year slaves were given Emancipation.

Because Ska wasn't such a big jump from Jamaican boogie or shuffle it sounded very Jamaican. Ska was pure dance music so it was easy for the sound system crowds to adapt as their own sound. Trombone player Rico Rodriquez has said "Once Ska was created, it exploded in Kingston, then all over the island."

The development of Ska came from the sound system operators seeing the crowd's reaction to new tracks. They could see what got the crowds going and what didn't.

The first Ska recordings were at Coxanne Dodd's Studio One 13 Brentford Road, Kingston which opened in '63.

As Winston finished, DJ took the mike and addressed the public.

"Hello deh, if yu jus' tune in, dis is Pirate Radio Skankdown, dreadly serious."

Dat was Rude boy Winston tellin' de history of Ska an' noh wi goin te pley ye som'. Dis is de orig-in-al fe De Ethiopians."

With the introduction complete he moved the record arm over and lowered the needle onto the record. A crackle came out of the speakers and across the airwaves as the needle skated across the outskirts of the '45. It came to the first groove and we heard Dillon's announcement followed by the brass section blowing out that sweet hypnotic melody:

Train to Skaville
Chike chike chike
Is this train to Skaville?
Is this train to Skaville?
Pick your seat

Chike chike chike

Everyone on board

Chike chike chike chike chike chike
Pshhh

Beep beep

Free man free
Free as a bird in a tree Beep beep

Is this
Is this
Is this

Train to Skaville

With the track finished, DJ told that The Ethiopians were founded by Leonard Dillon, born in Port Antonio.

He moved to Kingston in '64 and met Peter Tosh who liked his material and introduced him to The Wailers who introduced him to Sir Coxanne Dodd. He recorded two mento songs under the name Jack Sparrow at Studio One in '66 that didn't go anywhere. Dillon put The Ethiopians together with Stephen Taylor and Aston Morris, the latter of who left at the end of '66. Working in a factory, Dillon and Taylor persuaded their boss to finance a recording at Dynamic studios.

This was to be their first success, with the '67 Ska hit "Train to Skaville" on the W.I.R.L label making the UK top 40. Two other big hits was "Everything Crash" in '68 and "The Whip". There was a fascination with locomotives as they also had a single and LP titled "Engine 54" and another song "Train to Glory".

The Ethiopians went on to record Rock steady and Reggae with the "Reggae Power" album in '69. They always kept close to their roots, and inspired by Rastafarianism, sang about social issues in Jamaica – laying the foundations for Roots Reggae.

"Which way?" asked Axe Man.

7 Bellies stood swaying in the corridor, his feet rooted to the spot. It's one thing having a skin full sitting down, but standing up and contemplating walking in a moving train is another. He was trying to take control of his body, telling his feet he wanted to walk forwards. Only for that message to travel from his brain to his feet it had to first go through his stomach with many other thoughts coming in-between. More beer, pie and chips, The Devil's Arms, more beer, pie and chips. Well maybe not so many other thoughts, but nonetheless they delayed the message.

"Get tha's arse inte gear, thee's dying a thirst," said Axe Man.

7 Bellies stood like a rhinoceros, staring at its target about to charge. He still couldn't move his feet, but over

the years of being faced with this problem on a nightly basis he'd developed a technique to overcome this small detail. Concentrating, and after what seemed like five minutes, he willed his neck to move his head forwards, this being the shortest route for his brain to send a message. He still managed to think more beer in-between, however the message reached its destination and moved his head forwards.

This would inevitably move his shoulders forwards which would take him to slowly lean forwards until he would be off balance. Then it was just a matter of relying on the natural reaction of stopping yourself falling. Your feet automatically move forwards to counter balance the body. This was a technique that usually worked, or he otherwise fell round on his seven bellies.

Chapter Three

MURDER

7 Bellies' technique worked and Mad Axe Man followed him down the corridor in to the next carriage where from one of the cabins they heard what sounded like someone jumping up and down, singing, "I'm gobbin' on life"

Another voice was heard to be singing, "I'm taking my life"

As the first voice sang again "I'm gobbin' on life"

They sung together, " I'm just gobbin' on life"

Mad Axe Man asked, "What the bloody hell's going on here like?"

7 Bellies answered, "Whao that's Animal and Semi."

"Sounds like a couple Punks te thee," said Axe man.

"Yeah they are maan," said 7 Bellies.

"Does tha nor where t' beer and Thunderbirds is like?" asked Mad Axe Man.

"Whao it's down this way, I got it stashed in a real cool place and that," answered 7 Bellies.

"Aye well it just better be there or tha's in big trouble."

They entered the next carriage, where a sharp dressed man with a tongue to match stood in the doorway and welcomed them with these words:

"Yo dudes you wanna buy shoes. Then slip slide right in through the door. This place has got everything and more. All you need from birth to death, or if you're in love, marriage. Here at the Zoot's bargain train to Skaville carriage."

"Naa thanks Zoot maan we're on a mission," said 7 Bellies.

"A bloody wild goose chase thee reckons," added Mad Axe Man. "If tha's leading thee up a blind alley, thee'll wrap tha's bollocks round tha's neck."

"Whao keep cool maan," reasoned 7 Bellies. "It's just a bit further up, we're nearly there."

As they left Zoot's carriage and entered the next they came face to face with a figure all dressed in bright spotty clothes red boots and a top hat. "Hello pretty boys, I'm now juggling rings, do you want to see me spin a ring on my finger, or I can toss them up and catch them by putting my hand through the middles, ooh I've had my arm in rings up to my shoulder."

"Whao hello Jerry," said 7 Bellies as they walked on and told Mad Axe Man that Jerry Juggler was a bit of a shirt lifter but harmless enough. Mad Axe Man with an appalled look on his face said "What, a gaylord, a puff, a gender bender, a bloody babber stabber?"

7 Bellies answered "Oh I don't think he's a real one, just a bit limp in the wrists, probably all that juggling."

Mad Axe Man, remembering where they where supposed to be going, asked again, "Just where exactly is this beer?"

7 Bellies, somewhat disorientated from all the beer they'd drunk, plus the moving train, answered, "Nearly there, I think it's in the next carriage… or in the next one… or the one after that."

Mad Axe Man losing his patience said, "Thee's had about a bloody nough of this, tha's taking the piss, tha must think thee was born under a bloody Christmas tree."

Just then everything went pitch black. 7 Bellies reacted by saying, "Oh the lights have gone out, you got 50p for the meter?"

Mad Axe Man answered, "The lights haven't gone out, we're going through a tunnel tha daft bugger."

"Well I can't see a bloody thing maan," said 7 Bellies.

"It takes thee back te when thee were down pit tha nors." When Mad Axe Man didn't get any reaction he asked 7 Bellies, "Where is tha, what's tha lurking about at?"

Thinking 7 Bellies was hiding he said,"Aye let's play murder in't dark eh? 7 Bellies thee's coming te get tha 7 Bellies." Then a blood curdling *Aaagghhh* was to be heard, followed by a thunk... then... silence.

The blood curdling *Aaagghhh* fell on the ears of Sir Johnny O.B.E Flannel, whose compartment was in the same carriage. Johnny reacted by saying,

"What time's happy hour? Is it time to sing? I don't know I can't see a thing. What was that noise, it sounded like a thunk. Oh I must be blind drunk."

"If everyting is not wrong – everyting is alright. Dis is DJ Dread an ye listen te Pirate Radio Skankdown. Seh why don' wi get on down an' do som' more skankin', Winston pley I som' music."

"Dat right DJ, ya de DJ and I de selector."

Winston picked out another Bad Manners single, telling listeners "Special Brew" was released September '80. The song was written while recording their debut album "Ska 'N' B" when they'd ran out of material to fill the album. They were sitting, drinking crates of Special Brew and had a tune with words that sounded like a love song. That was too sloppy for Manners but a love song about beer was something else. The song was written in five minutes and reached number three in the charts. Winston finished by saying it was the B side he was going to play, a song that's almost an instrumental telling of a steam engine. He set the needle on the record.

And Buster announced:

IVOR THE ENGINE AND HIS FANTASTIC JOURNEYS THROUGH OUTA SPACE...

Shake a leg

Ivor the engine

Ivor, Ivor, why are you following me

IS THIS THE END OF IVOR THE ENGINE OR WILL THERE BE MORE CONCLUDING EPISODES... LISTEN.

The Hawkwind was approaching Folkstone in Kent near Dover when the red light shone again in the engine, giving Michael the cue to ask his father who else made their mark in the early R&R years. Seamus answered.

Charlie Edward Anderson Berry – Chuck Berry – famous for his duck walk, is another one of the pioneers of R&R, he is appropriately named "The prime minister of R&R". It is quoted by John Lennon that "if you tried to give R&R another name you might call it Chuck Berry".

He was influenced by Louis Jorden and T-Bone Walker, a blues guitarist/singer who was playing with his teeth and in strange positions inspiring a young kid called Hendrix to pick up a guitar. Berry had been playing the blues since he was 14 and as a young man joined up with The Johnnie Johnson Trio and within a short time became the leader of the band. He approached Muddy

Waters for advice who pointed him to Leonard Chess at Chess Records.

Berry wrote the first single by an Afro-American to reach the top 10 in the hot 100 with the'55 R&R record "Maybelline". It was based on the '38 "Ida Red", an old country and western song from Bob Willis. "Maybelline" went to number one in the R&B charts and number five in the hot 100. Maybelline is about a girl driving a Cadillac Coupe de Ville, with Berry chasing in a V8 Ford.

His next hit was inspired by Berry's sister Lucy who was always playing classical on the home piano. Berry wanted to play his own style which is what "Roll Over Beethoven" is all about." Move over Beethoven /Tchaikovsky, here's R&R." It reached 29 in the top 100 Chart in '56. The same year Berry starred in the film "Rock, Rock, Rock," and in '57 he toured with The Everly Brothers and Buddy Holly,

Another song was inspired in '58 by another piano player – Johnnie Johnson, who had by now acquired a taste for alcohol. Berry told him, "Johnny B Goode". Goode was spelt so because Berry was born in Goode Avenue St Luis. The song has been quoted as having the most famous opening riff in R&R history. It's about the American dream, a poor country boy who couldn't read or write so good but sure could play guitar and from hard work, one day might have his name in lights. The song reached number two in the R&B chart and number eight in the pop chart.

In '59 Berry starred in the film "Go Johnny Go" and in'64 "No Particular Place To Go" reached number two in the US and number three in the UK. '72 Gave Berry his only number one in the hot 100 chart and also a number one in the UK with "My Ding a Ling". Berry has inspired countless musicians including Angus Young of AC/DC and Bruce Springsteen who is also a big fan..

Mad Axe Man woke up grinning, still high from the night before as he thought to himself, it feels like thee's on a fucking roller coaster. That was some night in The Devil's Arms last night thee can't remember a fucking thing.

He lay uncomfortable and felt he was not in his bed. Then where was he? Had he gone back to someone's house? It was something he often did after a night in the Arms. He opened his eyes and immediately closed them again, feeling a blinding pain from the light which shot straight through his head.

His senses were coming back and not only did he now have a hangover but it tasted like someone had shit in his mouth as well. To make things worse it felt like he really was on a roller coaster, the room was moving, making him dizzy and nauseating him.

He tried to remember what he'd seen for that split second that his eyes had been open, but he hadn't recognised anything. It wasn't 7 Bellies' place – he lived in a wig wam in his mother's backyard. She'd kicked him out the house years ago because of his alternative lifestyle, basically choosing not to work, and live off social benefits, all of which he drank at The Devil's Arms.

He wasn't at Coke's place either because he lived in a flat which smelt musty from not being cleaned or decorated in years. That split second his eyes were open he'd seen light coming in from both sides as if he was in a passage way or a corridor. So he wasn't at a festival – that was usually fields of mud and tents. So where was he?

He thought again of The Devil's Arms. He always went to The Devil's Arms. Then he remembered a meeting. That was it: Pirate Radio Skankdown, all the cast were there, they were planning something. He had a vision of himself riding down a train track on his Harley. Then like a flood it all came over him at once. York, Selby, Leeds, they'd hijacked a steam train, they were going to Skaville. It all went dark, there was a tunnel....

More of his senses were coming back. He now felt a wet sensation down his leg. Then slowly as the possibilities began to swirl in his mind, a realisation began to form and an embarrassing thought entered his head as he said out loud to himself, "Oh no thee has'nt pisse'd thee self as thee?"

He lay there feeling sorry for himself. He was totally sick and miserable. He tried pretending it wasn't hapening, that it was just a dream... but it was a fucking noisy, uncomfortable dream he thought. He felt the train rumbling along, rocking him side to side. And now, he felt, not only was his leg wet but it was sticky too.

Then like a jolt, murder in the dark shot through his head. He automatically called out –

"7 Bellies! 7 Bellies man!" He sat up, opened his eyes, and got the fright of his life as he saw he was covered in blood. "What the bloody hell has thee done?" He called out again "7 Bellies! 7 Bellies man!" As he jumped up, he shouted, "Oh SHITE."

"Michael an' Saemus deh, not only feeding and driving de engine but informing us an' de listener' at Pirate Radio Skankdown all 'bout R&R," said Winston.

"Jah... Rastafari and dis is ya host DJ Dread, seh Winston ya was tellin' earlier 'bout de firs' wave of Ska, haf ya got any more interesting facts fe de listeners?"

Winston said that during the slave years at carnival time the slaves were allowed to take on the role of Lords, Kings, Dukes etcetera. This was a tradition which was kept and followed on by Ska producers, musicians and performers which is why we have Prince Buster, King Hammond, king Tubby, Lord Tanamo, Sir Coxxanne Dodd and Duke Reid.

Mad Axe Man staggered back to their compartment and burst in saying, "Lads, lads."

Pot Belly was first to react and answered, "What's a matter Axey, where's 7 Bellies?"

"Thee don't nor."

Coke came around and looked up. Seeing Mad Axe Man he *sniffed*, "Like what's all that blood maan?"

"Thee don't nor, we went through a tunnel, t'were all dark, thee must have fallen over and passed out or something, 'cause next thing thee nors, is thee wakes up on t'floor all covered in blood, and like 7 Bellies had disappeared."

Coke, looking bewildered, *sniffed*. "Weird maan," and being really concerned for 7 Bellies asked, "and like, where's the beer and Thunderbirds?"

"Thee don't nor we never got to it."

Pot Belly, looking Mad Axe Man up and down, put two and two together, got five and started accusing. "You've killed 7 Bellies 'cause he drank all the beer. Watch him Coke I'm going to go tell Mr Dread." Pot Belly jumped up and ran out of the compartment, leaving Coke and Mad Axe Man looking at each other in disbelief.

"Dat interesting facts deh Winston, I an' I feel de show settlin' down noh wi leave dem Babylon behind, wi can relax an' tek tings eeasy, Winston wha' wi got lined up fe de show, who com' nex'."

"Oh we got –" Suddenly there came a knocking at the door.

"Mr Dread, Mr Dread, something awful's happened," said Pot belly as he burst in through the door.

DJ took his radio show seriously and worked on it professionally, so was not used to being interrupted while on air. He looked with a screw face as he said, "Wha' dis Pot Belly, ya no in dis sketch."

"It's Axey, it's 7 Bellies, he's covered in beer, 'cause he drank all the blood, so he killed him, and now he's all dead."

"What ya talk about, who's killed who and drank all his blood, ya make no sense mon."

"Axey's killed him, Axey's killed my 7 Bellies bruvver man, he drank all the beer and he's covered in blood."

"Let me get dis straight, Mad Axe Man drank all de beer, den him kill 7 Bellies and cover him in blood."

"Yeah, a fink so, oh I don't know, you'd better come Mr Dread, come and tell Axey off."

"Wi in de middle of a show Pot Belly, mi cyaan com' pley one a ye games."

"It's not a game Mr Dread, it's true, it's true."

"Wha' ya tink Winston?"

"It all soun' a bit confusin' DJ."

"It all soun' very confusing, why if Mad Axe Man kill 7 Bellies, it would be..." Colour slowly drained out of DJ's face. His heartbeat raced, and his knuckles went white as he clenched his fists. His eyes were wide with fear as in his head he heard The Selecter's Gabba shout out **MURDER** followed by Pauline Black singing **MURDER OOW MURDER, OOW MURDER, I SAY MURDER –**

DJ shook his head, saying, "Tank yer Selecter but wi don' nor dat."

Winston, thinking he was talking to him, said, "Wha' dat DJ?"

"Err nuttin, mi seh nuttin, err mi no feel good, seh Winston why don' ye pley an' introduce de nex' track."

Winston, always eager to share his knowledge, told the listeners that he was going to play a track from a man who was and still is the first and only Jamaican artist to enter the US charts with purely Jamaican music – making the top 10 too. He had the first Reggae song to top the UK charts. The year was '68, the song was The Israelites – a re-release of which made the top ten in the UK charts again in '75 – and the artist was Desmond Adolphus Dacres, better known as Desmond Dekker.

Born in St Andrew, he grew up in Kingston and attended the Alpha Boys School. He worked as a welder in Kingston alongside Bob Marley. He was always singing and was encouraged by his workmates to audition, which he did in '61 for Coxanne Dodd's Studio One and Duke Reid's Treasure Isle. Neither was impressed.

He auditioned for Leslie Kong's label Beverlys in front of Derick Morgan long before Morgan himself, who was later to become the label's biggest star. However, Kong waited until the right song came along before he released a single. That was in '63 and the song was "Honour Your Mother and Father". It was a hit.

When Desmond first went to England his record company bought him a suit. The first thing he did in true rude boy style was to cut off the bottom six inches of his trousers to emphasise his white socks and loafer shoes. Another song, "007 Shanty Town", idolising the rude boys, made him an icon with the Jamaican rude boys and the British Mods who followed his tour.

With this told Winston announced: "Dis track taken from de Early Beverly Sessions, '63 to '68, from de album "Rudi Got Soul". Winston flicked a switch and "Rude Boy Train" was sent out through the air waves.

The rude boy train is coming now
The rude boy train is coming now.
Dippy dippy doey, dippy dippy doey

As the track played, DJ Winston and Pot Belly left the studio with DJ saying, "Com' wi mus' check dis out, weh ya carriage Pot Belly."

"It's just next door Mr Dread".

The three of them left the studio and walked down the corridor into the next carriage. On reaching the compartment they entered. DJ's opening line was, "Irie."

Sniff "How's it going maan," replied Coke.

"Noo then how is tha?" greeted Axe Man.

"I an' I fine te Pot Belly com' interrupt de show an' tell I someting 'bout ya drinkin' blood covered in beer an' killin' 7 Bellies."

Rude boy boat is coming now
Rude boy boat is coming now
Dippy dippy doey, dippy dippy doey

Looking at Pot Belly, Mad Axe Man reacted. "Well tha's a lying little toe rag thee didn't bloody do it right. We went through a tunnel, it were all dark, thee must have fallen over and banged thee's 'ead, 'cause next thing thee nors, is waking up on t'floor covered in blood and 7 Bellies was gone. Thee was a bit confused like and thee came straight back ere."

DJ stood recounting everything Mad Axe Man had just told him. He then asked Coke, who was starry eyed and still out of his tree, what he knew about all this. Coke reacted with a *sniff*. "About what maan, like we're going to Skaville and that yeah."

Rude boy plane is coming now
Rude boy plane is coming now
Dippy dippy doey, dippy dippy doey

"Right," said DJ. "You tree stey here, don' nobody leave dis carriage Winston an' I go look fe 7 Bellies."

Coke, suddenly waking up, *sniffed*. "Yeah maan, like how is he?"

Pot Belly asked, "What if we want to go to toilet Mr Dread? Can we leave to go to toilet? Can we, can we?"

"I an' I be back wid all dis sorted out 'fore den. Winston... com'."

Rude boy get up a circuit chart
Rude boy get up a circuit chart
Dippy dippy doey, dippy dippy doey

As they stood out in the corridor Winston asked, "Wha' 'ye tink DJ?"

"Mi don' nor, I an' I don' waan believe it tru', wha' wi need is a detective, someone te solve dis murder err mystery err dis suspense." As DJ was saying mystery and suspense, he heard a voice in his head. Again it was The Selecter's Pauline Black singing, "**I say murder.**" DJ shook his head and said, "Cool it Pauline". Winston, not hearing what was going through DJ's head, gave him a puzzled look. And from out of nowhere the man in blue stood before them saying in his New York accent, "Excuse me gentlemen, but I couldn't help overhearing murder, mystery and suspense."

Rude boy a loot an a shoot an a wail
Rude boy a loot an a shoot an a wail
Dippy dippy doey, dippy dippy doey

DJ was somewhat startled and irritated from the interruption. The man in blue could hear it in his voice when he spoke. "Wha' dis, Winston and I, in de middle of a show wid one fe de cas' missin'."

"**Murder**" shouted Gabba in DJ's head, who froze with fright and immediately went pale, he shook his head as the figure in blue spoke.

"Perhaps I can be of assistance."

"Mi don' see hoh, ya a janitor." Then, calming down and feeling ashamed, he apologised. "Sorry mi don' mean te soun' rude, aldough mi was a Rude Boy, I a Rasta noh."

"Mi still a Rude Boy."

"Yes Winston, still a Rude Boy, so mi no racist or prejudice, mi don' judge people by de colour fe him skin fe him dress, wi all bruddah's an' sistah's, so tell I janitor, hoh can ya be fe assistance?"

Double o seven is back on the scene
Double o seven is back on the scene
Dippy dippy doey, dippy dippy doey

"Well in these blue overalls with matching blue hat with janitor printed in big yellow letters, I do look a bit like a janitor."

"Ya look exactly like a janitor."

"In fact, I just fought a battle with a turd you wouldn't believe the size of. I had to break it in half over my knee and shove it round the U bend with my bare hands. But under this blue cap and overalls are my trilby, my raincoat and my badge that says Matt Davis, Special Agent."

"No mon, it seh Matt Davis Toilet Duty," pointed out DJ.

"Oh sorry, I got demoted," said Matt, as he remembered back to New York and told The Weasel case.

It was 11pm Friday night and I was ready to hit the sack, but as usual I was just home from work, tired hungry and smelling like a wrestler's jock strap. It felt like I'd been wearing my clothes for a week, and when I thought about it... I had. I took a shower and put on my lucky Scooby Doo boxer shorts. Why did I put them on? Because I was in need of some luck.

I'd been working on a case around the clock for three months, trying to track down a gangster code named The Weasel, called so because he was as slippery as a... as a... well he was a slippery elusive character and we couldn't catch him.

Where was my wife June? Or was it Jane? I couldn't remember. I seemed to remember we'd got divorced somewhere along the line, married nine years. I saw her three weeks. I made myself a coffee, something I'd only recently learnt to do. I'd always thought it came out of a machine outside the office. Too tired to cook, I threw left over cheeseburgers in the microwave, set the dial and pressed the button. Modern technology is moving so fast these days. Why, I hear you can even get pocket sized calculators now.

With coffee and cheeseburgers down me, I lay on the bed and closed my eyes. The phone rang. It was the office. The Weasel had been spotted in a stolen pink Cadillac the other side of town. It was my case and the office wanted me on it now.

I grabbed the car keys and ran out, running down the street I realised I was only wearing my lucky Scooby Doo boxer shorts. It was the first lead we'd had on The Weasel in six weeks so there was no time to go back to the apartment and dress. I was Matt Davis, Special Agent, and I had a job to do.

I turned the key and the feds' Pontiac T-bird kicked into life. It would take me ten minutes to reach the other side of town, but I knew a shortcut that could get me there in fifteen.

The office had radioed me the stolen Caddy's plate – P155 O double FF – piss off shouldn't be too hard to find. I cruised down 42nd street, looking.

I went up 43 and across 44. The street was lined with hookers. I saw Mrs Jones, my next door neighbour, and gave her a wave. Going up 45 I spotted the Caddy turning at the end of the street. I put my blue flashing light with siren on and floored the accelerator. The chase was on.

The Weasel shot across 47 and turned down 49. If I knew the town like I thought I did, I could take 48 and cut him off outside the city park. Damn. As I got there he'd U-turned and was going back up 49.

I administered a hand brake turn, spun full circle and carried on into the city park, demolishing a statue of Abraham Lincoln.

I drove straight through the park out on to 50. There he was two cars in front of me. I overtook and pulled alongside the Caddy. The weasel pointed a revolver and fired. I swerved over the highway, my hand fumbling in the glove compartment. Rubik's Cube, socks, tin opener... pistol. I returned the fire.

He jumped a red light with me hot on his tail, turning left and then right, straight across the entrance to the city bus station and round the back. I had him: there was no way out.

Except the bus route that went straight out the back up to 4th Avenue. Damn, I'd lost him.

I kept up my speed racing down 4th Avenue and up 5th where I spotted him again. Pedal to the metal, I caught him at the end of 6th.

I rammed him over into a row of trash cans, jumped out, pulled him from his seat and told him to spread 'em. It was only now I realised The Weasel had done it again. It was no longer a pink Cadillac but a yellow Ford Mustang and somehow The Weasel had turned into a nun.

The state police circled me and told me to lay down my weapon.

There I was, 12 midnight, with a written off feds' Pontiac, a demolished Abraham Lincoln to my credit, standing in Scooby Doo boxer shorts, pointing a gun at a nun telling her to spread 'em.

"They threw the book at me... my telephone... my stool... my desk... and me... out of the Special Agents. And that's how I ended up being demoted to Matt Davis, foot patrol."

Rude boy get up a circuit chart
Rude boy get up a circuit chart
Dippy dippy doey, dippy dippy doey

"Tcha mon," said DJ understandingly, "ya an old member fe de show, mi no recognise ya in ya disguise, ya still Matt Davis Special Agent te mi. Ya investigate dis 7 Bellies Mad

Axe Man ting, Winston an' I mus' go back te de studio an' do de show."

Double o seven is back on the scene
Double o seven is back on the scene
Dippy dippy doey, dippy dippy doey

Matt Davis stood in the corridor, weighing up his tactics. He was saying to himself, No time to dippy dippy doey, I got a case to solve. Now let's look at this the same way we unblock a toilet. Start from the bottom and work our way up to the top. Or sometimes you have to start from the top and work your way to the bottom. The top and the bottom of this case is: 7 Bellies is missing, presumed murdered by Mad Axe Man. As I can't interview 7 Bellies I have to start with Mad Axe Man and he's at the top of my list. Top of the train, from there I'll work my way down to the bottom.

"*He he he...* jah jah children, ya listen te Pirate Radio Skankdown wid Desmond Dekker deh mi sorry fe ya experience som' interference earlier when Pot Belly com' in an' interrupt de show. I an' I haf a likkle hiccups wid 7 Bellies an' Mad Axe Man. Don' worry 'bout a ting 'cause every likle ting goin' te be alright. Mi tink deh a perfectly natural explanation fe dat."

This was followed by silence as again DJ froze and the colour drained from his face. He heard voices in his head – this time The Selecter's Pauline Black with Gabba singing together:

Murder, I say murder, ooh yeah murder,
I say murder, oow yeah murder, that's what I
really want to do.

Winston shook him out of his trance by nudging his shoulder and saying, "Hello everybody wi seem te haf

som' technical problem deh, DJ's microphone no work."
Winston gave the microphone a tap and a *donk* was heard
over the air waves.

"OK tank ya Winston as I seh a perfectly natural
explanation I an' I jus' bump in te an old friend who gonna
check it out. Who bettah te ge' te de bottom fe dis dan...
him like wha' lieutenant Colombo is te private detectives,
him like wha' Tommy Cooper is te magic, it dat bungling
dithering appear' him don' nor wha' him doin'... it Matt
Davis Special Agent.' DJ then tuned in to the misfits'
compartment to listen in.

After making his way up to their compartment,
Matt entered and introduced himself. "Good afternoon
gentlemen. Matt Davis toilet duties Special Agent. I'm
here to investigate the disappearance of a Mr 7 Bellies
and ask for your cooperation in clearing up this matter."

Mad Axe Man protested, "Thee didn't bloody do it
reight?"

Pot Belly accused, "You did, you did, you killed my 7
Bellies bruvver man."

Coke, still looking bleary eyed, caught some of the
conversation and joined in. "Yeah like where is 7 Bellies I
haven't seen him for like ages maan."

Matt Davis, feeling his authority slipping away, took a
step forward and said, "I'll be asking the questions and I'd
like to start with you Mr Pot Belly. You say Mr Axe Man
here killed your 7 Bellies brother man. What evidence do
you have?"

"I know he did, he must have done, we was playing Oh
yeah alcoholy and 7 Bellies drunk all the beer and Axey
said he would kill him."

Mad Axe Man in his protest admitted it. "Well course
thee said that, thee were annoyed at time, but it were just
a figure a speech like."

Matt Davis looked earnestly at Pot Belly and asked,

"Mr Pot Belly I address this question to you. Did you see Mr Mad Axe Man here kill your brother 7 Bellies?"

Pot Belly was forced to admit that no, he didn't – adding that they'd gone down the train somewhere looking for some beer and Thunderbirds that 7 Bellies had hidden somewhere with only Mad Axe Man coming back covered in blood.

Matt Davis looked Mad Axe Man up and down and confirmed, "Mr Axe Man you are in fact covered in blood and the empty holster in your belt indicates your axe is missing which could be the murder weapon. Mr Axe Man, I put it to you. Did you kill 7 Bellies?"

Mad Axe Man protested his innocence again. "No thee bloody didn't reight, tha's not taking that gutter snipes word for it is tha?"

Matt seizing the moment believing he'd got the case solved asked "Then how do you account for the blood on your clothing, your axe and Mr 7 Bellies both being missing".

"Well it's like thee told DJ Dread and Winston. We went te get some beer and Thunderbirds that 7 Bellies said he'd hidden somewhere in a safe cool place. Then it all went dark, we went through a tunnel and thee must have fallen over and banged thee's 'ead, 'cause next thing thee nors, is thee's waking up on t'floor covered in blood and 7 Bellies were gone."

Matt questioned further. "And your axe was missing?"

"Mad Axe, looking lost for words, answered, "Iye thee suppose so."

"Do you have any witnesses to this?"

Mad Axe Man, now frustrated, feeling accused and not having the answers, swore. "How does thee bloody nor, it were pitch black thee couldn't see a bloody thing."

"Think. Did you see anyone while you were with 7 Bellies? Anyone at all who can account for your statement, it could mean a lot."

"Well now thee thinks about it Iye, we did see some people."

Matt asked, "And do you know who?"

"Not really, the were a couple a Punks like jumping up and down somewhere, then the were someone trying to sell us something. Iye he'd turned his carriage into a shop, looked like Ali- Babba's Emporium."

Matt, writing this down, pressed. "Anyone else? Can you think of anyone else?"

"Aye, some bloody puff dressed up in spotty clothes."

"And you spoke to these people?"

"Well not really. 7 Bellies did though."

"But they did witness you with Mr 7 Bellies?"

"Iye thee reckons so."

Pot Belly, seeing this was not going the way he wanted, butted in. "We know he was with him, he went out with my 7 Bellies bruvver man and he killed him Mr Toilet Duties, he killed my 7 Bellies bruvver man."

Matt told Pot Belly to calm down as Mad Axe Man denied killing 7 Bellies again. Although his axe was missing and he was covered in blood, making him the number one suspect, his statement still had to be checked out to see if there was any other evidence and both the body and murder weapon had to be found.

Coke, feeling it was time he contributed something to the proceeding said, *sniff*, "Wow it sounds like Cluedo. Whodunit maan? Was it the butler or Mr Peacock *ha ha*." Pot Belly queried, "Who's Mr Peacock? I don't know a Mr Peacock."

Matt answered, "He's a player in a board game," then addressed Coke sternly, "You don't seem to be taking this very seriously Mr Cain. Do you know something we don't and if so perhaps you'd like to share it with us."

Coke *sniffed*. "Well, like life is too serious maan, and yeah I would like to share something with you, but I haven't got much left *sniff* if you know what I mean, and like it's a long way to Skaville maan."

Coke not being a suspect, Matt disregarded his innuendo and turned his attention back to Mad Axe Man. He requested a blood sample and that they all remain in the cabin while he checked Mad Axe Man's statement. Then he exited the cabin.

"Overcome de devil wid a ting call love, Pirate Radio Skankdown here an' dat was Matt Davis an dem raasclaats dat mess up I show. Matt him straighten dat out so I an' I can get on down an' do som' more skankin'. Seh Winston it dark outside."

"Dat 'cause we goin' tru' de Channel Tunnel. It 31 miles long, an 'cause wi noh 250 feet undah de English Channell mi goin' te pley a nudder track fe dat Mr Blubber Belly and him Bad Manners."

Winston said that, lucky for the listeners, on the "Looney Tunes" album Ivor made a comeback. He was having another adventure with Buster telling the story backed by the band to take you on a musical journey, as he lowered the record arm over the fourth track on side two of the album.

And Buster Bloodvessel announced...

THE CONTINUING STORY OF IVOR THE ENGINE AND HIS ADVENTURES UNDER THE SEA... shake a leg,

Ivor The Engine,

You're getting deeper Ivor,

It's dark down here,

Turn on your floodlights,

ah ha, the buried treasure,

But look out, Ivor, there is a giant squid upon us,

But Ivor fights and escapes unmarked,

A lobster... run Ivor,

Oooooooooooh it's putting the willies up me,

Aaaghh Ivor, Ivor The Engine whooaggh,

Ivor, Ivor,

Look closely Ivor there's the buried treasure,

Now let's head for the surface,

Ivor The Engine
And how he escaped with
A full quarter of a million in gold bullion.

As Ivor headed for the surface so too did The Hawkwind, coming up in Coquelles, Pas-de-Calais. Michael and Seamus had just finished frying a brunch of eggs, bacon, beans and a fried slice on the polished shovel in the furnace, all washed down with cans of Guinness as they approached the first disused tunnel they would be hiding in for the day.

The Hawkwind left the main track. As it slowed, Matt looked out the window observing that they were driving past what on first sight appeared to be a shanty town on the other side of a long running wooden fence. On a second look he saw that it was allotments, and that the structures were little sheds the gardeners had built – mostly from posts, old doors, pallets and left over planks – to house their few garden tools and wheelbarrows. Then he saw a pile of railway sleepers stacked along the side of the track followed by a wall of bricks and then darkness as the train entered the tunnel and pulled to a halt.

The cast had strict orders that no one was allowed to leave the train. It was the rule that when the train stopped, everybody slept. Only Michael and Seamus the engineers would work through the morning, cleaning out the furnace and draining the boiler to cool the engine. They would then themselves sleep until dusk when they would start preparing the engine, checking the dampers which allowed air to flow in to the fire box. They would fill the sand boxes which would distribute sand on to the rails and stop the four big driving wheels from spinning.

By 9.30pm, the 5,000 gallon tender would have been filled with water, while rags soaked in paraffin would be lit on a shovel and thrown on to the coals in the furnace. And, like he would every night, Seamus would recite Jerry Lee Lewis and say, "Great balls of fire." It would take two and a half hours for the water to reach boiling point.

Chapter Four

SOMEBODY GOT MURDERED

It was midnight, and with all the local train services closed down for the night, it meant The Hawkwind, now primed and up to temperature, could leave the tunnel to further their journey.

As the train backed out of the tunnel, Matt, being ever alert, looked out the window to observe the whole landscape and horizon, which was lit up by the full moon.

For a moment Matt felt lost. He didn't recognise anything from where they were. It was as if the whole landscape had changed. They had driven straight into the tunnel this morning and reversed straight out at midnight, but something struck him as being out of place or rather not being in place at all.

The stacked pile of sleepers weren't there anymore and neither was the fence. The shanty town had completely disappeared – all the little garden sheds were gone and trees had simply vanished.

Matt assured himself they were all there this morning.

As Seamus threw an arm full of garden hoses clear from the train, Michael was dragging planks of wood and branches by the handful and pushing them in the furnace. The Hawkwind steamed ahead. Seamus blew the whistle as The Hawkwind rounded a bend to warn any night time scavengers that might have wandered on to the track. The red light came on showing Pirate Radio Skankdown was back on the air and Winston wanted them to tell some more about Rock and Roll. So Seamus did:

Richard Wayne Penneman – Little Richard – was another one of the artists responsible for laying the foundations of R&R and Glam Rock.

His first hit was in October '55 with a song called "Tutti Frutti". The story goes that a producer, Robert Bumps Blackwell, was trying to break him in to the Rock and Roll market when after about half a day in the studio with musicians from Fats Domino's band they couldn't get a song that would do it. During the break Little Richard played a practice song which went,

> *"A wop bop a loo mop a good god damn* (which was a sort of capello drum intro)
> *Tutti Frutti loose booty*
> *If it don't fit, don't force it*
> *You can grease it, make it easy"*

"A wop bop a loo mop" had come from Richard while having to wash so many dishes at a Greyhound bus station. It was something he would answer his boss back with; he could get away with it because his boss didn't understand it.

The original title, "Tutti Frutti Loose Booty", was one of his songs he'd perfected singing around the gay clubs. The producer thought that was the song they were looking for but the lyrics weren't appropiate for the American public. A young woman Dorothy Labostrie, who was always hanging around the studios, and who fancied herself as a songwriter, was given the song to change the lyrics. An hour later it was recorded as "Tutti Frutti".

"A wop bop a loo lop a lop bam boo
Tutti Frutti over routie, tuttie frutti over routie
all rooty (pronounced aw rooty – meaning alright)
Tuttie Fruttie all rooty, tuttie frutti all rooty
Tooty frutti all rooty"

It went up the rhythm and blues charts in Nov '55 and reached number two in early '56. The song broke a black artist through to the white market. However, he was not entered into the main charts.

In those days there was no copyright so it was common as soon as anybody had a hit for others to also record it. White singer Pat Boone, a successful pop singer, had 38 top 40 singles (mostly R&B covers) including Fats Domino's "Ain't That A Shame". He covered Richard's "Tutti Frutti", and had a bigger hit with it than Richard. It entered the main charts.

Richard said of Boone, "His version was on the whites' dressing table (keeping appearances for their parents) while mine was in the drawer. They liked mine better."

Between Blackwell and Richard they decided to record the next song so fast that Boone wouldn't be able to copy it. "Long Tall Sally" went to number one in the R&B chart in March '56 and stayed in the top six for 19 weeks. However Boone did copy it and got a number eight.

Little Richard scored another number one with "Rip It Up" and a number two with "Slippin Slidin", both in '56.

He scored another number one with "Lucille" in '57 and a number four with "Good Golly Miss Molly" in '58. The piano intro was from "Rocket 88".

Rock and Roll was developing at a time when in some states audiences were still segregated between balcony and dancefloor. But as far as the kids were concerned that was a parental and governmental issue, because by the end of the show black and whites would be dancing together.

It is quoted that Richard said of himself, "I'm the king and queen of Rock and Roll."

In the 60's he had The Rolling Stones and The Beatles open for him. Jimmy Hendrix also joined his band for a short time.

"Jah jah jah jah jah jah jah Rastafari, evah loving evah faithful, DJ Dread here at Pirate Radio Skankdown an' dat was dem rock an rollers Michael an' Seamus again. Seh Winston why don' wi tell de listener' 'bout Reggae?"

"'Cause dat com' affa Rocksteady."

"Tcha mon den tell 'bout Rocksteady."

Winston did:

In 1965/66 American soul became slower and so did Jamaican Ska. Some said it was because of a particular hot summer in '66. Some said the Rude boys also played a part: they would play Ska records at half speed so they could emphasise their tough dance moves which would be to just stand and rock-steady. Another story is that during a session where the bassist didn't turn up, Jackie Miitto the keyboard player took over the bass but couldn't keep up with the up-tempo Ska beat so slowed down.

Whether it was the hot summer, the influence from American Soul, Rude Boys, or the above story, the fact is that Ska slowed down that year with the bass being heavier than in Ska, taking over the guitar, and lyrics taking over the melody. A singer took the front line, and the horn section who had been the soloists took a step back. Ska up to then had mostly been fast and instrumental. Now, it slowed down and turned into the songs of Rocksteady.

As with Ska, the first to actually play Rocksteady is disputed, but Alton Ellis was the first to use "Rocksteady" (which was a dance) for a song title, "Get Ready to Rocksteady". The song was played regularly for the next two years, earning Ellis the title The Godfather of Rocksteady.

Another first was Hepton Lewis who was trying to sing a Ska song called "Take It Easy" which was too fast for him. He asked the band, guitarist Lyn Taitt, bassist Jackie Jackson and pianoist Gladston Anderson "Gaddy" to slow down for him. It was Gaddy who said "This here boy is Rocksteady". The name stuck and they had a hit.

Rocksteady songs were often about social issues and Rude Boys were still a social issue. As in Ska, they were either praised or condemned in songs like Alton Ellis's "Don't Trouble People", Derick Morgan's "Tougher than Tough", Prince Buster's "Judge Dread", Clarendonian's "Rude Boy Gone a Jail", Dandy Livingstone's "A Message To You Rudy", The Rulers' "Don't be a Rude boy", The Soul Brothers "Lawless Street", Desmond Dekker's "007 Shanty Town", Justin Hinds and the Dominoes' "No Good Rudie", and The Wailers who were for a time themselves Rude boys, sung "Hooligan" (considered to be the first rude boy song), "Rudi got bail" and "Let him go".

Probably some of the most well known Rocksteady tracks are "The Tide is High" by The Paragons and "Feel like Jumping" by Marcia Griffiths. This has also been covered by Bad Manners. Another fine example is the social comment on striking – "Everything Crash" by The Ethiopians and Winston's favourite, "Baba Boum Time" by The Jamaicans.

It is said by everyone involved that Rocksteady was a happy time for Jamaicans – boys and girls dancing together, people having fun – the music united everyone. It was a fruitful time, there was no greed, jealousy or hatred between singers and musicians who sung and made music for the love of it, from which the music industry grew.

Rocksteady peaked in '67. Since Haile Salassie's visit to Jamaica in '66, the Rastafarian movement was growing daily. Jamaicans were becoming aware of black consciousness, politics and protest. African drumming, righteousness and spiritual awareness all began to influence lyrics, and the music and rhythm from then on changed. In '68 it turned in to Reggae.

"Music is de biggest gun, Pirate Radio Skankdown an' rude boy Winston deh givin yu de roots of Rocksteady," said DJ as he and Winston touched their clenched fists together and drunk from their bottles of Red Stripe.

"Irie Winston, can wi noh tell 'bout Reggae?" asked DJ.

Winston said that to keep the show in chronological order they should now talk about Reggae. But he had made a running order for the show and had promised Animal and Semi a slot to talk about Punk. He wanted to get them on air before they were too drunk. He then added that although Reggae came before Punk it wasn't until the mid-seventies before it hit the mainstream – which was the same time as Punk.

Both movements had a lot in common. Witnessing high unemployment and feeling suppressed by governments, both groups were protesting through music. They were also to influence each other with Bob Marley making reference to The Damned and The Clash in his "Punky Reggae Party", The Clash covering Junior Murvin's "Police and Thieves" and Stiff Liitle Fingers covering Marley's "Johnny Was". It was also common during the first Punk gigs in the Roxey that DJ Don Letts would play Dub Reggae before the bands came on stage.

"Hold on deh Winston if yu go tell evrytin' mi haf nuttin lef te tell."

"Sorry DJ, OK mi tune in te de Punks compartment."

Animal was known as Animal for his animal behaviour. He lived in filthy squats, not washing, not changing clothes and only having money for drink and gigs. Semi was short for semi-conscious, for that's what he was when he hadn't drunk himself unconscious. Which is what he usually did.

They were two Scottish Punks, now in their forties, and had witnessed the beginnings of Punk and followed the early bands and those that followed thereafter. They were drinking McEwens lager, waving Scottish flags and scarves. Sitting with their feet up on the bench wearing 14-hole Dr Marten boots that looked like they'd never seen polish since the day they left the shop. Originally they had been black, but now they were so dried out they were white and cracked in places.

The rest of their attire didn't get much better. Animal was wearing torn tartan trousers with a bum flap; Semi a kilt; and they were both wearing T-shirts so old the print had worn off. Their black leather jackets were self-painted with groups that were just still readable –The Sex Pistols, The Clash, The Damned, Crass, The Angelic Upstarts, Stiff Little Fingers, Sham 69, Flux Pink Indians, and UK Subs.

They were drunkenly arguing about what was originally a four piece punk band called The Epileptics who formed in Bishop, Stratford. Animal stated that on vocals was Colin Latter, bass Derick Birkett, guitar Kevin Hunter and drums Martin Wilson. Semi argued that Latter and Birkett moved to Hertfordshire, London, where they picked up a drummer and two guitars and changed their name to Flux of Pink Indians.

In 1981, Flux of Pink Indians signed and released their debut EP, Neu Smell, on Crass Records which reached number two in the indie charts. Animal and Semi were drunkenly reciting a track from that EP. The track was called Tube Disaster which went as follows,

Intro poem

*Can ye smell the neu smell, a travelling through
the air
Aye I can lad, it's coming from over there
Over the hills, down in the valley there's new
buildings there
There's a nuclear power dump site someone
doesn't care
Parliament says it's safe, so why not bury it
there.*

*I love tube disasters
I want to marry a tube disaster
I want another one like the last one
'cause I live for tube disasters yeah*

*Build up some speed
Don't shut your eyes
Make sure that everyone in the train dies
You don't get no prize, no time to say goodbyes
Just smile everyone
You'll be on TV tonight that's right*

*I love tube disasters
I want to marry a tube disaster
I want another one like the last one
'cause I live for tube disasters yeah*

*Go through a wall, forget about the brakes
It's so much easier than the pills you can take
I go through Moorgate and I'm wide awake
But no bloody drivers gone and made a mistake
    that's yet
is it me that needs a home?
not likely, vicarious living rids your boredom*

I love tube disasters
I want a marry a tube disaster
I want another one like the last one
'cause I live for tube disasters yeah

Outro Poem
And oh as yes the sky did turn to night
I shield my eyes and hide from the bright of day
And cast the stone, deep into the field of man
And hide in shame and low the flag, raised in
vain
And close my mind to this lost day
And shield my body with ferns of grey
And ask no more of life unsaved and smile no
more
And lay here saved become the tombstone of my
grave

"Make sure everyone on the train dies eh?" Quoted Matt Davis as he entered their compartment.

"And who might you be?" asked Animal.

"Excuse me gentlemen, let me introduce myself. Matt Davis Special Agent."

"Gettifu ye badge says toilet duties," interrupted Semi.

"Err that's true but I used to be a special agent and I'm acting as one now and would like to ask you two gentlemen a few questions."

"Questions eh?" imitated Animal. "What kinda questions?"

'Ïye, an if we get em reight, do we win a prize an that, like a bottle a whiskey?' asked Semi.

Matt Davis, feeling he was being ridiculed, put on a stern face and asked, "What's your reason for being on this train?"

"Ey yer blind as well as daft, we're going te Wembley te see Scotland kick the hell outa England."

"Well if you're going to Wembley, then you're on the wrong train, this train is going to Skaville."

"Ne kiddin," said Animal "Och we musta got on the wrong train somewhere Semi."

"Err you seem to be a bit confused, I'm a bit confused myself, but I'll tell it to you straight, tell it like it is, lay my cards on the table so to speak, give you all the facts –"

Animal Interrupted. "What are you on pal?"

"I'm investigating a possible murder and I need to know if you two gentlemen saw anything unusual this morning."

"Iye, I saw a cow doing a jobby whilst walking aboot in a field," said Animal.

"Very clever things are cows yer know," added Semi.

"What about two gentlemen going by the names of 7 Bellies who looks like an overgrown ZZ Top singer guitarist wearing John Lennon sunglasses?"

"Iye a recken we did see him, what aboot him?" asked Animal.

"He wasne doing a jobby though," added Semi.

Matt persisted, asking, "Was he with another man looking like Animal from the Muppet Show?"

"Exactly like him. You're bloody good you are Matt," complimented Animal.

"Iye, a suppose that's why he's a detective special agent and that," added Semi.

"Well that's solved that one then," said Animal. "Reckon that calls for a celebration, another drink there Semi."

"Don't mind if I do, will yer join us for one pal?"

"Hold on gentlemen," said Matt. "All we've established is that they came by here. Did you speak with them?"

"Ne we was giving it a bit of "Gobbin' On Life" at the time," answered Animal.

"Iye from The Alberto's" added Semi. Who went on to tell "Gobbin' on Life" was a track from the Snuff Rock

EP, Stiff '77 which sold 25,000 copies. It was by Alberto Y Lost Trios Paranoias a Manchester cabaret act from '73 - '82 which if you ever saw them you would describe as The Village People on acid. Each member dressed and played the part of a personality from music cults as Rock and Roll, Country and Western, Rock, Psychedelic, Folk, Punk. They went on to break all box office records at the London Royal court Theatre and in '75 topped the bill supported by Blondie, The Police and The Stranglers.

Bored with what was then making the charts and the all so hyped up music scene and industry. They decided to take the piss out of it writing songs using comedy and imitating personalities of the above music cults. "Anadin" was a take on Lou Reed's "Heroin", "Kill" The Damned, "Snuffin Like That" The Clash, "Snuffin in a Babylon" Reggae and "Gobbin' On Life" The Sex Pistols.

"I'm familiar with a Colt.45, a Magnum.44, but I never heard of a Sex Pistol before. Must be something new out on the black market." Matt made a note of it in his book.

"We're Punks yer know," said Animal.

"Punks eh, yes we got them back in New York too. Gangsters, hoodlums, young male hustlers, ruffians, petty criminals, and in the prisons those who bend over for Mr Big in the showers."

"Hey we're none a that pal," argued Semi, "we're anarchists, I'll have you know I shit on the steps of the Glasgow Magistrates, by the way."

Matt was appalled and disgusted by this show of disregard for law and order and was just about to say so when Animal said, "Iye that's one of Semi's famous stories, but what he does ne say, is that he was still wearing his trewsers at the time, on his way in to face a too drunk te fuck charge. *He he he.*"

"Drunk and disorderly," corrected Semi.

"And that's Punk is it? Excreting in your trousers in public?" asked Matt.

"Ne ne," retaliated Animal. "If ye wanna know what Punk is then ye have to go back to the beginning of the Punk movement and that starts with John Joseph Lydon, who was born to Irish parents in Camden Town London. He grew up in Finsbury Park, by the way." Animal then went on to tell them.

As a child, Lydon dressed in Dr Martens and Ben Sherman shirts, being part of the first Skinhead movement during '66 to '69. Lydon spent part of his youth in gangs of 30, 40 kids who would break into factories and have fun breaking machines.

During '74/'75 England had its highest unemployment rate ever and national strikes were rife. School leavers who had believed everything they'd been taught – "Education was the key to success" – were at a loss when they walked out of the school gates to "No Future".

Disillusioned and bored, Lydon and a group of friends as well as other small groups such as The Bromley Contingent made up from youths from Bromley, a suburb and other surrounding towns south of London, started rebelling against everything. "If it was quiet, they wanted it loud." "If it was black, they wanted it white." Basically, they did the opposite to everything that had always been just to get a reaction, just to get noticed.

The hippy scene had just passed so flares and long hair was out. Mods and Skinheads had also been and gone so being smart was also out. Cutting chunks of your hair out so it had no style at all, wearing base ball boots, ripped T-shirts and a tie around your legs was in. It got you noticed and no one could work out which style you were part of. Truth was, they weren't part of any style. They were being original, which in the beginning was what Punk was all about.

The drawback was that football firms and second generation Teds would beat them up for looking scruffy.

This meant they couldn't go to pubs, so they took to going to gay clubs where they were accepted for who they were. Here they were introduced to sex wear and started adding rubber, latex, vinyl and leather to their attire. They dressed to shock. A shop called Too Fast Too Live Too Young to Die on the Kings Road became a hang-out for these gangs. It was owned by Malcolm Maclaren and his girlfriend Vivian Westwood, who were selling fifties style clothes with new added colours and fetish wear.

At 17, a green-haired Lydon (wearing a ripped T-shirt held together with safety pins sporting Pink Floyd with their eyes cut out and I hate written in biro above) was walking down the Kings Road when he was approached and asked by Bernard Rhodes to a meeting with Malcolm Mclaren that night at a pub called The Roebuck.

There he was asked if he wanted to join and sing in a band of people he didn't know. They called themselves The Strand. They went back to Mclaren's shop and Lydon karaoke'd, twisting and toughting himself like a hunch-back to the juke box over Alice Cooper's "Eighteen". and he was in. The Strand were playing covers of Rod Stewart, The Faces and The Who – they'd been playing two years and hadn't written anything themselves. Lydon, with his anti-everything attitude saw them as a band with no originality, no style and no point.

All that changed when two or three weeks later he started bringing in his own songs to rehearsals. Lydon came up with "Anarchy in the UK" and for a time they played under the name The Swankers.

Maclaren changed his shop name to Sex, Lydon became Johnny Rotten and The Strand became the Sex Pistols. Punks now had a platform to stand on and the music came to be known as Punk Rock which was a means to express themselves.

Groups like the Bromley Contingent and other small groups who were ex-fans of Bowie, Roxy Music and Glam Rock – who up till then had been the only ones who dared to be different – now had something to focus on. A band, fronted by Lydon, was singing about how they felt. These small groups totalling around 150 who up to then hadn't known each other, now all started coming together at Pistols gigs. These were the first Punks, giving the Pistols an instant following.

Matt, realising he had lost the thread of his interview again, brought it back.

"Gentlemen, gentlemen, can we please get back to Mr 7 Bellies and Mr Axe Man?"

"Hold on a minute, I think they were having a bit of an argument," said Semi.

Matt, finally thinking he was getting somewhere, pressed on. "Now this is very important. Can you remember the exact words which were spoken?"

"That's an awful difficult one there. Let's have a wee think aboot it," said Semi. "Och I've got it,

7 Bellies said 'It's doon this way, I've got it stashed in a real cool safe place and that' and Axe Man said 'Iye well it just better be there or tha's in big trouble.'"

Matt, writing all this down, asked "They're the exact words you heard?"

"Iye, the exact words, are you calling me a liar pal?"

"No, of course not. I'm trying to trace their last movements, words and actions in order to piece together this puzzle."

"I thought you were investigating a murder," said Semi. "Another drink Animal?"

"Thank you very much gentlemen, you've been very helpful. Here's my card. If you think of anything else you can contact me. I'm usually... cleaning one of the toilets."

"Fools die for want of wisdom, yu listen te Pirate Radio Skankdown de show dat gettin' out a tohn. Ya jus' hear

Matt Davis gettin' him investigation overway deh," said DJ.

"Wid Animal an' Semi talkin' 'bout Punk," added Winston.

"Tcha mon, Winston dem nor jus' much 'bout Punk as yu nor 'bout Ska, bu' I no overstaan' it all in dem Scottish accent," said DJ.

"Wha' dem seh is," said Winston, who went on to explain.

Punk started in London, building up in the mid seventies long before it became "Punk Rock" – the title given to describe the music by author and painter Caroline Coon. Punk was visual and it was about individualism, the message being, "Be who you want to be".

It started off as a subculture and would possibly have stayed a small underground scene if it hadn't been for the media hyping it up and blowing everything out of proportion. The media made a scandal out of everything – and if there wasn't one, they'd make one up.

Punk Rock ran opposite to everything that had previously been a standard formula. They stripped it down to the bare essentials: two guitars, bass, lead and a small drum set was enough. You didn't need to be a talented musician, either. Power chords played at break-neck speed and distortion replaced complex chord structures and guitar solos.

Not being able to sing was also no problem because Punk was angry and frustrated; the lyrics were usually shouted rather than sung down the microphone. Songs were usually under two minutes long and there was no beating about the bush with hidden messages – it was all about straight to the point lyrics. Punk was about openly attacking the status quo and the British Government.

They were also protesting against the music industry. Basically, the message was that you don't have to go the way everybody else is going, the way it's always been. The message was "Break loose".

Recording went with the DIY attitude of Punk – a four track portastudio or home tape recorder was enough to catch the statement. It was supposed to sound live and raw, not mixed and polished up.

They released on small independent labels. Stiff Records adopted a Punk attitude with their slogan: "If it ain't Stiff, it ain't worth a fuck."

"Good afternoon I'm –" but before Matt could get any further he was interrupted by the fast rhyming of Zoot.

-"Yo dude slip slide right in. Shut, close the door and seal. Now we've got privacy I'll make you a deal. What you come to buy, something new, something old. Diamonds, pearls, silver or gold."

"The name's Matt Davis, Special Agent."

"Well you're wrong if you're expecting me to sing – I've got receipts for everything."

"I'm investigating the disappearance of a Mr 7 Bellies, which could be a possible homicide."

"Murder on the Train to Skaville – Why, dat terrible."

"It's also the title of this book but what I'd like to ask you is, what's your reason for being on this train?

"I got a dream, if you know what I mean. I'm going to Skaville, to open a Zoot's bargain basement store. I've got one in England. When I've got one in Skaville, I'll move on and open more."

"Erm, did you see a Mr 7 Bellies with Mr Axe Man this afternoon?"

"For sure I saw those dudes. I thought I've got nothing to lose. So I tried to sell them on commission. But 7 Bellies said he was on a mission."

"Mission eh? That's very interesting. Could put a whole new light on the matter, and did Mr Axe Man say anything?"

"Why yes, but it didn't make any sense. I got it here on tape for twenty nine dollars and ninety nine cents."

"You taped the conversation?"

"To a Special Agent I wouldn't lie. Now are we going to deal? Are you going to buy?"

"Twenty nine dollars and ninety nine cents eh? You drive a hard bargain, Mr Zoot."

"The tape is only the beginning. For fifty dollars you get a Sony Walkman to play it in."

"Twenty nine ninety nine plus fifty, why that's..."

"Seventy nine dollars, ninety nine cents. I make a special deal for you. Call it a hundred and I'll throw in the batteries too".

"One hundred dollars? This better be worth it."

"There you are just press play, and hear what they say."

Matt Davis pressed the button and heard 7 Bellies say, "*No thanks Zoot, we're on a mission.*" Which was followed by Mad Axe Man saying, "*A bloody wild goose chase thee reckons, if tha's leading thee up a blind alley, thee'll wrap tha's bollocks round tha neck.*"

"Thank you Zoot, this is hard evidence. If my translation is correct, Mr Axe Man was threatening Mr 7 Bellies to strangle him with his own... testicles... Erm, have a nice day."

"Togetherness is bettah dan fightin'," said DJ as Winston cut back to the studio. Winston could see DJ was about to go into one of his trances with fear from the murder of 7 Bellies, so he opened two bottles of Red Stripe and gave DJ one. Quickly, he tried to change the subject, clinking the bottles together and touching clenched fists. He said, "Irie, seh why don' yu tell de listener' 'bout Reggae?"

"I an' I," said DJ, coming back from a near panic attack.

"Yu de DJ," Winston reminded him.

"Yeah man," said DJ, sitting up and taking a drink from his Red Stripe before announcing, "Dis is Pirate Radio Skankdown de hottest show in tohn; Bringin' yu Roots an'culture fe all 'roun'; So why don' y'all sit down."

DJ laughed at himself and his little rhyme, then said, "I an' I tell yu de roots fe Reggae".

Reggae is slower than Ska and usually faster than Rocksteady. It started creeping in between '67 and '68, and was first known as a dance called Reggay during the Rocksteady period. The first time the term Reggay appeared in a song was in the Rocksteady hit "Dance Do the Reggay", written by Toots Hibberts for his group The Maytals. This was released in '68 on the Beverly label in Jamaica and on the Pyramid label in the UK. The first recorded Reggae song is documented as being The Pioneers' "Longshot Bus' Me Bet" in '67.

There are several reasons and circumstances that shaped how Reggae came about. Derick Morgan states they didn't like the name Rocksteady; that it was Jamaicans' version of American Soul. He was one day playing around with "Fat Man", a song he'd first recorded for Duke Reid in '59 and changed the beat to the organ and rhythm guitar playing up front. This sounded like "Reggae Reggae".

Another story concerns Edward O'Sullivan, aka Bunny "Striker" Lee, a Chinese Jamaican record producer who claims he came up with the organ shuffle (a new rhythm) and started using the word Reggae which was soon followed by everyone. "Say What You're Saying" in '67 by Clancy Eccles and "People Funny Boy" in '68 by Lee "Scratch" Perry are also credited as the first songs to make the crossover from Rocksteady to Reggae.

Electricity also played a big part in the development of Reggae, which came at a time that studios were becoming more sophisticated. Newer, smaller studios were also setting up, usually owned by musicians, giving a wider scope of ideas from Dodd and Reid who up until then had the monopoly.

Reggae was new, so there was lots of room for experimentation. The electric bass and organ were brought in to play by a new generation of musicians who weren't all accustomed to playing styles of the past. With the bass being played dominantly, it took the place of the drums and guitar, along with the organ taking the lead (with the drums coming in third). The organ was played with a technique of stabbing the keys; one theory for this technique was possibly developed on a faulty studio organ where the keys were sticking and had to be stabbed hard to play.

The National grid had by now connected up to regions out in the country. It meant that jukeboxes, radios and travelling bands like Byron Lee brought the new Reggae beats to a far greater audience than its previous runners. This enabled the whole island to be a part of a new Jamaican sound. Country people were now also getting involved, bringing in wider influences, that up until then had mainly only been heard in and around Kingston. This new impulse brought in with it snatches of African drumming and guitar with elements of Mentos Banjo.

Ska and Rocksteady had reached America, Canada and England. With Reggae songs like "Young Gifted and Black" by Bob Andy and Marcia Griffiths reaching number one in the UK during 1970. "Love of the Common People" by Nicky Thomas hit number nine. Both were on the Trojan label, and it wasn't long before London's international tourists took this new Reggae music with them to the rest of the world.

As DJ finished telling all this he leaned back in his seat, stretching his back. "Maximum respect DJ, dat was jus' like fadah use te tell us," said Winston.

"Tcha mon Winston, I fadah teach I an' I roots an' noh I an' I tell de listener', so if yu jus' tune in deh dis is Pirate Radio Skankdown bringin' yu Ska, Reggae, Roots an' comedy."

Jerry Juggler never really fitted in at school or at the several jobs he tried. He couldn't see the point of doing something for a living that you didn't like doing; a job that gave no job satisfaction. Shift work, sleeping during the day and working through the night, working 50 weeks, going on holiday for a fortnight, coming back and working another 50 weeks. He always went on exotic holidays, seeing different parts of the world, and was fascinated by different cultures, different foods, wines, music. So one day he decided why not turn it around and work for two weeks and go on holiday for 50?

He put his savings together, sold some of his belongings, bought a rucksack and set off to travel the world. He'd always believed only people who were born in circus families could juggle and it was an art form that was passed down from father to son. However, in the eighties, just as Rubik's Cubes and skateboards had been, juggling was suddenly all over the place. Jerry had always had an ambition to juggle so before he left on his travels he bought a how to juggle book that included three beanbags.

He practised daily while travelling through Holland, Germany, Austria and Switzerland. By the time he reached France he was an accomplished juggler. He met street artists who performed in town squares, markets, and in front of terraces who were making enough money for food and wine. He joined up with them and played festivals for a while before putting his own show together and going solo. He joined different circuses and theatres – performing as a clown, juggler, magician and uni-cyclist. And so he found a way to make a living with job satisfaction. His travels didn't stop in France, either.

He travelled through Spain, Morocco, Portugal, Japan, Australia and America.

It was during a visit back in England visiting family that he chanced on calling in The Devils Arms for a drink where he met DJ Dread who was fascinated by all his travels, himself only having seen Jamaica and England. Jerry could tell a good story and talked in inuendos and double entendres.

Having stood up and performed hundreds of shows in front of live audiences Jerry was a born entertainer which is why DJ not only gave him regular slots on Pirate Radio Skankdown, he now wanted him to open the live stage show in Skaville.

"Hello pretty boys, I'm Jerry Juggler. It's ever so exciting to be here in Skaville. Oh aren't you all looking butch in your big boots and braces, sporting your short hair cuts. I wear braces myself; my braces are for keeping my big spotty shorts up, not that they stay up for long though, one quick flick of a clip and they're straight down. Do you want to know what I keep in my shorts? That's right, my balls. I'm so glad so many of you have turned out to see the Pirate Radio Skankdown show, I'm so chuffed, I want to get my balls out, and play with them in front of you all. What's that? You've all got balls of your own to play with? Ooh you naughty boys, not like my balls you haven't, look, they've got lights in."

"Excuse me."

"Ooh you frightened me, look my balls have dropped."

"Err sorry to interrupt. Matt Davis Special Agent. I'm investigating a possible murder and would appreciate it if you would answer a few questions."

"Murder, ooh do you think the killer will strike again."

"It's not definite yet, all we have is a missing person, but a lot of facts are adding up to it looking like murder, you must be Jerry Juggler."

"I am but I haven't done the dirties on anyone."

"Erm, are you alone?"

"Yes, well at least I was until you... came along."

'It's just that I was stood at your door for a while and I distinctly heard you talking to someone. Some big men by the sound of things. Are you hiding anyone in here?'

"Ooh you eavesdropper. big men... ooh you silly, I was practising my speech. I'm opening the show in Skaville and I don't mind telling you, I'm shitting myself."

"Well I guess that'll be one less toilet to clean."

"I beg your pardon?"

"Oh sorry, just thinking aloud, tell me Jerry... you don't mind me calling you Jerry."

"Ooh no you can all me what you like."

"Er Jerry, tell me, do you know a Mr 7 Bellies and a Mr Axe Man?"

"Of course I do. They've been on Pirate Radio Skank-down since... about the third show, they're usually on the alternative hour."

Just then, above the noise of the train wheels on the rails and the rattling of the carriage, there was a sort of scuffling noise like a body being dragged down the passageway. A rubbing along the corridor wall and door could faintly be heard. However Matt, in deep conversation, appeared not to have heard it.

"Erm and have you seen these two gentlemen this afternoon?"

"Ooh yes very rude and arrogant they were, and arguing too."

"Arguing you say."

"Yes bickering, quarrelling, at... ends with each other, ooh."

"Do you know what the argument was about?"

"About a queer."

"Queer you say."

"Yes, I heard Axe Man say, *just where exactly is this queer.*"

"I thought they meant me, so I jumped straight into bed, pulled the duvet over my head and pretended to be asleep."

"Strange action to take."

"Axe Man was bulging."

"Bulging you say."

"His eyes, he looked furious."

"Did you –"

Matt stopped in mid sentence, putting his forefinger to his lip and holding his hand up as if to tell Jerry to be quiet for a moment. Matt moved to the door and put his ear to it. Still holding his hand up at Jerry he took the door handle in his other hand and quickly pulled it open. He stepped out in to an empty passageway.

"Erm sorry to interrupt but I thought I heard something. Now erm did you hear anymore of the argument?"

"Ooh yes I heard it all. 7 Bellies was saying *we're nearly there* but Mad Axe Man was impatient and said *I've had about a...* then he said a naughty word."

"I'll need to have it for the statement Jerry."

"He said *I've had about a bloody nough, take this, you'll be pushing up bloody Christmas trees.*"

"Erm another argument, another threat, did you hear any more?"

"No, they passed me by, and went further down the train."

"Well thank you very much Mr Juggler."

"Ooh, one more thing... comes to mind."

"And what's that?"

"A while later Mad Axe Man came limping back."

"Limping you say."

"Yes, I notice these things."

"And did you notice which leg?"

93

"Yes, his right one."

"And he was alone?"

"Yes."

"Okay, so we know they both came as far as here... Say, how long before Mr Axe Man came back?"

"Oh erm, let me think. Wash my hair, blow job, brush, comb, mirror, make up, dress, erm... about four and a half hours."

"FOUR AND A HALF HOURS? Well that's sure time enough to kill somebody, probably time enough to hack them in to pieces and flush them down the toilet too. Erm... I think that's how he did it."

"I think I'm going to be sick."

"You'd be amazed at what people flush down the toilet, why I've found –"

Just then Jerry retched forwards and threw the contents of his stomach up. Matt, busy writing his notes down, looked up and said, "Erm sorry, I think that will be all for now," and left, still writing down his notes.

Chapter Five

NIGHT TRAIN

The Hawkwind was steaming along. Michael, still burning wood and coal to keep the boiler up to pressure, dragged out a moped.

"Get away out of it," he said to his father.

"In this day and age I'd believe anything," said Seamus.

"Well how do you think it got here? We didn't load it on at the last stop," said Michael, confused.

Seamus laughed as he said, "Young scallywags will have thrown it over a bridge as we rode under. In my day it was rusty old bicycles but times have changed – now it's stolen mopeds."

It was Seamus who saw the red light come on this time. Looking at Michael, he nodded towards it.

Michael took the hint and asked, "Father how did we get to be called Teddy Boys?"

Seamus said that after World War Two, Saville Row tailors on the Kings Road, London, tried to reintroduce clothes inspired by the style of the Edwardian period. In '53 a newspaper headline shortened Edwardian to Teddy; young men wearing these items of clothes became known as Teddy Boys which was further shortened to Teds.

A typical outfit would be a long drape jacket with velvet trim collar and pocket flaps, plus a white shirt high-necked loose collar, slim-jim tie, a brocade waistcoat, drainpipe trousers and brightly coloured socks. Your choice of shoes were Brogues, Oxfords or Crepe-soled, known as brothel creepers (and later known as beetle crushers). It was all topped off with a hairstyle of a quiff at the front, side combed back, known as a D.A – a duck's arse.

Teds dressed to mock the high class, showing they too could afford to wear expensive clothes. The suits were tailor made, and Teds who were usually lower class garage attendants, factory workers etc, paid for them by weekly instalments which would maybe take a year to pay off. It was a time when materials were still scarce and some items were still rationed. It offended many people because of the cost; most middle class and lower class were still making do with the clothes they had, along with hand-me-downs. Many people only had work clothes for the week and a Sunday best.

"Forward evah, backwards nevah, DJ Dread here, yu listen te Pirate Radio Skankdown. Dat dem engineer Teds deh, tankyu mon. Noh mi waan pley yu sometin' fe de Wailers but firs' mi waan tell yu who dem ar'an'how dem com' tegedder." DJ then went on:

Nesta Robert Marley, born 6th Feb '45, started his recording career as a soloist at 17 after being encouraged by Desmond Dekker who he worked alongside as a welder. Marley wrote three songs in '62 and took them to Federal Studios where Leslie Kong recorded 'Judge Not' and 'Do You Still Love Me'. Kong paid him £20. This was later followed by 'One Cup of Coffee', which was put out under the name Bobby Martel, and 'Terror' as Bob Martin. None of them were hits and Kong took Marley off his books.

Not to be deterred, Marley thought he could make it better with a group and teamed up with his childhood friend Bunny Livingstone. They were later joined by Winston Hubert McIintosh (Peter Tosh) followed by another male and two girl singers. They started out calling themselves The Six Teens, The Teenagers, The Wailing Rude boys, The Wailing Wailers and finally The Wailers.

On July 6th 1963 at Dodds Studio One, backed by The Skatalites, they recorded "Simmer Down", a song aimed at the Rude boys telling them they're licking (hitting) too hard. That evening they attended one of Dodd's Sound Systems and were surprised to hear the morning's recording being played on an acetate. The crowd loved it and demanded it to be played again and again. When Coxsone released it at the end of that year, it went on to sell 70,000 copies and made number one in Feb '64.

Between '64 and '66 they were to record over a hundred tracks for Studio One, singing Mento, Calypso, Folk, Doo Wop, Gospel, Soul and pop covers including Bob Dylon and Tom Jones songs. They also sang in the language of the Kingston Ghetto which was indecipherable to outsiders.

They then recorded for Kong's Beverly label, followed by their own Wail 'N' Soul 'M' after which they moved onto Lee Perry's Upsetter label with over another hundred recordings, and at the same time another of their own labels, Tuff Gong.

Leaving Perry they moved to JAD, a company consisting of Soul singer Johnny Nash, Arthur Jenkins and Danny Simms (where either as The Wailers or Marley on solo acoustic versions they were to record well over 200 tracks). They then released a one-off on CBS before ending in '72 on Chris Blackwell's Island.

The Wailers had been through Ska, Rocksteady – and since Haile Salassie's '66 visit to Jamaica were devoted Rastafarians, still wailing out for the people in the ghettoes through their brand of Roots Reggae. They were well established in the Caribbean but it was with Blackwell's belief and support in them they put out the album "Catch a Fire", which aimed to break them through to the white Rock market. It was released December '72 and was followed by American and European tours in '73. That same year they put out the album "Burnin" after which both Livingstone and Tosh left to follow solo careers.

Obviously Marley felt the loss of Livingstone and Tosh but it had always been Marley who put his heart and soul into every show. He saw himself as a messenger in his belief of Rastafari and had a job to do. The remaining Wailers now became Bob Marley and The Wailers joined by his wife's group the I Threes, who sang back-up harmonies. It was with this group that they went on to reach international stardom, giving Marley the title of the first Third World Super Star.

DJ had finished his Red Stripe and was drinking another, feeling relaxed and enjoying himself. He had forgotten the events of earlier and felt the show was now Irie and wanted to say more. He addressed Winston, "Winston pley I de backin' track mi waan tell de listeners 'bout dis song."

Winston picked up the '70 album "The Best of The Wailers" with DJ telling him that it was put out by Leslie Kong on his Beverly label. Bunny Livingstone warned him not to put it out under that title believing they still had a long career ahead of them and their best was still to come. He added that if Kong thought that it was their best then it must mean he was near the end of his life. Kong went ahead with releasing it and died a week later.

Winston selected the track "Stop The Train I'm Leaving," which as DJ said was written and sung by Peter McIntosh who was to later say of it, "It was about failed schemes and time to move on". The song was first recorded with the title "Stop That Train I'm Leaving" with

Lee "Scratch" Perry at his Black Ark studio with Perry's house band the Upsetters and the rhythm section of the Barrett brothers, who were about to become permanent recording and touring members of The Wailers.

Like much of The Wailers' material, over the years some songs were re-recorded for different labels and producers. A slightly different version of this song was recorded again in '72 for their "Catch A Fire" album.

With that said, Winston lovingly lowered the needle on to the album and Peter's soulful harmonic voice could be heard singing –

Winston commented, "DJ in a way dis song 'bout us, de opening "Stop The Train I'm Leaving" is de same as yesterdey mornin' when yu com' runnin down de platform."

"Tcha mon, I an' I walk roun' Leeds wid de babylon on I tail all de mornin', den mi give de raasclaat de slip *he he he*, an' com' jump on de train de las' secon'."

"All mi life mi been teachin, teachin an preachin tru Pirate Radio Skankdown, words and songs of Ska and Reggae. I an' I try te teach de people wi can live togedder in peace and harmony One Love yu nor, but dem Babylon mon, everytime I start a new station dem cut I down, Babylon nuh waan peace Babylon waan power." DJ then defiantly added, "But wat dem don' nor, is wi lickle but wi tallewah."

"Some goin' eas', and some going wes', and some going te Skaville *he he he*. I and I done I bes' in Hingland, mi don' nor wedda mi righ' a wrong te leave but it won' be too long 'fore wi fin' out."

Listening to The Wailers is like a religion to DJ, because they recorded so much material there's always a song for every type of feeling or mood you're in – and for every time of the day or night. DJ, feeling calm and at peace with the world, said, "Irie Winston, lay some sweetness on I."

"Yu waan I kiss yu Leeroy?"

"No bloodclaat, pley anuddah track."

It was only now as Winston looked down at the controls he saw he had neglected to press transmit during the last transmission meaning only DJ and himself had heard Peter Tosh's "Stop The Train I'm Leaving". Fearing a scolding from DJ he said nothing.

Matt Davis was walking up the corridor on his way to DJ Dread and Winston to report his findings. His intentions were to interview Mad Axe Man about the statements of threats he'd collected when he heard, aagh aagh aagh.

Thinking someone was being attacked he turned around to investigate and headed back down the corridor when he heard aagh aagh aagh again. Sensing he was getting closer he speeded up his pace only to stop dead in his tracks when his eyes fell on an object on the corridor floor. It was an axe covered in blood. The murder weapon, he thought to himself.

Following procedures, he told himself to play it by the book, bag it and label it for forensic evidence. He'd just done this when he heard aagh aagh aagh coming from behind the door he was standing by. He kicked the door open and burst in saying "Freeze, this is the FBI!"

Winston selected a track the Mods would dance to: "The Godfather of Soul", James Joseph Brown's "Night Train" from '62 reaching number five in the R&B chart. The song, originally a 12 bar blues on a 78 was released on the United label by Jimmy Forest in 1952.

Winston said the song was also featured on the "Quadrophenia" soundtrack and if you ever get chance to see Brown on film then look op the T.A.M.I (Teenage Music International Performance) from '64 and check out his footwork. He then played the record remembering to press transmit, and tuned into the cockney Mods' compartment.

Miami, Florida
Atlanta, Georgia
Raleigh, North Carolina

GBH, christened Gerald Brian Harris, was teased about his name at school so much that just hearing any one of his names sends him into a violent outrage. So much so that he is now only referred to as GBH or Grevious. He is in his early thirties, still has a violent short temper, usually forgets to breath between sentences and being an ex-boxer is always ready to bring out the fists.

In the Mod culture GBH is a face, wearing a petrol blue three-ply tonic mohair suit and a pair of gleaming brogues.

Miami, Florida
Atlanta, Georgia
Raleigh, North Carolina
Washington D.C
Oh and Richmond, Virginia too

Sparrow, the only class schoolmate he had, and probably even then only because he did his homework and carried his books for him, is still his goffer. Sparrow in the Mod culture is known as a ticket wearing a Fred Perry with Stayprest trousers and pods.

On the hat stand hung their fishtail parkers with sewn on patches of The Who, The Lambrettas, Secret Affair, The Jam, Purple Hearts, The Chords and button badges saying "We are the Mods", "British Mods rule OK" and "We put the Ska back in Scarborough".

Baltimore, Maryland
Philadelphia
New York City
Take it home

And don't forget New Orleans
The home of the blues
Oh yeah night train
Night train, night train

"Ere, Grievous."

"What?"

"He's an auwite sort a guy ain't he."

"Who?"

"That Sylvester Stallone."

"Oh yeah, he done auwhite for himself he has,with that string of Rocky and Rambo films, written, directed and starred in 'em himself he 'as."

"Yeah, you know he started out in porno?"

"YOU WHAT?"

"Yeah, the Italian Stallion he was."

"YOU WHAT? That Rocky heavy weight champion of the world, that Rambo green beret killing machine, was a porn star? Poncing about on camera... with his wedding tackle out? The big baby with a speech impediment crying, 'Yo Adrian, I did it", the made-in-Hong Kong action man with moving eyes and a girly sewing kit in his big knife?" *Pant pant pant.*

Just then he saw the red light come on which told him it was time to tell his version of how the Mod culture evolved. He took a drink from his Holsten Pils, drew on his cigarette and began.

The term Mod comes from the word modernist, the name used to describe Jazz musicians and their fans in the fifties. The roots of the Mod subculture originated around London's Soho '57, in coffee bars which stayed open longer than pubs. This attracted middle class and art student youths who would hang out there. Another attraction was pinball machines and the jukeboxes which played Jazz and Blues. The art students were interested in

Italian and French art films and Italian magazines, where they looked for new styles and ideas for clothes.

In '59 Colin MacInnes wrote the book Absolute Beginners about a modernist who wore sharp fitting Italian clothes. In the early sixties, American African music, Soul and R&B were added to the jukeboxes as working class youths from different backgrounds and classes had started to descend on the coffee bars. They adopted the sharp Italian styles, French haircuts and, taking inspiration from the modern Jazz stars, started dressing up. They became what would be named later as the first Mods.

It was an expensive life being a Mod. All their money went on records, clubbing and clothes – some had up to 15 suits. Because fashion changed from week to week a Mod had to stay one step ahead. As soon as anything became popular it was time to move on to something different. These Mods were known as the "faces". When dancing they had the moves; a face didn't blend in with the crowd, a face would stand out. The majority of Mods were followers; these were known as the "tickets". Being a Mod wasn't just dressing up as a Mod, it was a lifestyle, it was a way of life. Anyone else was known as a "number" – and together they made up the numbers.

To Matt's surprise and relief, no one was in danger. He stood face to face with Sir Johnny O.B.E Flannel who greeted him with. "Aagh aagh aagh Iyyl drink to that" On seeing Matt Davis having just kicked his door open Sir Johnny asked himself " Who's this then? it's a boy from the blue, Blue Loo by the smell of him."

Matt only got as far as introducing himself and to say he was investigating before he was interrupted.

"Matt Davis Special Agent FBI, I wonder, who am I? It comes back to me now and again. But for now, why don't I play you my police series, top ten. Number ten, he's always sucking, no not a stick of rock, but a lollipop. Always one for the ladies, it's Kojak with who loves you baby. Moving down to number nine, he's out there fighting more crime –"

It was here that Matt Davis interrupted him by impersonating him. He said, "Number one, it's Matt Davis Special Agent investigating what looks like the murder of Mr 7 Bellies." But again, he was interrupted with:

"Murder, if it's murder you've come to talk about, why didn't you say. Let's have a look and see what I can play. I could murder a beer myself, what's that on my top shelf? My top ten murder stories, books and films. Number ten: It's that Agatha Christie classic Murder on the Orient Express –"

Matt interrupted, once more impersonating him with, "Number one it's the Pirate Radio Skankdown classic, Murder on the Train to Skaville. Now if you insist on avoiding my questions I will have to charge you with obstruction of justice which will be a sentence of thirty days in the slammer."

To which Johnny replied, "Thirty days in the slammer. That sounds like my kind of party. Slam 'em down and spin around...and it lasts for thirty days."

Daily wear for the Mods would be Levis, Wrangler jeans or Stayprest trousers, Fred Perry shirts, shoes were pods. For the clubs, a suit (known as a "whistle") would be worn. These would be tonic mohair suits that had been personally tailored to the customer's demands, so no two suits would be the same.

Everything was an option, from the number of buttons on the cuffs (sometimes up to ten), the angle and number of pockets, length of vent, side vents, colour and type of material. Talk about two tone suits, these Mods sometimes ordered up to three-ply coloured fabrics.

With two fittings these would take at least a month to make and would be paid in weekly instalments, with a pair of black loafers, coloured socks (never white) and sometimes topped off with a narrow brimmed trilby and a German fishtail parka to keep their suits clean and dry. All that was needed now was the transport to take them away from their working class environment for the weekend or to the clubs that had sprung up all over the West End.

Public transport stopped too early for the Mods, who stayed out all night. A solution was found in the shape of the Italian scooters from Lambretta and Vespa which were also bought on higher purchase schemes. These were chosen because of their sealed panels, which covered all greasy and oiled working parts which made them the ideal transport.

A scooter wasn't just a means of transport. Like their clothes, it was their pride and joy. Here they could also be individual and set themselves apart from one another by customising them with mirrors (as many as 30), fog lights, chromed side panels and bumpers. Crash bars and luggage carriers were also added and finished off with a two tone paint job.

During the early sixties Mods were slowly building up in numbers. They had been listening to Blues such as Muddy Waters, John Lee Hooker, but by '63 they slowly shifted to The Stones, The Kinks and The Animals, who were all making news in the British pop scene playing versions of American R&B. After hearing these songs, the Mods would look up the originals.

Then they were drawn to the new sound which was now making its way across to England. It was Soul, which was coming out of Detroit, Michigan, first called Tamla and set up on Jan 12th, '59 and changed to Motown on April 14th, '60 with the name "Hitsville USA" above the studio. Motown was a label that recorded African American artists playing Soul R&B. Just down the road another label, Stax, had above their studio "Soulville". The Mods, coming from a working class environment, could relate to these sounds.

"I'm talking about thirty days behind bars," said Matt, trying to make the consequences clear.

"It gets better and better. Johnny's dream is coming true, Listen and I'll tell you. All my life, I've been propping up bars, while I've been sinking down jars. Now I get to be behind them, it sounds like paradise. How long do I get, if I punch you between the eyes?"

"We're talking thirty days in prison. That's thirty days without alcohol."

"Thirty days in jail without any ale. Tell me what to do Matt Davis, how can I help you?"

"Good. Now, did you see Mr 7 Bellies pass by here this afternoon with Mr Axe Man?"

"Question time. Who's going to be first on the line?"

"Mr Flannel, did you see the two men in question?"

"I've been in here, drinking my beer, singing my song. I didn't see anyone."

"Then how about this axe covered in blood? I found it outside your compartment in a pool of blood."

In the clubs the Mods would be taking amphetamine pills (speed) such as Purple Hearts, Dexys and Bombers (the street name being leapers) to fuel their all night dancing to the sounds the DJs were playing. Music included the Stax house band, Booker T and the MGs, who played on loads of records backing for Otis Redding, Sam and Dave, Eddie Floyd and Wilson Picket.

In '62, they had a USA hit of their own. The instrumental "Green Onions" was first released on Volt and then on Stax, and went on to reach number three on the pop chart and number one on the soul chart for four non-consecutive weeks, meaning it went up and down in the charts reaching number one on four separate occasions.

GBH then reeled off a list of artists, song titles, chart positions and year the first Mods would dance to them.

Curtis Mayfield, lead singer of The Impressions, "It's Alright". US pop chart, number four. R&B chart number one, 1963.

In '64 Rod Stewart joined The Hoochie Coochie Man. In '65 he was billed as "Rod the Mod" in an ITV documentary when in another band, Steam Packet. A TV crew followed them about on tour. In '69 Rod would join The Faces who started out in '65 as a Mod group The Small Faces, who reached number 14 with their debut single, "Watcha Gonna Do About It?"

Soloman Burke (The King of Rock & Soul), "Everybody Needs Somebody". Number 58 in the US pop charts, 1964.

Ramsey Lewis Trio, "The in Crowd". Number 13 in the US pop charts, '65.

The Who, "My Generation". Number two in the UK, '65

Smokey Robinson and The Miracles, "Going to a Go Go". Number 11 in the US pop chart, number two in the R&B chart, '66.

The Capitals, "Cool Jerk". Number seven in the US pop chart, number two in the R&B chart, '66.

Gerry Spencer Group, "Keep on Running". Number one in the UK for four weeks at the beginning of '66.

Temptations, "My Girl". US number one, '65. "Get Ready", US number 29, '66

Small Faces, "Tin Soldier". Number nine in the UK chart, '67.

Four Tops, "Standing in the Shadow of Love". Number six in the US chart, number six in the UK chart.

Four Tops, "It's Just the Same Old Song". Number five in the US.

This was the scene until 1967 when Mod started to become commercialised by clothing companies. Until then the style had been all about originality, with youths putting together their own clothes. By now the word Mod was also an everyday term for anything new – television was even using it in the show Ready Steady Go.

Groups the Mods had followed were now changing their musical direction, The Who's "Pictures Of Lilly" got to number four, "I can see For Miles" reached number ten and The Small Faces' "Itchycoo Park" hit number three. But it wasn't the Mods who were buying the records.

The hippy psychedelic marijuana scene creeping in was far from the high energy amphetamine fuelled life the Mods had been leading. It was songs like these that signed the end for them.

Different areas split into different scenes: Swinging London, the now ever-so-fashionable Mod scene, and Psychedelic.

"Murder, blood, axe, murder" Repeated Johnny "Outside my compartment, well that just stinks. I think I'll drown myself in drinks."

"Have you heard or seen anything unusual this afternoon?" asked Matt.

"This afternoon, let's have a drink and go absurd – and I'll try and remember what I heard. Here we go, aye let's play murder in't dark eh. 7 Bellies thee's coming to get tha 7 Bellies, aaagh aaghhhhh. Is it time to sing? I don't know, I can't see a thing. What was that noise it sounded like a thunk? Oh I must be blind drunk."

After getting his breath back Johnny said to Matt, "That was it, that's what I heard."

Matt, deciphering Johnny's statement, quoted him back. "Let's play murder in the dark eh, I'm coming to get you, 7 Bellies, I'm coming to get you. You heard a noise, it sounded like a thunk, erm… like the sound of an axe striking at a body or perhaps like the thunk of a body falling to the ground?"

"I don't know, it was just a thunk, I was blind drunk."

"Okay so you were blind drunk and the axe was found right outside your compartment. This evidence and statement could, in fact, make you the murderer. Sir Johnny O.B.E. Flannel I ask you to remain here in your compartment while I take this blood soaked axe to my toilet, bathroom cabinet, err laboratory, for forensic tests."

Chapter Six

SOMEBODY'S DEAD FOREVER

"Greetings, evah living, evah faithful, Jah Rastafari, yu listen te Pirate Radio Skankdown de show dat bring ya Ska, Reggae an', seh Winston wha' Mods haffe do wid Ska an' Reggae."

"Mi tell yu dem all connected DJ, if yu listen dan yu hear GBH tell dat in '67 de Mods dem commersialised an' feel no original."

"Ya."

"De Mods dem go follow Desmond Dekker, Prince Buster, The Pioneers, Laurel Aitken, Derrick Morgan and Symarip."

"How dat come 'bout?" asked DJ.

Winston explained that by '67, Britain had large numbers of West Indian immigrants, many of them Jamaican. They brought with them that infectious Ska, Rocksteady beat and, in '68, Reggae.

White working class youths living together with blacks as second class citizens in the same economically depressed areas felt they had a lot in common. Hard Mods, leftover from the original scene, saw these musical styles as something new, raw, underground and non-commercialised. They attended West Indian night clubs or private house/flat parties playing Blues and Ska.

They kept the clean, sharp look of the Mods and shaved their heads as their Jamaican counterparts did. And because they were working class, they first wore steel-toed work boots, any brand of jeans, white work shirts and braces. These items and flying jackets were bought from ex-Army stores.

Later, work boots were substituted for Dr Martens, Brogues and loafers, while shirts became Ben Shermans and jeans became Levis, which they would spend three hours sitting in a bath to shrink to size. Harrington jackets replaced the US air force jackets, and the Gentleman's Crombie overcoat, complete with red pocket handkerchief, was adopted for the winter, topped off with a pork pie hat. The Mods adapted the rebellious sounds of the Rude boys and became the first Skinheads.

Music known as Ska, Rocksteady and Reggae in Jamaica became to be known in England as Skinhead Reggae. It must be stressed at this time there were black and white Skinheads; there were no politics, just mixed races listening and dancing together to Jamaican music.

Traditional Skinheads are known as Trads or Trojans named after the Trojan record label. The era of the Skinheads peaked in '69.

"Dat all very interesting, so tell I Winston, wha'ppen on de train te Skaville since wi las' talk te de listeners?"

"Well DJ, Matt Davies, him out deh investigatin' de disappearance fe 7 Bellies, an' de fact dat Mad Axe Man him cover in blood an' him axe is missing."

DJ, having just listened to the backgrounds of Mods and Skinhead Reggae had forgotten all about earlier proceedings and was now suddenly in shock. With his thoughts all a whirl he ad-libbed. "Tcha Mon Winston wi all nor 'bout dat episode, well actually wi don' nor 'bout dat episode." He then began turning white again as he heard The Hotknives "Jack The Ripper" in his head. They were singing –

***My friend Jack, My friend Jack, Stab him in the
back, murder***

"Weh dat soun' com' fe?"

Winston, looking at DJ with some concern, asked him,
"Wha' soun' DJ?"

"Dem soun' mon, dem singin' murder."

"Mi hear nuttin DJ."

"Mi cyaan' get murder out I head, Winston pley I som'
music."

Winston quickly introduced Symarip.

Symarip, who started out as The Bees, recorded
"Jesse James Rides Again" in '67. They then changed their
name to The Pyramids and because of legal contractual
obligations changed their name another time, reversing
Pyramids and played secretly under the name Simaryp
which somewhere along the way was changed to Symarip.

They were the first band to aim specifically for
the Skinhead Reggae scene, writing a classic album
with the title track that became an anthem: "Skinhead
Moonstomp". The track was based on Derick Morgan's
"Moon Hop". The album also contains other Skinhead
gems such as "Skinhead Jamboree" and "Skinhead Girl".
The original album cover also featured five Skinheads.

With the introduction complete, Winston selected the
track "Must Catch a Train Tonight", sending it out to the
listeners. Off air, he asked DJ what was troubling him.

***Must catch a train tonight
I've got a date
Must catch a train tonight
I can't be late
I'm feeling mighty fine la la laaaa
Oh oh la la la, Oh oh la la la, Oh oh la la la
tonight***

"Mi jus' waan nor wh'appen," answered DJ.

As if on cue there was a knock at the door. Matt Davies entered and introduced himself. "This is Matt Davies, Special Agent."

"Tcha mon I an' I nor who yu ar, yu don' haffe introduce yu self every time," said DJ.

Matt replied, "I do it for the benefit of the listeners. Besides it's how my scripts always start. If you don't like the way I start my scripts perhaps you should have a word with the editor. As a matter of interest, who does write my scripts?"

Winston, laughing, answered. *"Hee hee hee.* It DJ, Matt. DJ himself write yu script."

"Cool it Winston, dat classified," scolded DJ.

Matt, looking DJ up and down, said "You seem... a bit... how do I say? on edge, if you don't mind me saying."

"Yu don' seh, an' mi do mind," shot DJ, as quickly as The Man With No Name firing off his Colt 45. Then he asked, "Noh ar' yu goin te tell I an' I yu fin' 7 Bellies alive an' well, so wi can finish de show an' go a Skaville."

Winston, supporting DJ's anxiousness, added, "DJ is undah som' stress."

DJ fired out another shot. "Winston." But the way he shot that one word out gave it a whole row of meanings. One being, shut the fuck up.

Just then Pot Belly burst through the door and blurted, "Mr Dread, Mr Dread."

"No mon Pot Belly," said DJ, with a look that could kill. He then changed the direction of his eyes and addressed Matt. "Tell I."

Matt managed to say, "Well," before he was interrupted by Mad Axe Man who came running in panting two seconds behind Pot Belly. There was blood on his nose and fingers. He said, "Don't listen to him, tha's talking shite, what's thee told tha?"

DJ, becoming more and more frantically annoyed by the second, said to both Pot Belly and Mad Axe Man, "Out, mi waan hear wha' Matt haffe seh."

But Pot Belly had something important to say too and tried again, only managing to say, "But Axe's k –"

"OUT," shouted DJ before Pot Belly could finish his sentence – only to be overruled by Matt who had decided to take control of the situation.

Matt said, "Well actually it might be better if they both stayed. I've got some very interesting facts, evidence and statements with my own conclusion, ideas, thoughts, theories… and doubts, which all add up to making this a very interesting and very... confusing case. Not to mention a great Skankdown production. Oh but I did... just mention it."

DJ, now hysterical with the suspense and Matt's neverending long drawn out sentences with as many pauses as he feels necessary thrown in to keep you on the end of your seat or to drive you mad, before getting to the point, begged. "Don' do dis te I. Matt, haf yu fin' 7 Bellies?"

Must wash my hands and face
Wanna look pretty
Must brush my hair and shoes
Don't wanna look ghastly
I'm feeling mighty fine la la laaa
Oh oh la la la, Oh oh la la la, Oh oh la la la
tonight

Matt replied, "Err nope, I've followed the trail he took with Mr Axe Man here and got some witnesses. Here are their statements. Number one is from Misters Animal and Semi Conscious.

Mr Conscious states that he heard Mr 7 Bellies say... erm, if I may refer to my notes..." As he flicked through his notebook DJ sat drumming his fingers on the table until Matt continued. "Agh, here we are." He read. *"Yeah it's down this way Axe Man, I got it stashed in a real cool safe place and that,* which we conclude is the bottles of beer and Thunderbirds which they set out together to fetch."

Pot Belly interrupted, "We know they went to get the beer, and only Axey came back, because he murdered him, and now he –"

"If I may finish," Matt interrupted, with no one really listening to what Pot Belly had to say.

"Mr Conscious also states he heard Mr Axe Man here threaten Mr 7 Bellies with these words: *'I'ye well it just better be there or tha's in big trouble'.*"

Pot Belly tried again. "There see, they didn't find the beer and he murdered my 7 Bellies bruvver man and now he –"

"Thee hasn't murdered anybody, tha's in big trouble wore just words," protested Mad Axe Man, who interrupted Pot Belly.

Matt continued, "The next witness they passed was a Mr Zoot Sharp and he actually managed to tape a threat from Mr Axe Man to Mr 7 Bellies. This is hard evidence, which I had to purchase at an extortionate rate thanks to the sales tactics of Mr Sharp. Listen to this." As Matt pressed play on the portable tape machine, the distinct voice of Mad Axe Man was clearly heard threatening, *"If tha's leading thee op a blind alley, thee'll wrap tha's bollocks round tha's neck".*

Matt, gloating now, said, "Got you there Axe Man. What have you got to say in your defence?"

Who defended himself with, "Thee didn't bloody do it reight, wrap tha's bollocks round tha's neck is a common saying bakome, thee mother used te say it te thee all time, but yer don't mean it literally."

Matt, thrown off slightly, pressed on. "Erm, well, that still remains to be seen," before adding, "erm, preferably not." Carrying on with his report, he went on to say, "Moving further down the train I interviewed a Mr Jerry Juggler where the story takes a strange twist." Matt read from his note book that Mr Juggler had heard these words *"Just where exactly is this queer"*.

"Beer, thee said beer, the bloody shirt lifter," said Mad Axe Man.

Matt, still with his head in his notes, read on. "He then went on to state you threatened Mr 7 Bellies with, and I quote *'I've had about a bloody nough, take this, you'll be pushing up bloody Christmas trees'*."

Mad Axe Man, amazed at how circumstances and events had come to this, swore. "Is everybody round the bloody twist or what like, thee said thee's had about a bloody nough of this, tha's taking the piss, tha must think thee was, born under a bloody Christmas tree," and finished with, "that spotty puff's talking out his arse."

Winston, coming to Axe Man's defence said, "Yu mus' admit it soun' quite similar."

DJ, looking at Matt, asked, "Wha' yu mek fe al dit mon?"

Pot Belly chirped up accusingly. "He murdered him, he murdered him, and now he's –"

"Cool it mon, let Matt seh wat him fin'," interrupted DJ – again before he could finish his sentence.

Matt cleared his throat and looked at his public like he was a lecturer standing before a hall full of university students about to explain the depths of his work. The long lonely hours of surveillance, his only company being a cold coffee and an uneatable hot dog.

The complexity of forensics, how everything is important from a bite out of an apple, to... a pair of foul smelling socks. The vitality of being first on the scene and studying it from every angle to get the whole picture, what was going through the victim's mind, what was going through the –

"Wha' yu fin?" asked DJ, interrupting his thoughts and bringing him back from a huge shining hall full of eager, young, bright-eyed university students, to a dimly lit, cramped up railway carriage with a Skinhead, Dreadlock Rasta, delinquent kid Rocker and an accused-for-murder wannabe Hells Angel.

Realising that because of his past failures he would never have made it to the top in his chosen profession, not to mention never being able to give that lecture, made him think of another time he failed.

It was 10.00 pm 4th July and where was I? In my flat, on my own. Sure I'd been invited to parties

But what about Percy the goldfish? I couldn't go out and leave him on his own. I thought about taking him with me, but that would only cause suspicion. He was a witness to a case I was working, and I didn't want anybody, spiking his drinks at the party. This case was big and I couldn't get it out my mind.

Here I was on 4th July and still working. I tried to relax and switched on the TV. James Bond 007, I turned over to Dirty Harry. I just couldn't get away from work. And until this case was solved, I wasn't going to get any sleep either. I paced around the room and stopped by the window. I could see a triangle of rain in the beam of the lamp post across the street. For some reason I stared at this with a blank mind for over an hour. Then, BANG. Something triggered off in my head. There it was, staring me in the face all the time.

It was raining on the day Percy witnessed the robbery. We had on record the robber was wearing a blue mac. Tonight it was raining, and if the robber was out, he'd be wearing a blue mac. I put on my trilby and raincoat. It was 4th July and me and Percy were going out on the town.

I walked the streets for about five blocks, newspaper under one arm, Percy under the other... looking. But what was I looking for? I needed a drink, so stopped at a bar. I had myself a Tenants Pils, Percy a whisky. I took a cigarette from the packet on the bar and told the bar tender to light me. I inhaled, coughed, and remembered, I don't smoke.

This case was getting to me. I stubbed out the cigarette, drunk up, and ordered another round. That's when I noticed they were playing karaoke at the end of the bar. And I could hear somebody ... killing Gene Kelly's "I'm Singing in the Rain".

A beetle crawled out from under the ashtray and across the bar. BANG went off in my head again. But I couldn't put my finger on it, so I swatted the bug instead.

Percy was swimming round and round trying to catch my attention. When I looked at him, he was looking straight in the direction of the singer. A man fitting the description of the robber was... killing.

"I'm singing in the rain", and wearing a blue mac. We had him, I arrested him as he left the stage

You just couldn't kill a song like that and expect to get away with it. This is Matt Davis, Special Agent, just been demoted to typing pool.

"Wha' yu fin?'" asked DJ impatiently.

Matt, coming back from the past to the present, frowned and carried on where he had left off.

"Well according to Mr Juggler it was four and a half hours later before Mr Axe Man came back. He passed Mr Juggler's compartment again, only this time he was... (Matt holding his words back on purpose for maximum suspense before going on to say)... alone and limping... (Here he stalled again, leaving his listeners to let this sink in and ponder over this latest uncovered information).

Mad Axe Man couldn't believe how everyone was hanging on to Matt's every last word. He decided to break the silence with "Well I'yl go to our house, course thee was bloody limping, thee'd fallen over. Tha's not taking that gender bender seriously is tha?" Then, he addressed Matt with, "Yer slack twat... limping."

Matt took these insults like water off a duck's back. He continued, "We'll come back to that later if I may. I have a theory on what you were doing during this four and a half hours between passing by Mr Juggler's compartment for the second time."

"I'ye an just what is tha's theory like."

"It is my theory that you murdered Mr 7 Bellies by striking him with your axe. Then, you chopped him into pieces."

"I'ye and thee suppose thee fried them pieces up and sold 'em as 7 Belly burgers eh?"

Oh oh la la la, Oh oh la la la, Oh oh la la la tonight

DJ, unable to contain his surprise at this latest revelation, said, "Wha', 7 Belly burgers, don' tell I dis tru'."

Matt, now faced with another possibility, slowly dismissed Mad Axe Man's suggestion (but made a note of it for later reference) and followed his instincts. "Erm, I hadn't thought of that. It is my theory that you disposed of Mr 7 Bellies or rather the pieces of him, down the John."

"Down the John, John who?" whined Pot Belly. "I don't know anyone called John."

Mad Axe Man tried to shed some light on the matter by suggesting "Shitehouse, bog, W.C. water closet, karzy, outhouse, privvy, the loo, lavatory, Mary Whitehouse –"

"Him mean de toilet, Pot Belly," said DJ, cutting him off before he could go any further. Then, looking at Matt for confirmation, he asked, "Don' yu Matt?"

Matt nodded. "Yes."

DJ asked, "Is dat how he do it?" He then confronted Mad Axe Man with "Axe Man, ye kill 7 Bellies an' flush him down de toilet?"

Mad Axe Man, for the umpteenth time, protested his innocence. "Look thee didn't bloody do it reight, is this a bloody conspiracy or what like?"

Matt admitted, "Well there's no actual evidence to support my theory. On searching through all the toilets, cisterns and U-bends the only human remains I found were the ones commonly known as stools."

"Stools, stools, you found stools in the toilet, how did they get there?" asked Pot Belly, not for the first time totally confused.

"Tha means turds Pot Belly," answered Mad Axe Man. "Like when thee's been for a bab or te drop a log like, had a shite, take a dump, a Bungle's finger."

Matt continued. "On my investigation of the toilets I did, however, find these words scribbled on some of the walls and doors. If I may refer to my notes?" He flicked through the pages of his notebook, and on finding what he was looking for said, "Ah, here we are." He began to read.

"You flick ash in our bogs,

And we'll shit in your ashtrays.

Here's another.

Some come here to sit and think,

Some come here to shit and stink,

Some come here to scratch their balls,

But I come here to write on walls.

Good eh?

When everything's wrong, and nothing ain't right,

Just sit tha self down and have a good shite."

Matt, smiling to himself, went on to say, "You'll like this one."

Here I sat, broken hearted,

Paid a penny and only farted".

"It'd cost tha more than a penny to fart these days," interrupted Mad Axe.

"You have to remember it's an old train," answered Matt, before continuing.

"And finally:

Here you sit in this marble hall,

Reading the writing on the wall,

If no paper can be found,

Just slide your arse along the ground."

DJ, who didn't know how these words were relevant to the case, enquired, "Yu tink dem som' sort a clue' or riddle' fe de killer?"

"Nope, just graffiti I thought was funny," answered Matt.

DJ protested. "Don' do dis te I Matt, wi got no time fe joke'. Murdah is nuh fun." Disappointed, DJ asked, "So yu tell I yu fin' nuttin in de toilets?"

"Nothing at all, nothing at all that is... except for these, which I will be holding on to as evidence until this case is closed."

Must catch a train tonight
I've got a date
Must catch a train tonight
I can't be late
I'm feeling mighty fine la la laaaa
Oh oh la la la, Oh oh la la la, Oh oh la la la
tonight

As he dragged a huge duffel bag in from the corridor and pulled out twenty bottles of Newcastle Brown Ale, he read aloud from a label: "The one and only premium bottled beer with its own unique colour, taste and strength, and may I add a healthy 4.7% alcohol content."

DJ Dread, Winston, Mad Axe Man and Pot Belly all looked at the bottles, then at each other, than back to the bottles, then to Matt, who was enjoying the moment and squeezing out the awe till the last second before he conjured – like a magician – and pulled out a further six bottles of Thunderbird. Again, he read:

"Thunderbird, the American classic fortified apple wine with flavours producing a tasty 13.1% alcohol. All in the toilet cistern of carriage number five. No wonder it wouldn't flush. So, it would appear that Mr 7 Bellies did in fact stash some beer *in a real cool safe place and that*'."

Pot Belly, standing up to Mad Axe Man, said, "You murdered him for nuffin Axey – you murdered my 7 Bellies bruvver man for nuffin and now you've ki –'

"Pot Belly, let Matt finish an' give all de evidence him haf'," interrupted DJ.

Matt continued, "Further down the train I found the hardest evidence of all...." (Again he waited for the suspense to reach a climatic peak before he went on.) "... A blood soaked axe, in a pool of blood."

"JEHOVAH, de murdah weapon!" cried out DJ.

Matt agreed. "At that time I thought so too; it was right outside Sir Johnny O.B.E Flannel's compartment and on interviewing him I got this statement." He read from his notes.

"This afternoon, let's have a drink and go absurd
And try and remember what I heard, here we go,
Aye let's play murder in't dark eh,
7 Bellies thee's coming to get tha,
7 Bellies ....aaaaaagggggghhhhhh
Is it time to sing
I don't know, I can't see a thing
What was that noise, it sounded like a thunk
Oh I must be blind drunk."

DJ complained. "Mi don' overstaan a ting mon, wha' him seh?"

Matt explained, "To break it down, to simplify so to say, make it easy to understand, what Mr Sir Johnny O.B.E. Flannel is saying is that he heard Mr Axe Man here threaten Mr 7 Bellies. Let's play murder in the dark; I'm coming to get you, followed by a bloodcurdling scream, and then a noise – a thunk – which could have been the axe striking Mr 7 Bellys or his body hitting the ground."

Mad Axe Man, still protesting his innocence, denied it. "Thee didn't bloody murder 7 Bellies, when thee said let's play murder in't dark thee wore just lurking about like, like we did when we wore bairns. That thunk wore probly thee falling down and knocking thee self out."

Pot Belly, not having any of this, said, "Officer, arrest that man. He murdered my 7 Bellies bruvver man and now he's ki–'

"Matt, is he guilty?" DJ asked, jumping in.

"Well if you've been listening closely you'll have noticed that when I said I'd found the blood soaked axe, DJ said 'Jehovah! The murder weapon.' I said at that time I thought so too. But as a result of forensic tests I've found the blood on the axe and the pool of blood both to be A Rhesus."

Everybody looked at each other with an expression on their faces that said what's A Rhesus?

Matt saw the puzzlement and answered. "Which is Mr Axe Man's own blood. This matches the statement from Mr Juggler about Mr Axe Man here limping past Mr Juggler's cabin. If I may examine your right leg, Mr Axe Man?"

"Tha's not a bloody puff an' all is tha?"

Matt persisted. "Your leg, please," to which Mad Axe Man reluctantly responded by stepping forward, lifting his leg up and putting his foot on the desk. His bike boot toe end touched Winston's turntables, who up to now had said very little since the intrusion at his studio.

That was up to now, that was before some antichrist had not only dared to blaspheme against all that was pure and sacred, but had stepped over the threshold and put a dirty great foot on the holy turntables too. The turntables that played Ska, Rocksteady and Reggae, bringing love, peace and harmony to the masses.

Winston saw it as if the devil himself had crashed through Saint Peter's gates with a dumper truck, and followed by an AC/DC tarmac crew. Angus Young performing a Townsend jump kick from the cabin followed by a Chuck Berry duck walk in overdrive across the floor while thrashing out a riff on his Gibson lead guitar, never missing a stroke.

With the rest of the crew belting out their instruments and the devil himself being a reincarnation of Bon Scott – who wore the tightest pair of jeans humanly possible, teamed with white plimsoles and a naked torso – takes to the stage, climbing up on the roof of the dumper truck and screaming "I'm on a Highway to Hell."

Well, thought Winston. Mad Axe Man did want to be a Hells Angel, but with his long hair, tight leather pants and biker boots he looked more like a Hills Angel.

Winston couldn't hold his anger in, and not knowing which swear word to use, used them all and let rip. In under a second, he'd managed shit, bugger, bastard, fuck, tit and wank, and then went on to call Axe Man a greasy, long haired dickhead of a bloodclaat, bambaclaat, goat fucker and raasclaat pig. He finished off by saying he didn't have any respect for other people's property.

Matt stepped in, saying that this would only take a moment. On examining Mad Axe Man's right thigh he discovered a cut through his leather trouser leg and confirmed it. "Just as I suspected – a deep laceration to the upper thigh where you actually fell on your own axe." Mad Axe Man, finally feeling off the hook with just as bemused a look on his face as the rest of the party, said in a relieved tone, "Well bloody hell, fancy that, cut thee's leg with thee's own axe and thee never felt a thing."

"Well, due to the alcohol content I found in your bloodstream it's not surprising. You must have consumed a vast amount before going out to play murder in the dark."

"Aye well tha knows we were knocking 'em back a bit like... tha could say we had a few."

"A FEW," said Matt astonished. "You've drunk enough to be embalmed." This was giving his medical opinion.

DJ, still none the wiser, asked, "Haf him murdah 7 Bellies or haf him no murdah 7 Bellies?"

Matt summed it all up and gave it to them straight. "With all the evidence, facts and statements, I've come to the conclusion that Mr Axe Man here did..." (Everyone was becoming acquainted with his technique of giving it to you straight as he gave another one of his long pauses before finishing his sentence.) "... not murder Mr 7 Bellies."

There was silence and looks of surprise, confusion and relief – in that order – from all the faces in the carriage. That is until DJ, thinking they could celebrate, finish the journey to Skaville and put on the best show anyone had ever seen, broke the silence by saying, "So 7 Bellies him alive den?"

Must catch the train everybody, everybody, everybody
Must brush my hair and my shoes

"I didn't say that," answered Matt, "I think Mr 7 Bellies is probably very dead and murdered by... Mr Sir Johnny O.B.E Flannel – who was blind drunk at the time. Here's how I think he did it. When the train entered the tunnel, Mr Flannel struck Mr Axe Man unconscious then killed Mr 7 Bellies with Mr Axe Man's axe. He then disposed of the body; I don't know where yet, erm, perhaps in one of the air vents, but I haven't checked them yet –"

"Well it'd have te be a bloody big air vent," interrupted Mad Axe Man.

"Take it or leave it, I'll carry on regardless," said Matt, and he did, going on to say, "he then wiped the axe clean of his own prints, cut Mr Axe Man's leg and left the axe lying next to him in the pool of blood, putting all suspicion on Mr Axe Man."

DJ's hope, as with the rest, now faded away. He asked, "Is dat yu t'eory? Is dat wha' yu believe?"

"Nope. Why, if that was the case then Mr Axe Man here could have killed Mr 7 Bellies, disposed of his body, cleaned the axe, cut himself and lay down outside Mr Flannel's compartment to make us believe the ludicrous story I just told you."

Everyone stood in silence not knowing what to believe or what to think anymore.

Pot Belly, still convinced of Mad Axe Man's guilt, took advantage of the silence and seized his moment. He blurted, "He did, he did kill my 7 Bellies bruvver man and made it look like Mr Flannel and now he's killed Coke as well...."

"Oh no dit is getting worse by de minute," said Winston.

DJ felt sick to the stomach. This was not love thy neighbour, this was not his dream, Pirate Radio Skankdown was supposed to spread Bob Marley's message of "One Love" and here they are killing each other within the first 48 hours.

"A whole bag of fuckery" said DJ who was now most definitely cracking up. He was holding his head as if he had a terrible headache but was actually trying to cover his ears to block out the remix that was playing in his head. It was a remix of The Selecter's, "Murder" and "Too much pressure", Alberto Y Lost Trios Paranoias "Gobbin' on Life", The Hotknives "Jack The Ripper" and The Angelic Upstarts' "The Murder of Liddle Towers", which went something like this:

Murder, oow oow murder, I say murder, that's what they want you to do.
Too much pressure this pressure's got to stop
Livin' is a cliche' it's all been done before
Death is the only thing we got left to live for
Murder ... I'm saying murder
Too much pressure this pressure's got to stop
Life is cheap, but death is free
Die die die, come die with me
Too much pressure it's got to stop it's got to stop
Murder... I'm saying murder
My friend Jack, My friend Jack, stab him in the back, murder
Too much pressure it's got to stop it's got to stop
Too much pressure it's got to stop it's got to stooooooooooooooooooop

MURDER

Chapter Seven

ONE STEP FORWARD,
TWO STEPS BACK

Matt Davis was the first to speak. He said, "So Mr Axe Man, you're still under suspicion for the murder of Mr 7 Bellies. And now it's been brought to my attention that you are responsible for the murder of Mr Caine, too. How do you account for these accusations?"

Mad Axe Man defended himself. "It's just a coincidence like, thee suppose thee's jus been int rong place at rong time like. If it wern't fer bad luk thee wouldn't ave nowt, thee's always holding fork when tha's dishing out gravy, bloody hell if thee fell in a barrel a tits thee would come out sucking thee's thumb." Looking sorry for himself and feeling the whole world was against him he then went on to say, "Thee nors all fingers ar pointing at thee, but thee swears thee didn't do it reight. Coke and 7 Bellies ar thee's mates, like we've known each other fer donks."

"Donks? What's donks mean?" asked Pot Belly.

"Yes Mr Axe Man, please elaborate on donks," requested Matt.

Axe Man answered sarcastically, deliberately articulating as if Matt was as delinquent as Pot Belly.

"DONKEYS' YEARS, A LONG TIME, WE'VE KNOWN EACH OTHER FOR MANY YEARS."

"Alright Mr Axe Man, you don't have to get cynical."

"Thee's jus protesting thee's innocence."

"I sincerely hope I can verify that Mr Axe Man. But now, I need to know everything that happened leading up to the last time you saw Mr Caine."

Mad Axe Man told that after DJ and Winston had left Pot Belly, Coke and himself, stating they would be back with all this sorted out. As the door closed they all looked at each other speechless.

Feeling uncomfortable, it was Mad Axe Man who broke the silence by saying, "Well int tha or tha going to say nowt then?"

Coke reacted with a *sniff*. "Nowt," he said, and then cracked up laughing.

Pot Belly, annoyed at Coke, said, "I don't fink your funny."

To which Coke replied, *sniff* "Don't be so serious maan."

To which Pot Belly responded with, "You fink Axey murdering my 7 Bellies bruvver man is not serious then?"

Coke retaliated, *sniffing*, "Like we're going to a festival maan, it's going to be bigger than all the other festivals we've ever been to. Bigger than Glastonbury and Reading, it will wipe the floor with Monsters of Rock, Acid Daze, it will make Stonehenge look like Lego bricks. It's going to be even bigger than Woodstock. This is going to be the mother of all festivals maan, live on stage, the Pirate Radio Skankdown show in Skaville. It's going to be a real good trip maan."

Pot Belly, sounding sad and disillusioned, said, "Well it hasn't started off as a real good trip maan has it?"

"Tha's not wrong there," added Axe Man. "Accused of bloody murder and confined to our cabin within first hours. How long does it take te get te Skaville anyway? Thee's never heard of it afore tuther night."

Pot Belly tried to shed some light on the matter by suggesting, "Int it near Potter Brompton somewhere?"

Coke answered. *Sniff.* "Naa, that's Scarborough maan."

"Honestly Pot Belly, tha's as thick as shite," said Axe Man.

"Well you don't nor where it is," countered Pot Belly.

"Ha ha ha ha *sniff,* nice one Pot Belly," laughed Coke.

"So like just where the fuck is Skaville then, Mr Geography?" asked Mad Axe Man.

Coke took a deep breath, trying to collect his thoughts and bide himself some time before he *sniffed* and said, "Well we've got to go to Dover maan, and then through the Channel Tunnel, over to France then right across Europe."

"What?" interrupted Mad Axe Man. "Thee can't wait that long for a bab, thee's off te find thee self a bab house."

Pot belly didn't understand what Mad Axe Man was saying but understood enough to know he was planning to leave the compartment. He recited, "Mr DJ Dread said *don't nobody leave this compartment till he's found my 7 Bellies brother man and got all this sorted out.*" He then added, "And Mr Matt Davis Special Agent Toilet Duties said *you had to remain here.*"

"And Axe Man says, tortoise is sticking thee's head out, thee's off fer a shite."

"Tortoise, have you got a tortoise? Can I feed it?" asked Pot Belly, having lost the thread of the conversation.

"Thee doubts tha'd want te feed this tortoise," said Mad Axe Man.

Sniff. "Yeah, well I could do to siphon the python myself," said Coke.

"Siphon the python? What do you mean, siphon the python? Python, that's a snake in't it? I don't like snakes, have you got a snake Coke?" asked Pot Belly.

"Yeah, It's my trouser snake and I'm taking him for a piss."

"You two will get into terrible trouble when Mr DJ Dread and Mr Matt Davies toilet duties find out."

"Thee'll be in even bigger trouble if if thee don't. Thee is touching cloth as it is, and thee hasn't got a change of duds," argued Mad Axe Man.

Sniff. "Which way, Axe Man?" asked Coke, clearly still out of his tree as he pulled himself up and walked his hands along the wall to the door.

Mad Axe Man, training his tortoise back in, very carefully and very slowly stood up, saying "This way."

They left the cabin, taking the first right and passing a cabin whose curtains with a big anarchy sign painted on them were closed. Mad Axe Man told of the Punks who were jumping up and down earlier like a couple of lunatics, and asked, 'What's this hanging on't door Gettifeyebassa?'

Sniff. "Gettifeyebassa," said Coke in a Scottish accent.

"Oh that's Scottish for get the fuck out of here you bastard."

"What?" said Axe Man.

"I think they mean do not disturb; that'll be Animal and Semi."

"Thee didn't nor tha could read and speak Scottish."

Sniff. Yeah maan I know them. Maybe we should call in and have a drink?"

"Good idea; only one problem."

Sniff. "What's that?"

"Thee has te empty thee's reject box first."

At this time, Semi was working his way through the trays of McEwens lager with Animal.

"Another beer?"

"Aye, Iyl get em in," said Semi.

"Och, keep yer hand in ye pocket it's my roond," said Animal, reaching across the table and grabbing another two cans. Suddenly the the red light came on, signalling to them that it was time to talk about the second wave of Punk.

Animal spoke:

By '77, the first wave of Punk was over (The Pistols, The Clash and The Damned are recognised as being the first three UK bands). What set out as a D.I.Y. approach to the music industry, with ideals of originality, individuality, self hate, personal anarchy and not selling music as a product, had sold out to the very cause it had set out to oppose.

What was the new wave had become the same as the old wave. It was unfortunate that it all happened so quickly but the people who started it off had lost control. Andrew Czezowski – who hired the Roxy Club at 41-43 Neal Street, Covent Garden (which became to be known as The 100 Club because it was open for 100 days) to give the first Punk bands a venue and kids the chance to see bands for a reasonable price (three bands for 40p) – could no longer afford the rates The Roxy were asking. At least, not without putting the entrance fees up. This wasn't what punk set out to be.

Punks weren't stars and the kids could talk to the bands who, when they weren't playing, were on the streets or in the clubs themselves. When Punk started it didn't matter what you looked like either, black, white, long hair, short hair – but now it was fashionable you had to have short hair, tight trousers and plastic clothes.

True Punks with original ideals even slagged off The Pistols, who had signed up with big labels including A&M, E.M.I. and Virgin. In reality they were caught in a catch 22 – a band could not survive and support itself without selling records. Punk had become commercialised, fashionable and all the big record companies were suddenly signing up a Punk band. A second wave of punk was beginning.

Many bands inspired by the Sex Pistols had a different sound. "Siouxsie and the Banshees", "X Ray Spex", "Generation X", "Sham 69' 'The Slits', 'The Adverts', 'Subway Sect', 'Buzzcocks', 'UK Subs', 'The Vibrators' àll started in '76, with the exception of 'The Addicts' who formed at the end of '75 and 'Eater', who although formed in '76, were playing Punk before ever hearing or seeing 'The Pistols' or 'The Damned'.

Members from some of these bands were just a few months earlier in the crowd at Pistols gigs. Some were members of what had been Bromly continent – Steve Sevrin, Siouxsie Sue, Billy Idol, Shane McGouwen.

This second wave was working class, using all the energy and aggression of Punk Rock while turning down the volume and eliminating the distortion. They played clear notes, added catchy guitar solos and wrote populist lyrics.

Some of these bands and definitely all that came after (with the exception of anarcho Punk bands Crass and Flux Pink Indians) were jumping on the bandwagon and cashing in. It was no longer about letting the music industry see that anyone could get up and have their say with songs that were between one and two minutes long – songs that weren't even asking for three minutes of glory.

This second wave did want the glory. It became known as Street Punk and what the big labels were putting out was three minute commersialised pop rock. Everyone involved was in it for the money.

Coke was staggering on his feet, walking his hands along the walls of the corridor in a drunken stupor. He had saliva running down his chin as he giggled to himself at the sight of Mad Axe Man in front of him. Mad Axe Man was clenching his buttocks together with all the concentration he could muster and walking on his toes, like a ballerina in black leathers and biker boots.

Entering the next carriage, Coke saw and read a sign hanging on the door.

Sniff. "Shop closed, back in half an hour."

"Oh, that's like Zoot's Bargain Basement carriage. Tha can buy owt, an' if tha hasn't got it tha'l hav it by end't day, guaranteed," explained Axe Man.

Sniff. "Nice one, we can pick up a couple of crates."

"Good idea, only two problems."

Sniff. "What are they, then?"

"One, thee's off fer a shite. And two, tha's closed."

"Oh yeah," said Coke, disappointed.

They moved on in to the next carriage where Coke stood looking at the flowered pink curtains.

Sniff. "Who's in here then?"

"Thee goes bah name Jerry Juggler."

Sniff. "Nice one, like he'll be good for a bit of entertainment and that."

"Bad idea. Only three problems."

Sniff. "Let me guess. Err, he doesent drink, err –"

"One, thee's a gender bender. Two, he guttersniped on thee. And three, it sounds like Matt's in there interviewing him, and we were ordered to stay in our compartment."

On entering the next carriage they heard, "My Top Ten Rehab Tips Of The Day, Number Ten: Start the day with a glass of fresh orange juice followed by............... a whiskey chaser."

Sniff. "Sounds like Johnny Flannel's on board; we can call in and have a chat," said Coke.

"Thee needs te call in and have a shat first. Come on, what's tha lurking about at?"

Mad Axe Man, still with buttocks held together as tight as a vice, tip-toed forwards, while Coke, leaning on the wall walked at 45 degrees, into the next carriage. A wave of relief came over Mad Axe Man as he saw the answer to his pleas – a toilet – only to have that relief just as quickly taken away by Coke. Coke said, *sniffing*, "Well it's like covered in maintenance tape maan."

"Aye, and some bugger's stuck a sign on saying out of order."

Sniff. "Yeah and what's this? Restricted area by order of the janitor. It's crossed out and it says Matt Davis Special Agent in biro."

"Bloody hell, thee's busting fer a shite. Thee's gonna stick thee's arse out window."

Sniff. "Naa maan, that's dangerous."

"It's not as dangerous as shiteing thee's pants."

Sniff. "Come on maan, there must be another one further down the train," said Coke as he dragged his feet along the floor, still walking his hands along the corridor wall.

Mad Axe Man hung back, taking something out of his pocket before leaning over the maintenance tape.

"Tink right an' yu be right, Pirate Radio Skankdown an' dat was dem Punks Animal an Semi deh. I an' I don' really see wha' dat haffe do wid Ska an' Reggae but Winston here assure' I it all connected," said DJ.

"Dat right DJ, it all coming togedder now."

"Soon come Winston, soon come. Wi a radio show, wi mus' pley music."

"Dat why wi noh tune inte dem cockney Mods GBH an' Sparrow te tell us 'bout de Mod revival an den wi pley anudder track," said Winston.

"Grievous."

"What?"

"It's a kind of an auwhite train ride so far, don't yer fink?"

"You know what Sparrow, I fink you're white. It makes a nice change to be sat here with a few beers playing cards on a Saturday night. A nice change from what we usually do on a Saturday night. What do we usually do on a Saturday night, Sparrow?"

"We usually sit in The Devil's Arms with a few beers playing cards."

"Do we? Well that's exactly what I mean Sparrow. A nice change to be away from The Devil's Arms and them rowdy lot."

It was here they saw the red light come on. GBH, who was quite proud of his knowledge of the Mod culture, sat up and opened a bottle of Holsten Pils. He lit a cigarette and began to talk.

In Nov '78, The Jam released "All Mod Cons" which sparked a Mod revival. In '79, the compilation album "Mods' May Day" was released – as was The Who's film, "Quadrophenia", which was set in '64 – the peak of the first Mod generation. Booker T and the MG's "Green Onions" was re-released and reached number seven in the UK, which seemed to confirm it: Mods were back.

Originals from the first time round were joined by a new generation of Mods who wore white bowler shoes as per Paul Weller's trio, or cherry red Dr Martens. Army or camouflaged trousers were worn and heavily mirrored scooters were back in fashion, complete with fox fur on the aerials.

The Jam were joined by a list of other new bands that had sprung up on the scene. These included Purple Hearts (named after the amphetimine barbiturate mix from the sixties) who had been around since the Punk movement in '77, and who supported the Buzzcocks for their first gig. They had a chart entry at 57 with "Millions Like Us".

Secret Affair, who played their first gig at The Reading University in Feb '79 opened for The Jam. They also took a leaf out of the Punk movement, signed to Ariste and started their own label, "I Spy". Their debut single "Time for Action" sold over 200, 000 copies and reached number 13 in the charts followed by "Glory Boys" and "My World". In 1980 they released Laurel Aitken's "Rudi Got Married" which made number 60 in the charts..

Another Mod band, The Lambrettas, put out a cover of The Coasters' "Poisen Ivy", which they'd scored a number one R&B chart hit in '59 with. The Lambrettas played a Ska version and put it out in a black and white sleeve with the logo of a Mod in a parka looking like Walt Jabsco and substituting Two Tone for Two Stroke. It earned them a number seven in the charts.

Other Mod bands on the scene were The Chords, The Merton Parkas, The Scene, The Jolt, The Fixations, Small Hours, The Mods, Squire, and Begger.

The difference between this Mod revival was the first Mods were going forwards, where as this generation were going back to the 60's, which probably because of no progression soon caved in on its self, or got lost under the Two Tone movement which was growing by the minute.

"'Eer, Grevious."

"What"

"The Jam."

"What about 'em?"

"They made some good records didn't they?"

"YOU WHAT? Some? They made untold amount o' blinding records"

"How did that all start then"

"Well it's a good thing you ask, Sparrow, 'cause they were my favourite band. I'll tell you –

The Jam started in Woking, Surrey in '73, with front man Paul Weller playing with various line-ups until the mid seventies when it settled with Bruce Foxton and Rick Butler. They started playing covers of early Rock and Roll until Weller heard The Who's "My Generation". He then became fascinated with Mod music which prompted him to go out and buy a black suit, fish-tail parka and and save up for a scooter. Weller, inspired by Townsend, moved from bass guitar to lead rhythm and persuaded Foxten to play bass with Butler on drums.

During '77 they played on the London pub circuit alongside the Punk movement.

The Jam were also having their say, playing high volume lead and bass with machine-gun drums and Weller spitting out lyrics through clenched teeth. But where as the Punks were scruffy, violent, playing distorted, creating chaos and genuinely not giving a fuck about anything, The Jam were wearing suits and playing a clean professional sound, writing three minute youth anthems with political observations.

They shone out against the Punks and with albums titled, "This Is The Modern World", and "All Mod Cons", The Jam became head of the Mod revival. And did you know, said GBH, quite enjoying himself, that "Town Called Malice" was a double A single, "Precious" being the other A side. On 18 Feb '82, both were played on Top of the Pops in the same show. The only other band to ever accomplish this feat was The Beatles.

Another interesting fact is "That's Entertainment" and "Just Who is the 5 o' Clock Hero?" were the bestselling import singles in the UK of all time.

"Blinding times," said GBH, with Sparrow nodding his agreement.

"But all good things must come to an end, and so did The Jam. In 1984, when at the age of 24 and after four number one singles – "Going Underground", "Start", "Town called Malice", and "Beat Surrender" – plus a number one album, "The Gift", Weller disbanded the group, saying there was nothing else for them to accomplish..

"He never stopped being a Mod though. Years later, Paul Weller, in an interview with Jonathan Ross, was referred to as once being a Mod. He answered, 'I'm still a Mod, I'll always be a Mod. You can bury me a Mod.' I suppose that's how he got the title 'The Modfather'."

"Rasta de rebel, de promise keeper fe de poor, an' de bearer fe hope fe a more righteous tomorrow. Irie mon, yu listin te Pirate Radio Skankdown, dat was GBH deh – him sure nor a ting a two 'bout dem Mods."

"Irie DJ," agreed Winston. "An' noh wi pley a song wid lyrics jus' like Punk or Reggae, stating 'I don' get wha' dis society waan, mi goin' overgroun'."

"Tcha mon Winston, Pirate Radio Skankdown go overgroun' te get away fe de Babylon."

"Dat right DJ, an' now me tek yu back te March 22, 1980, an'wi leave dem Madness holding up deh 'Baggy Trousers' at number two, an' wi pley De Jam's number one, 'Going Underground'."

Some people might say my life is in a rut,
But I'm quite happy with what I've got,
People might say that I should strive for more,
But I'm so happy I can't see the point,
Something's happening here today,
A show of strength with your boys brigade and,
I'm so happy and you're so kind,
You want more money of course, I don't mind,
To buy nuclear textbooks for atomic crimes,

"Na, what was we talking about Sparrow?"

"Well we was havin' a game a cards wasn't we?"

"Oh yeah. Nice to get away from the Devil's Arms and all them rowdy lot, hey Sparrow."

Just then Coke and Mad Axe Man entered their cabin. Both looked worse for wear, Mad Axe Man up on his toes holding a very stern face of concentration as if standing before a judge about to be sentenced.

Coke, still unsteady on his feet, had walked his hands around the door frame and was hanging on to the wall for support. He looked over his shoulder at the hat stand with a stupid grin on his face.

And the public gets what the public wants,
But I want nothing this society's got,
I'm going underground, (going underground)
Well the brass bands play and feet start to
pound,
Going underground, (going underground)
Well let the boys all sing and the boys all shout
for tomorrow

GBH and Sparrow sat at their table and looked up at the hippy and wannabe Hells Angel who both loomed over them. As far as Mods were concerned, Hippies and Bikers fell in to the Rockers category – who had a long history of fights with Mods going back to the '64 "Battle of Hastings Two".

Not knowing if they were in a threatening position or not, Sparrow was trying to work out an escape route, while GBH was planning to fight his way out. It was like a gun slinger's draw at high noon; everybody's eyes were darting from one to another's, trying to anticipate who was going to make the first move.

Some people might get some pleasure out of
hate,
Me I've enough already on my plate,
People might need some tension to relax,
(me?) I'm too busy dodging between the flax,

The tension was as tight as a mountain climber's rope who's slipped and is hanging from it over the edge of a cliff. Only now he realises the white rope has a blue line through it, being an old rope with a snag in, and not green as he thought when he took it out of the shed in the darkness of the morning's early hours.

He's now hanging, knowing the rope is not going to hold out for long. He sees strand by strand breaking and twirling apart. The mountain face is 10 metres out of reach, meaning he has to climb 20 metres up the rope to reach the face before he can take any tension off the rope. He looks down and sees the rocks a thousand metres below; all waiting to break his fall – when the tension broke....

...as Coke, addressing the hat stand, *sniffed*. "Hi guys, don't suppose you know where I can have a wazz maan"?

"YOU WHAT?" asked GBH.

"Ey up lads, does tha nor where there's a Mary Whitehouse, like thee has to open thee's bomb doors tha nors," said Mad Axe Man.

"YOU WHAT?"

Sniff. "You know maan, take a leak," said Coke.

"YOU WHAT? YOU WHAT? YOU WHAT?"

"Aye, take a dump, drop a log like," added Axe Man.

What you see is what you get,
You've made your bed you better lie in it,
You choose your leader and place your trust,
As their lies wash you down and their promises rust,
You'll see kidney machines replaced by rockets and guns,

"DOES THIS BLEEDIN LOOK LIKE A KARZY?" replied GBH, who was rapidly metamorphosing into the equivalent of a warewolf. He was now the crazed boxer he used to be. The boxer who never heard the bell at the end of a round; the boxer who didn't stop beating someone even when they were out cold. The boxer who had to be pulled off his opponent by four men and dragged to the changing room.

Hair was growing across his hands. The veins in his neck were sticking out like tree roots. And he was about to rip their heads off when Coke, seeing a stack of crates under the hat stand, said, "Oh wow, you got some beer!"

The blood boiled over in GBH's head. He burst out with "YOU WHAT? Got some beer, we got crates of the stuff, going down to Skaville ain't we? You gotta have something to do on the way down there ain't ye, which is why we've got some beer. *Pant, pant, pant.*"

And the public wants what the public gets,
But I don't get what this society wants,
I'm going underground, (going underground)
Well let the brass bands play and the feet start
to pound
Going underground (going underground)
So let the boys all sing and the boys all shout
for tomorrow,

By now Sparrow had realised they were under no threat at all, and if so could handle these two misfits anyway. It would be as easy as drinking a pint of lager. The hippy looked like he'd fall over if you took his hands away from the wall, while the wannabe Hells Angel, who was still standing on his toes, looked like he would shit himself if you just touched him.

Coke and Mad Axe Man, oblivious to the danger they were in, spoke together. Coke *sniffed*, "How's it going maan? And like is there any chance of a beer?"

"Aye," said Mad Axe Man, "and has tha seen 7 Bellies? Only thee's under suspicion of murdering him like."

We talk and talk until my head explodes,
I turn on the news and my body froze,
The braying sheep on my TV screen,
Make this boy shout, make this boy scream,
Going underground,
Going underground,

"DO WHAT JOHN? LEAVE IT OUT. There I was –"

"We," interrupted Sparrow.

"WHAT?"

"There we was," corrected Sparrow.

"Oh yeah, there we was, sitting in our carriage having a quite game of cards and a drink – getting away from The Devil's Arms and all you rowdy lot. Then in the middle of the night two of you come waltzing in, looking for a beer, looking for a lavvy, telling me you're accused of murder. NO, you can't have any beer. NO, I don't know where there's a karzy, and now I'll give you a tip – it's a dead cert. If you two don't disappear before I stand up I'll be accused of murdering the bloody pair of you."

Then, looking at Coke, who was still hanging on the wall, he said "Naa, Spiderman. HOP IT and take Twinkle Toes 'ere with you."

Well the brass bands play and feet start to pound
Going underground
Going underground
So let the boys all sing
And the boys all shout for tomorrow

Going underground, the brass bands playing pow pow pow
Going underground let the boys all shout for tomorrow

Spiderman and Twinkle Toes found themselves back out in the corridor, still no nearer to a lavatory. Feeling a bit peeved, Coke sniffed, "Like we only asked where the toilet is."

"Aye, tha'd think thee'd asked em te pay some poll tax," said Mad Axe Man.

Chapter Eight

TWO TONE TRAIN

Winston was telling DJ and the listeners that now the second waves of Punk and Mod had been discussed he could now talk about the second wave of Ska, which began with Punk band The Automatics in 1978 at a time when second wave Punk bands were fading out. The Automatics were a band of musicians handpicked and put together by Gerald Dankey, who had adopted the Punk name of Jerry Dammers.

In '78, during the "On Parole" tour in support of The Clash, they played a mix of Punk and Reggae which didn't quite work with the audience. In '79 they had changed their name to The Specials and swapped Reggae for Ska which worked better than anyone could have imagined. They had built up a large following, had a phenomenal live show and were predicted to be the next big thing, with a row of record companies chasing after them with contracts.

By the end of August they were the next big thing. They had climbed up the charts to number six with a song titled "Gangsters", which was a reworking of Prince Buster's '64 "Alcapone". The song was written after a trip to Paris where they really did have their guitars confiscated and were disillusioned with Bernie Rhodes and the whole corruption of the music industry.

"Gangsters" came out on Dammer's brainchild Two Tone, a new label with the distinctive logo of a black and white Rude boy called Walt Jabsco and black and white checks. The label was easily identifiable and stood for multi-racialism – The Specials being a multi-racial band. They had seen racism creeping in during their earlier gigs as The Automatics and made a ploy to do something about it.

The label was set up to sign other up-and-coming bands for single releases. Madness, a North London band with their own sound had supported The Specials twice, and were the first to be signed. They released "The Prince", a song playing homage to Prince Buster which reached number 16 in October. They were followed by another Coventry band, The Selecter who released "On My Radio" which reached number eight, also in October. Birmingham band, The Beat, who had supported The Selecter, then released the Smokey Robinson number "Tears of a Clown", reaching number six. They were followed by another Selecter support band, The Bodysnatchers, who released a cover of Dandy Livingstones "Let's Do Rocksteady" which reached number 22.

Not only was the label black and white, but so were the lyrics. The Specials wrote songs about political and social issues, educating the youth of the day. Unfortunately and quite unbelievably, the media often missed the whole message and saw them as a bunch of racist Skinheads.

In October, a 40-date Two Tone tour kicked off with The Specials. Madness and The Selecter skanking across Britain, turning it black and white as it went from town to town. The music was just as infectious as the first time round, getting everybody up and dancing again. Two Tone mania spread across England from the stage, radios and turntables and on to televisions, when on the 8th of November 1979, The Specials, Madness and The Selecter all appeared on that evening's Top of the Pops.

The new Two Tone stars played along side Purple Hearts, Secret Affair, The Lambrettas, UB40 and Dexy's Midnight Runners. Due to a Skinhead revival in '78 and the Mod revival in '79, there were Mods, Skinheads and a few Punks still hanging on, with Rude Boys, Rastas and Soulies all turning up at the early gigs.

The Two Tone movement revived the careers of Rico Rodriquez, Judge Dread, Laurel Aitken, Desmond Dekker and Toots and the Maytels, not to mention Prince Buster's back catalogue.

The Specials' number one "Too Much Too Young" live EP inspired Trojan records to re-release Harry J and the Allstars' "Liquadator" and The Pioneers' "Longshot kick de bucket" as a double A side, which reached number 42. Symarip's "Skinhead Moonstomp" was also re-released and made the lower end of the charts in1980.

The first five Two Tone bands all charting with their debut singles was the peak of Two Tone, but October 1980 saw the first of these bands – The Bodysnatchers – split. They were followed by the Selecter in February of '81. The Specials themselves split not long after their million-plus selling masterpiece "Ghost Town", which held number one for three weeks.

The Beat on their Go Feet label split in '83, while Madness, who had moved on to Stiff Records and leaned towards the commercial side of pop, called it a day in September '86.

With all these bands gone, the Scooter clubs were to keep the scene going. There was one band that briefly appeared on the Dance Craze album and film. Bad Manners, who had always been there – even before the Two Tone movement – were the least serious of them all yet outlasted the whole movement. And although Buster's gone through more than 200 musicians, the fat man's still belting out "Lip up Fatty" today. It seems like he always will be.

That left Rude boys with a period of two to three years with not much happening on the live music scene. It was a time to research and look through second-hand record stalls and discover lost gems from the first wave of Ska. I say two or three years because as early as '85/6, just as the second wave was ending, the third wave was already beginning.

"Tcha mon Winston, haffe ya swallowed a Two Tone bible o' sumtin'? I an' I remember dat jus' like yesterdey," said DJ.

Spiderman and Twinkle Toes slowly and carefully made their way further down the train, coming to the next carriage when it suddenly all went dark. Coke let out a scream, frightening Mad Axe Man, who asked: "What the fuck, is tha alreight?"

A scraping noise was heard, followed by a flash, then a flame of light with the smell of burning sulphur as Coke struck a match. It illuminated his face.

"Tha's in a tunnel," confirmed Axe Man. "Ey this all seems familiar. T'were in a tunnel that thee lost 7 Bellies, Deja-vu or what like."

Coke gave another scream as the match went out, leaving them in total darkness.

The Hawkwind was shunting along, the carriage rattling and rocking side to side. It was making them feel disoriented; they were losing all sense of direction. Mad Axe Man was begining to panic and called out –

"Coke, what is it like?"

Sniff. "Burnt my bloody fingers, didn't I?"

"Then tha should have a Zippo."

Sniff. "I gotta Zippo maan, I use it when I go for a pisso."

"Yer daft wazzak, thee means a Zippo lighter."

Mad Axe Man flicked his on and held it out so they could see each other. It was then they heard another voice – it sounded like it was being strangled. "Hello," it said, scaring them both half to death.

"What the bloody hell's that like?"

"Hello. Over here," said the voice again.

"Sounds like someone's playing bloody silly buggers, lurking about oer yonder," said Axe Man while pointing with the side of his head down to the end of the carriage.

They heard the voice again as The Hawkwind shunted out of the tunnel and into the moonlight, revealing a small, bent figure.

Sniff. "It's Slimey! Hello Slimey, like how you doing maan?"

"Hello, Coke."

"Axey, you know Slimey don't you? He was with Skankdown when Speed and me used to do the alternative hour."

"Aye, well that was afore 7 Bellies and thee, but thee reckons thee has heard of him aye."

"Hello Axe Man."

"Aye, err hello Slimey. What's tha doin skulking about int shadows like?"

"I like it here I do, it's quiet here, not like in the kitchen, with all them pans and cutlery clanking about. Ovens, cupboards and drawers opening and closing. Recipe man telling me what to do all the time. I come out here to get some peace. Why, what are you doing here? Haven't you got a compartment?"

Sniff. "Oh yeah we're right up the front maan."

"If you're up near the front, then why are you down here?"

"Aye well it's a bit of an emergency like. Thee's got an Australian volcano in thee's bowels."

"Do you need a Doctor?"

"There int no Docter that can help with this problem."

"It's terminal?"

Sniff. "It's worse than that; we've ran out of beer maan."

"Australian volcano you say? Never heard of that, is it some kind of Baileys ice cream dessert?"

"No, it's a vindaloo fer breakfast, washed down with Thunderbirds and Newcastle Brown."

"Then why is it called an Australian volcano?"

"'Cause it's not coming up spewing molten rock, lava and ash – it's going Down Under, and all the fires of hell and damnation are about te erupt."

Coke, now feeling they'd had enough of the small talk, decided it was time to get down to business.

Sniff. "So if you've got a kitchen maan, then like you've got brandies and wines to cook the meats in yeah?"

Slimey nodded.

Sniff. "Then let's go to the kitchen, maan."

"Good idea," said Mad Axe Man. "Only one problem."

"What's that?" asked Coke.

Slimey answered for him. He said, "Recipe man hates the skankdown cast." Which was true....

It all started with the television deal he got. The idea would be that he was filmed preparing meals. Recipe man had come up from the ranks of catering school through the cafés, where he prepared lunch menus of sandwiches and toasties, to a top restaurant, preparing three course menus. Television was going to make him a star; he would be famous enough to open his own restaurant to cater for the rich and the famous, top TV personalities, film stars and pop stars. Now, Recipe man was a cordon bleu chef.

What he overlooked in the contract, however, was that it was for a comedy show. In truth, he would be filmed preparing meals from leftovers – bits of ingredients found behind the cooker or taken from the cat dish. This

149

included frying an unravelled toilet roll and seasoning it with dead skin collected from bottom of the bed sheets.

All the ingredients and side dishes would be found and prepared by Slimey, who he was partnered with. Slimey, a third rate comedy actor, was the total opposite to Recipe man. Small, bent, everything from his fingernails to his hair was filthy. He was untidy, unhygienic, unkept and as far as Recipe man was concerned, unacceptable. The show flopped after the first episode and ruined Recipe man's dream of a chef's career. He was out on the street and after that one show, no one would touch him.

He was drowning his sorrows one night in The Devil's Arms when DJ Dread, who had loved the programme, recognised him and told him about his masterplan of leaving on the train to Skaville. He was in need of a cook. Recipe man point blank refused and wouldn't have anything to do with him, but DJ persisted, offering him his dream. He would be able to run his own kitchen on The Hawkwind. He could cook his own menu and could order whichever meats, vegetables, fish, fruits, herbs and spices he wanted. All the ingredients would be supplied by Zoot, DJ guaranteed him.

The only stipulation was that he had to work with Slimey and do a couple of sketches for Pirate Radio Skankdown. Recipe man hates down-and-outs, losers, wasters, has-beens or never-has-beens, but admittedly he could now include himself in this category. His heart and soul was in cooking and he loved running a kitchen, so with nothing else going for him, and having had three drinks too many – and probably against his better judgement – he accepted.

"Well it's worth a try, an tha might nor where thee can blow off this vindaloo," said Axe Man.

They entered Recipe man's kitchen and stood around looking at the cleanliness. Everything shone and sparkled;

everything was in its place. Recipe ran his kitchen like a tight operation and it was filled with delicious mouth-watering smells.

Sniff. "Hey good looking, like what's cooking maan?" said Coke to Recipe man.

"Supper's cooking and it's nearly ready. Now get out my kitchen. Slimey, where have you been?"

"I was taking my break in the corridor."

"Chefs and cooks don't take breaks. Only when your shift is finished. You can't leave a pan boiling unattended – cooking is like comedy, it's all about timing."

"Time to squeeze a curried sausage out. Has tha got a khazi round ere?"

Coke *sniffed.* "Yeah, like I need a leak maan."

"Curried sausages and leeks are not on this evening's menu."

"Thee means thee needs te empty out garbage."

Sniff. "I need to water the plants maan."

"In my opinion you two are the garbage and you can empty your flower power selves out into the corridor."

Sniff. "Well, how about a bottle of brandy to see us off like?"

"I'll see you off with this," said Recipe man, as he raised a meat clever above his head.

Sniff. "Cool it maan."

"Aye, what's tha's problem like?"

Recipe man impersonated Mad Axe Man's accent. He said, "Thees problem is, thee has to cook for the likes of tha and tha who's never worked a day in tha's life and who thinks life is a free ride." He swung the cleaver down into the meat board. "Now get out. Do I make myself clear?"

Out in the corridor Coke said, with a *sniff,* "What's he know? I once bought a bus ticket."

"Aye, and thee once worked all weekend stripping thee's hog down and putting it back together."

Winston lowered the needle onto side A, track two of The Specials debut album. John Bradbury's drum - signature rim shot with cymbol clash rang out setting the hot pace intro to the song. Horace's bass comes in joined by Roddy and Lynval's guitars with Jerry's Organ all accompanying Terrys pan vocals backed up by Neville on the chorus.

All you Punks and all you Teds
National Front and Natty Dreads
Mods, Rockers, Hippies and Skinheads
Keep on fighting 'till your dead

Who am I to say?
Who am I to say?
Am I just a hypocrite?
Another piece of your bullshit
Am I the dog that bit,
the hand of the man that feeds it?

Do the dog, do the dog
Do the dog, not the donkey
Do the dog, don't be a jerk
Do the dog, watch who you work for
Do the do the do the do the dog
Everybody's doing the dog

Take your FA aggravation
Fight it out on New Street Station
Master racial masturbation
Causes National Front frustration
Who am I to say
To the IRA
To the UDA
Soldier boy from UK
Am I just a hypocrite
Another piece of your bullshit

Am I the dog that bit,
the hand of the man that feeds it?

Do the dog, do the dog
Do the dog, not the donkey
Do the dog, don't be a jerk
Do the dog, watch who you work for
Do the do the do the do the dog
Do the do the do the do the dog
Do the do the do the do the dog
Everybody's doing the dog

"Out of many, one people, yu listen te Pirate Radio Skankdown, dat was I man bruddah rude boy Winston tellin 'bout Two Tone deh an' playin' de Specials. Seh Winston, one ting I an' I nevah overstaan' is how wi get dem bloodclaat National Front Nazi boneheads," said DJ.

Winston explained.

"How Nazi boneheads came about is something that doesn't interest me, but reading between the lines from reports during the second Ska wave of the Two Tone movement I've made my own conclusion."

In 1978, Margaret Thatcher, then leader of the Conservative Party spoke during an interview on television programme the World in Action. Her speech was on the prospect of raising the number of Pakistani and Commonwealth Britons. She talked about doubling the number to four million, adding that she was aware people were afraid of other cultures.

This was opposed by groups like the National Front and British Movement, who got most of their votes from blue collar workers and the self-employed who didn't want foreign competition. There was no thanks for those who were invited over here in the first place after the Second World War (caused by a fascist dictator) to work in the factories and help get Britain back on its feet.

Spiderman turned to Twinkle Toes and said, *sniffing*, "Oh well, we didn't come out empty handed."

"Whats tha mean like?" asked Mad Axe Man.

Sniff. "Like I only half-inched a bottle of Merlot Cabre dans le monde a trouve dans le sud de la France, didn't I?"

"Tha's talking bloody foreign, what's tha mean?"

Sniff. "What one's saying is that one took the liberty of helping one's self to one of Recipe man's red wines – a bottle of Chateau de la Hangover."

"Tha's a magician."

Sniff. "Only one problem," said Coke.

"What's that?" said Axe Man.

Sniff. "I forgot to take a corkscrew."

"Gis the fucker 'ere, thee's got a few tricks up thee's sleeve thee self," said Axe Man.

Axe Man took out a three inch screw and a screwdriver from his leather jacket pocket, and began to screw the first inch and a half into the cork. He then took out a pair of pliers and pulled out the cork. "Plop." He handed the bottle over to Coke who began gulping it down like it was going out of fashion. When he was about halfway through, Mad Axe Man interrupted him, saying:

"Is tha making love to that or what like?"

Sniff. "Here you go," said Coke, wiping his mouth with the back of his hand and handing the bottle over. Axe Man finished it off in one go.

With their alcohol levels topped up, Spiderman led the way, walking his hands further down the corridor walls with Twinkle Toes taking his time, still concentrating on his bowels some four metres behind. He said, "Does tha reckon tha can magic thee a toilet, thee's got a craving for a chocolate fudge."

Totally off his trolly but feeling on top form, Coke saw IT, and IT made him feel good. Finally he could do something good for once; do something for someone else.

He'd never been good at anything – sports, games, clubs, school – he didn't have one certificate. But now, halfway through his life, he had achieved something.

It made him feel like a winner, like he was on a roll, a winning streak. He could not fail, he felt like a top comedian, the lead singer of a mega band, a spokesman. Tonight he was the Master of Ceremonies and he had the crowd, Mad Axe Man, eating out of his hands. He had the knowledge, he had the power, he was in full control.

He took his hands from the wall and stood in the middle of the corridor. With his arms outstretched and fingers pressed together he presented. Sounding first like a fanfare, "De de de de de de derr," he slurred, "Alasyoung masterAxeManlooknofurtherforwhatyoudesireawaits behindthisverydoor." Then like a felled tree, he fell. Mad Axe Man not only felt like he'd won the pools, the jackpot and the lottery all in one but like a jammy bastard he'd won Bully's Star Prize and got the speedboat too. He cried out in relief. "A shite house, how the bloody hell did tha pull that out tha's sleeve?" Having only eyes for the toilet door he did not see Coke who was out for the count, sprawled on the floor.

In '79, Margaret Thatcher was elected as Prime Minister. Unemployment was one and a half million, her policies were to close down and sell off (privatising) many British industries, putting thousands of people on the dole. By '83, unemployment was at 3.6 million. Football violence had always been around; a scuffle here and there; nothing too serious but in the seventies, firms (organised gangs) were formed. With plenty of unemployed youth, out of boredom and with "No (forseeable) Future" there came an ideal oppertunity to belong to something and let off steam. Around this time – '78 and '79 – the police started clamping down on football grounds. Some of these gangs including National Front and British Movement supporters, whose methods were to cause trouble and gain media attention, moved in to the clubs and concert halls. This was the same time that the Two Tone multi-racial movement was building up. It became a target for these groups, who adopted the Skinhead look (which is originally black and whites sharing a love for Jamaican music) and went to concerts to cause trouble and recruit new members. This is where shit bugger bastard fuck tit wank journalists fucked up and reported Skinheads were fascists. One paper even reported on The Selecter, an all black group with the exception of one white – Noel Davis – and branded them a racist group.

There were some shuffling noises, and then there was silence... followed by "Orr... Err... Ooooh... Ooooh... Errr... Aaaaghhhhh... bloody hell thee's arse is on fire... Oooow Phwoor... bah hek is this Ganhi's Revenge or what like?" There was more silence, then: "Orr aahh... oow... orr no... not again." (As the sound of a two stroke engine starting up came... at first slowly...) Pe... Pe... Pe... Pe (Then started picking up speed) Pe... Pe... Pe... Pe... Pepepepepepepe PUGH... "AAAAAAGGGHHHHH!"

Chapter Nine

GHOST TRAIN

Matt Davis, DJ Dread, Winston and Pot Belly were all listening to Mad Axe Man as he told in full detail the events that led up to when he returned. Pot Belly asked, "Where's Coke?"

"Thee was hoping tha could tell thee."

"But he went out with you. And why is your nose bleeding? Have you had a fight?"

"What's tha talking about? tha nose int bleeding."

"You've killed him. You've killed Coke just like you killed my 7 Bellies bruvver man. I'm going to tell Mr Dread."

"Pot Belly, don't be daft. Like thee's in enough trouble as it is."

"And then you both came running here?" said Matt Davis, who then continued. "So while I've been out investigating the murder of Mr 7 Bellies –"

As Matt said "murder", DJ heard some lyrics from The Angelic Upstarts' "The Murder of Liddle Towers" in his head, subconciously twisting the lyrics to fit the circumstances:

"Why did he die?
Or did they lie?
I think he's dead,
So the detective said"

"Mr Axe Man here went with Mr Caine as far as the toilet just after Recipe man's kitchen."

"And that's where he murdered him, Mr Toilet Duties, along with my 7 Bellies bruvver man. Look, he's got blood on his nose! Coke must have put up a fight," said Pot Belly.

"Thee hasn't murdered anybody."

"Not so fast Mr Pot Belly. Here in, err, where are we?"

"Spain," answered Winston.

'Spain, a señor is innocent until proven guilty,' continued Matt.

"Aye, thee wish everyone'd remember that."

"Now, Mr Axe Man, please take this pen and paper and write what I dictate to you."

"No chance, piss tha's pants, thee's not tha's bloody secretary," objected Mad Axe Man.

"Mr Axe Man, I'm merely trying to compare what evidence I have in order to either clear your innocence or find you guilty. Refusing to comply not only makes you liable to obstructing justice but also adds to the overwhelming facts that are pointing at you."

Mad Axe Man's tolerance of these constant accusations had again just ran out. He exploded with a verbal attack on Matt Davis. "What facts? Tha's got no facts on thee 'cause thee's done nowt... so tha can facts off"

Matt, totally blunt to insults, carried on – he was a man taking no nonsense.

"Then you've got nothing to hide by writing this. Are you ready?"

"Aye, go on then, just te keep peace."

"Everything's in site."

Axe Man repeated whilst writing down, *"Everything's in site."*

"And save just a good shelf."

"Aye, and save just a good shelf."

"When it's not down and right."

"What the bloody hell is this like?"

"Just write it down, Mr Axe Man."

"When it's not down and right."

"Sounds a load a shite te thee."

Matt seemed to grow a couple of inches. His chest expanded, and with a smug look on his face he announced, "Got you Axe Man, you're busted."

"Eh?"

"Section 147 – a Mr Menia offence."

"What's tha bloody talking about?"

"You call murdering Coke and my 7 Bellies bruvver man mean? Surely he's more than a Mr Menia," protested Pot Belly.

DJ, not for the first time in shock, blurted out "MURDAH! Yu can tell him murdah by him handwriting, is dem som' kind a sadistic words a serial killer leave behind?"

Winston, who was always open minded added, *"Hee, hee, hee.* Down an' right, a load a shite, Mad Axe Man a poet an' him nevah know it."

"On the contrary Winston. Mr Axe Man knows very well he's a poet, and he's been using the public toilets as his art gallery to exhibit his poems.

DJ, confused and with a screw face, said, not for the first time, "Mi don' overerstan' nuttin."

Matt tried to make things clearer by explaining his method. "You may have been wondering why I requested Mr Axe Man to write for me."

"Thee was wondering that thee self," said Axe Man.

"Ya I an' I wonderin'," said DJ.

Matt explained: "It was merely to take a handwriting sample to compare to this poloroid photo of graffiti written on my office door. Err, one of the toilets. *Everything's in site and save just a good shelf when it's not down and right* is an anagram of some of the words and letters taken from when everything's wrong and nothing ain't right, just sit thee self down and have a good shite."

"But wha' dis tell us Matt? Dat him murdah Coke and 7 Bellies an' write a poem 'bout it?" asked Winston.

"There you see, he did do it," said Pot Belly.

"Gentlemen, please calm down and listen to the facts," said Matt, who then went on to explain how graffiti which appeared to be totally irrelevant to the case has been proved very relevant.

"This is hard evidence that convicts Mr Axe Man of writing the aforementioned graffiti. And if you look at this poloroid you will see it is written in red ink. The same red ink on his fingers which he probably used to itch his nose. This counteracts Mr Pot Belly's accusation of blood after murdering Mr Caine."

"Ooh you are clever, Mr Toilet Duties," said Pot Belly.

"Don't talk shite, it were a piece a piss man. Like red marker pen's sticking out thee's top pocket."

"Err, I hadn't noticed that," said Matt.

"Alreight so thee's busted for graffiti. It doesn't make thee a murderer. Is thee free to go now or what like?"

"Don't let him go Mr Toilet Duties – he's using tricks to cover his tracks," said Pot Belly.

"Bah ek thee's heard of mates stabbing thee int back, but tha's stabbing thee int chest Pot Belly."

"If him only guilty of graffiti, den who murdah Coke an' 7 Bellies?" asked DJ.

Matt thought he'd got it right but started doubting as he remembered he'd often thought he'd got it right. There was the time after arresting the cabaret singer where he'd been demoted to the typing pool. He thought he'd got it right that time too. He remembered:

It was another morning resigned to desk duties, but it wasn't just any morning. Because today is Tuesday, Christmas eve and I've got leave for Christmas day and Boxing Day. That's free time. I'm going to clean out Percy's bowl. "Agh Matt," said the Sergeant, interrupting his thoughts. "Today's your lucky day".

"What is it, Sergeant?"

"Jake has called in sick and we need someone to cover his beat. We're expecting the chewing gum gang out today."

"You mean the Hubba Bubba bubblegum gang? Harry, Barry, Larry and Gary?"

"You know the case."

"For sure, I've been typing it up from Jake's reports the last three months. Every time he gets within half a street from them, they take off like jack rabbits on mountain bikes.

"That reminds me, Sarge. You hear the one about the magician from Louisiana who couldn't pull a rabbit out of his hat?"

"No."

"He pulled a hare out his arse."

"This is no time for jokes. Today's Christmas Eve, the last shopping day, and the gum machines are all going to be full out in front of the stores."

"And you think the Hubba Bubba bubblegum gang – Harry, Barry, Larry and Gary – will strike again today?"

"That's what we think and we need someone out there. Unfortunately there's only you we can spare. You know Jake's beat."

"For sure. I grew up in them streets."

"Well look at it as a kind of one day trial promotion. But mess up this time and your career is down the pan."

"Yes Sergeant. I'll play it by the book."

"Jake's bike is in bay seven number two. Here's the key, your beat finishes at 14.00 hours. Type up your report and have a Merry Christmas."

"Thanks Sergeant. I won't let you down."

I took the keys and the lift down to the parking bay and opened up number two. Expecting a traffic division's Harley, what I got was a Laser 21 gear mountain bike. Oh well I'm out of the office and I got a job to do, this is Matt Davis Special Agent. Now how do you work these gears? All I had as a kid was a scooter. Here we go, 11th gear, that's fast enough for me, up to 4th Avenue, leaves all over the street. Happens about this time every year, something to do with the winter I heard.

Brrr it's cold, cold enough to freeze the balls off a glass giraffe, or is that, err, a bronze elephant.

Erm, no, a monkey. A brass monkey – yeah that's it… or is it? I can't remember. I just cycled past a woman eating a sandwich and singing whilst riding her bike. Not a bad trick if you can do it, perhaps she should be in a circus.

Ah my first criminal. An old woman just cycled across a pedestrian crossing whilst the green man was flashing. Play it by the book Matt, she's a criminal – FREEZE BITCH – that's a section 67 offence. I'm arresting you for cycling across a pedestrian crossing whilst the green man was flashing.

A man, flashing, where? Oh, I missed him.

Officer, my gum machine has just been robbed; there they go they're getting away on mountain bikes.

It's the Hubba Bubba Bubble Gum Gang – Harry, Barry Larry, and Gary.

Right maam, I'm going to have to handcuff you up.

Ooh, Officer –

To this street sign. I'll return for you later.

Which way did they go, storekeeper?

They went that away.

Okay, this is Matt Davis Special Agent in hot pursuit of four notorious kids.

Outlaws known as the Hubba Bubba Bubble Gum Gang – Harry, Barry, Larry and Gary.

They take a left, end of 4th Avenue, up 5th and swing a right onto Manhattan way.

I'm chasing some 50 metres behind. It's one, two, three, four and I'm number five.

Closing the distance to 40 metres and into St James' Park.

We've all just raced past a no cycling sign.

That's a section 66 offence.

It's Larry, Barry, Gary and Harry with Matt Davis coming up the rear, ooh err. I'm 30 metres behind now and we're all by the swings and heading for the bandstand.

I'm 25 metres and closing.

Harry's taken Gary, changing the order to Larry, Barry and now Harry with Gary in 4th position and Matt Davis still closing in, some 20 metres behind now. Round the bandstand, Larry swings out wide.

Barry sees his chance, takes the inside line and takes the lead.

It's now Barry, Harry, Larry and Gary who's dropping back from the pack.

I'm closing in on Gary, 10 metres, and we all race on up to the duck pond.

It's a long, long straight and slightly uphill.

Harry takes Larry, moving up from 3rd to 2nd.

It's now Barry, Harry, Larry and Gary with Matt Davis still in 5th position.

I've now closed the gap to six metres on Gary, five, four, three, and we reach the peak of the hill.

The duck pond is in sight and we all race across the bowling green, a section 240 offence.

Two metres, one metre, and I'm now neck and neck with Gary.

I'm in 17th gear and yes, yes, I've taken him.

It's now Barry, Harry, Larry and Matt Davis Special Agent in 4th place.

Barry takes the long sweeping right at the duck pond with Harry right on his back wheel.

Larry is some four metres behind Harry and I'm another four metres behind Larry.

Gary seems to have dropped out of the race.

It's one, two, three and four, all racing to the climbing frames.

Harry is pushing Barry to his limit and is now along his side.

It's Barry and Harry, neck and neck.

Oh Larry swerves to miss a discarded Coke can; litter offence section 119.

He's in to the verge, losing pace; I seize my chance and take 3rd place.

It's Barry and Harry still neck and neck, wheel and wheel.

With Matt Davis closing in five metres behind.

Past the climbing frames and heading for the ice cream stand.

Harry takes Barry and takes the lead and I'm now on Barry's back wheel.

It's Harry, Barry and Matt Davis Special Agent.

I pull up the side of Barry, take him, and take 2nd place.

It's just Harry and me, we're past the ice cream stand.

It's the home straight to the park gates.

I'm in 18th gear, 19th gear and I'm on his back wheel.

20th gear and it's 100 metres to the finish.

I'm side by side, 50 metres and 21st gear.

10 metres and I take the lead and race through the park gates.

It's Matt Davis, Special Agent, the winner.

I raced out the park and straight back to the station, reeling in my victory.

Okay, so I didn't catch The Hubba Bubba Bubble Gum Gang.

I thought, shucks they're only kids, and besides, it's Christmas. I filled in my report with *nothing to report, everyone in a festive spirit, Merry Christmas* and took my two days' leave.

Friday morning, there I was bright and early, feeling refreshed, revived and ready to face any new challenges the day had to offer. I was called in to the office and was informed by the sergeant about an old woman dying of hyperthermia who had just been cut free from a sign post. She had been there all Christmas. She'd been fastened by my handcuffs.

I was told I'd messed up again and was ordered to take leave of duty.

"If him only guilty of graffiti den who murdah Coke an 7 Bellies?" asked DJ again, shaking Matt back from the past to the present.

Matt answered "If you listened closely to Mr Axe Man's and Mr Sir O.B.E Johnny Flannel's statements, we now have two, possibly six suspects. Finding the murderer now will be like looking for a fart in a Jacuzzi."

"You fink a fart murdered Coke and my 7 Bellies bruvver man?" asked Pot Belly.

Everyone looked at each other in disbelief and then looked at Pot Belly. Then they all cracked up laughing, and they laughed and laughed until it hurt and then they laughed some more. And because laughter is contagious, Pot Belly joined in too – he didn't know why he was laughing, or what he was laughing at, but nevertheless he laughed all the same.

This scene went on for about five minutes because every time the last person would stop, one of the others would begin again and then everyone followed. It went round and round until everyone had tears streaming down their faces and were physically exhausted.

After getting his breath back and remembering how and why they had got into this situation, DJ asked, "Den who is de six suspects?"

Matt explained. "Mr Axe Man here has just stated that together with Mr Caine they both called in on Mr Sparrow and Grievous where the latter threatened... err, if I may refer to my notes... ah, here we are: *'if you two don't disappear before I stand up, I'll be accused of murdering the bloody pair of you'*."

They then moved on to Slimey skulking in the shadows and Mr Recipe man who threatened, *'I'll see you off with this',* as he raised and brought down a meat cleaver. Not forgetting that on exiting Mr Recipe man's kitchen they instantly consumed a stolen bottle of wine."

"So wha yu seh is...." said DJ.

"Which one of them did it, Mr Toilet Duties?" asked Pot Belly.

"So what I'm saying is, any one of them could have done it. They all had a motive."

"Like what kinda motive does tha need te murder someone?" asked Axe Man.

"Nearly all of them had and have been drinking heavily, including yourself Mr Axe Man. They all had their privacy interrupted, and one threatened assault with a deadly weapon," answered Matt.

"What you going to do now Mr Toilet Duties? Arrest them all?" asked Pot belly.

"I'll tell you what I'm going to do Mr Pot Belly. On investigating the disappearance of Mr 7 Bellies I started from the bottom, working my way to the top. But by the time I reached the top, the scent was cold and the murderer long gone... or had time to cover his tracks... or to arrange an alibi.

"This time, however, I intend to be hot on his tail, starting from the top and working my way to the bottom. So with no time to lose, and if you gentlemen will excuse me, this is Matt Davis Special Agent."

And with a *WHOOSH* he was gone.

"Where's he gone?" asked Pot Belly.

Mad Axe Man, putting on a voice from a horror movie, answered, saying, "Thee's gone out investigating, looking for suspects, looking for clues, looking for hired assasins, hit men, bogey men, monsters and murderers."

With that speech, DJ started going into one of his trances as he heard Thomas Mensforth (Mensi) sing another part of The Angelic Upstarts' "The Murder of Liddle Towers" in his head –

> *"Drunk and disorderly was his crime*
> *I think at worst he should be doing time*
> *But he's dead*
> *He was drunk and disorderly and now he's*
> *dead –"*

"Wwwhat wwwe sssuposed ttto do?" asked Pot Belly.

Winston, seeing DJ's reaction, said, "Mi tink you'd bettah go back te yu compartment an' give DJ here some space."

DJ, coming back to his senses, said, "Not dat I an' I over any pressure or nuttin, it jus' dat Winston an' I ar' tryin te put out a show."

"Aye thee knows where thee's not wanted. Come on Pot Belly."

The Hawkwind had reached Spain and was hidden in a tunnel on the outskirts of Madrid during the day.

It was now the middle of the night and the Skankdown fans had again done their best to fulfil their obligations by providing water and coals.

With the furnace fired up and the boiler primed, The Hawkwind shunted out of the tunnel. Matt, being ever alert, was leaning out of a window. He couldn't be sure but he thought he saw the silhouette of a figure move from the shadows before it was engulfed in a cloud of steam and smoke. Coughing and spluttering, gasping for air, he pulled his head back in and closed the window.

The red light came on in the cabin and Michael asked, "Father, tell me, if Rock and Roll started in America then how did it get to be a big thing in England?"

"Be Jezuz, haven't I told you that before son?" answered Seamus, who went on to tell.

Television played a big part, because at the same time R&R was taking off, in Feb '57 a programme that was set to run for six episodes ran for 96. It was the BBC show, "6.5 Special", so called because it was on at five past six. The show was produced by Jack Good and presented by Pete Murry, whose catchphrase was, "Time to jive on the old six five."

The opening theme performed by Don Long and his Frantic Five went to the sound of a steam train. Seamus sang –

"Over the points, over the points, over the points, over the points
The six five specials comin down the line
The six five specials right on time
Coal in the boiler burnin' up 'n' bright
Rollin' and a rockin' through the night
My heart's a beatin' 'cos I'll be meetin'
The six five special at the station tonight

The six five special better not be late
The 6.5 special platform 8
The train starts a brakin' hard as can be
The station is a shakin' like a tree
And I won't be missin' that special kissin'
When the 6.5 special brings my baby to me

Hear the whistle blowin' 12 to the bar
See the lights a glowin' bright as a star
Now the wheels a slowin' can't be far

Over the points, over the points, over the
points, over the points

When the 6.5 special brings my baby back
home

Over the points
Over the points
Over the points
Over the points

"Well that was about the gist of it, I tink it just repeated itself two or three times," explained Seamus. He went on:

Tommy Steele was an early guest. The show also put in educational topics which Good thought disrupted the music. The BBC didn't agree however, so Good resigned early '58.

Good moved to the ITV show "Oh Boy" which only played music. He produced it between '58 and '59. Cliff Richard performed on the show 20 times, and Marty Wilde 17.

September '59, Good moved again to "Boy Meets Girl" which featured Marty Wilde, Cliff Richard, Joe Brown, Adam Faith, Billy Fury and the Vernon Girls.

Another television show was "Drum Beat", which the BBC ran from April to August '59. It was produced and directed by Stewart Morris, and from the R&R scene it featured Cliff Richard and Billy Fury.

Matt Davis followed Axe Man's statement and found the toilet next to Recipe man's kitchen where he'd stated he last saw Coke. Matt stood observing the floor in the corridor, the toilet door, the walls, looking for clues, looking for evidence – anything that might give a sign as to what might have occurred.

He couldn't find anything out of place. The carpet tread was even, pictures of early 1900s English countryside were all hanging straight and in line with each other on the wall. The toilet door was still hanging on its hinges with no marks or scratches; there was nothing broken or hanging loose anywhere to give a sign that there had been a struggle, a fight or a murder. There was nothing to report.

As part of his duties, he cleaned the toilets. It was now an everyday occurance, and he didn't have to think twice about it. Actually he didn't even have to think once about it – he just did it; it had become second nature. He absentmindedly took the handle of the toilet door and in a single movement pushed it down and forwards, opening it in one practised, skilled, swift movement.

Unlike out in the corridor, if he was to make out a report of what he now had come face to face with, there was enough to fill a dossier. Nothing could have prepared him for this sight, even all the training and experience in homicide, and he'd seen some horrific scenes.

His eyes being his fastest senses took the scene in first and it was so unbelievable his mind couldn't comprehend what he was seeing. Maybe he had been breathing out as he entered, because what followed was a sensation that overcame him. It was equivalent to the opening of a rock festival with the stage and both sides, built nearly sky high from Marshall amps, blasting out Phil Spectre's "Wall of Sound". Only this wall was a wall of stench, and it literally knocked him off his feet. He found himself sitting out on the corridor floor. Stunned, he said to himself "HOLY SHIT".

DJ had a brave face on about the last events and opened the show. "De people dat tryin' te mek dis world baddah, dem no tek a day off, den why should I, yu listen te Pirate Radio Skankdown, Winston weh wi up te in de history fe Ska an' Reggae."

"Wi up te Madness DJ."

"Yeah mon everybody like Madness, Winston tell de people."

Winston spoke:

Madness is Mike Barson's creation which started in '76 when Punk was about and it seemed like anyone and everyone was in a band. Mike pulled in a couple of mates who at that time were listening to Motown, The Coasters, Kilburn and the High Roads (later to be Ian Dury and the Blockheads). They would sit around Mike's piano at his house playing to a Fats Domino LP. During the following months the band grew, but as they were all still learning their instruments there were constant frictions within the band and a frequent change of members.

They called themselves The North London Invaders and played their first gig 30th June '76 in the back garden of a friend's house. Graham McPherson, better known as Suggs, saw them at that gig and bragged that he could sing better than their singer. He later auditioned, drunk on a bottle of vodka, and could only remember all the words to "See You Later, Alligator". The other singer must have been bad because even a drunk Suggs was better. He became the new front man.

Suggs would often skive off from rehearsals, opting instead to support his football team Chelsea. He did this one time too many, and was eventually sacked from the band for not being committed. Luckily for Suggs they had a row of bookings while their singer was on holiday so he was let back in.

It wasn't until February '78 that they played their proper first gig. Even then they were still not the magnificent seven that we know now. That came in the beginning of '79 with the new name Madness taken from the B-side of Prince Buster's "One Step Beyond". It was with this formation that they went on to support The Special A.K.A on the 8th June at The Nashville which led them to Aug 10th – the date they released their debut single "The Prince" on Two Tone.

They then signed to Stiff Records that had now, with Punk, fallen behind changed their logo to "Fuck Art Let's Dance". This suited Madness down to a tee because with their nutty sound, what they were putting out was primarily pure dance music. If you listened carefully to the lyrics you could hear stories of life's observations.

Madness dominated the charts during the early eighties with 21 top 20 singles earning them singles band of the year three years running. It made them a household and school playground name. They became masters of making videos, with the "Complete Madness" video making number one at the same time as the same-titled album hit number one. At the same time, the single "House of Fun" was also number one. They produced seven top 20 albums and built up thousands of fans the world over – before the Nutty Train derailed in '86 and they called it a day.

"Dat was a raas dey fe everyone," said DJ.

Winston agreed and said that they left with a song released October 27th that, like their debut single, reached number 16. He then pressed a button which lifted the record arm and swung it over, lowering it on to the record. The listeners heard the Nutty Train starting up for one last time with a vocal percussion of noises and stamping feet which was the introduction to "(Waiting for) The Ghost Train".

> *A straw headed woman*
> *And a barrel chested man*
> *A pocket full of posies*
> *And a hat rim full of sand*
> *(Ooh ooh) waiting for the train*
> *That never comes*

"Meanwhile the 70's alcoholic DJ Top of The Pops presenter Sir Johnny OBE Flannel was drunk and talking to himself in his cabin "Oh no Johnny's booze is up, and Johnny needs something to sup. I think I will have to venture out, out and about in search of a bottle of stout.

> *A dog chasing the tumbleweeds*
> *Across the sandy floor*
> *Drift along the platform*
> *Through the ticket office door*
> *(Ooh ooh) waiting for the train that never comes*
> *(Ooh ooh) waiting for the train that never comes*

"Oh but who's this approaching. He looks like a stranger. Oow I think Johnny's in danger. He looks like the Grim reaper. Or is it Dr Death – phwoar he's got bad breath."

> *But don't tell me*
> *There's nothing coming*
> *You don't fool me*
> *I hear the ghost train*
> *Rumbling along the track*

Set them free
And I hear them

It's black and white
(Don't try to hide it)
It's black and white
(Don't try to hide it)

'Hola señor Johnny Flannell, si' acabu de comer paella, un plato de pescado. Es cierto que Sen'or Dread sabe organizar cosas. No podi'a creer cuando reibi'una post al de e'l que dijo que tuve que estur en la estaccio'n de Madrid a medianocte e'sta noche. Vamos a Skaville.

Pregunta Si Coke y 7 Bellies esta'n en el tren, van a asustarse cuando me ven."

The station master's writing
With a piece of orange chalk
A hundred cancellations
Still no one wants to walk
Keep the hungry children
From the skeletons in the back
Aim to keep an eye out
For the gypsy caravan
(Ooh ooh) waiting for the train
That never comes
(Ooh ooh) waiting for the train
That never comes

"What's he say – is my time up, do I now have to pay. Or is he talking a load of rubbish; let's see sombrero, poncho, he must be Spanish. Did I know you in the past, you look familiar. Perhaps you used to be a drinking partner. Are you a celebrity or are you a host? Oh I think you must be a ghost... Help, help."

"Adios, amigo."

I hear the ghost train
Rumbling along the track
Set them free
And I hear them
It's black and white
(Don't try to hide it)
It's black and white
(Don't try to hide it)
It's black and white
(Don't try to hide it)
It's black and white
(Don't try to hide it)
It's black and white
(Don't try)
It's black and white
(Don't try)
It's black and white
(Don't try to hide it)
It's black and white
(Don't try to hide it)
And I hear them
It's black and white
(Don't try to hide it)

Chapter Ten

DOWN IN THE TUBE
STATION AT MIDNIGHT

Further down the train the two New Age Travellers, Sticks and Bones, were getting well chilled out by mixing red wine and cola together to make Calamucho, a drink they'd picked up from a Polish guy on their travels.

Sticks is a drummer from Newcastle who always has his drum sticks in his belt even if he doesn't have a drum kit with him. He can drum out a rhythm on just about anything – tables, chairs, pots, windows, the possibilities are infinite. It was once said at a full moon festival in France where Sticks was playing on some scaffolding, "That guy's got rhythm in his soul."

He had his first taste of travelling at 19 when he got his truck licence and started transporting goods across Europe. He soon realised he could make more money selling things on the side – buying products in one country and selling them on in the next.

Another regular scam was truckers swapping goods and reporting them stolen. Sticks went one step further and reported his whole truck stolen in Czechoslovakia, while at the same time giving his resignation, saying the job was too dangerous. He then drove to Belgium, bought a false passport and got the truck re-licensed under a false name and address. This allowed him to drive anywhere in Europe without having to pay road tax or insurance.

Bones (a skeleton in skin), is a singer and a foul-mouthed self-confessed alcoholic with kidney problems, meaning with just one beer she gets very drunk. Bones was born in Ireland and brought up in London, and made her first acquaintance with the police when at thirteen she got caught joy riding after crashing into a lamp post. She dropped out of school at fourteen, ran away from a broken home and spent two years at Greenwhich Common in a tent with the peace group. From there, she moved on to the Glastonbury Michael Eavis camp where she met Sticks and stayed for three years. Some people get annoyed by her finishing every sentence with "innit".

Sticks and Bones formed the duo Global Skank, with other musicians loosely falling in here and there to form a band as and when needed.

For the last four years they have lived together in the back of a truck travelling around Europe from festival to festival, performing their act and blagging what they need along the way.

They honestly believe it's possible to blag anything, and live by this method (they could give Zoot some competition).

Because of English laws clamping down on the travellers' scene, they've travelled mostly abroad looking at England from a distance and going back only for a festival here and there. It was during one of these visits, as with the rest of the cast, that like a magnet they were drawn to The Devil's Arms. DJ Dread met and recruited them to tell stories of their travels or to sing a song on Pirate Radio Skankdown.

"What goes around comes around," said DJ, coming back on the air.

"Dat right DJ."

177

Winston spoke.

On August 8th '92, Madness got back together to play the farewell gig they never had. The event was called Madstock and it was held at Finsbury Park, London. The Prince's lyric "An earthquake is erupting" was made true when Madness opened up with "One Step Beyond" and 36,000 pairs of boots started stomping. Three eight and nine storey flats were evacuated when a balcony and several windows cracked as residents literally believed there was an earthquake. Madness were back.

"Yeah mon Winston, wi a mash it up wid Aswad, wi a laugh it up wid Ian Dury an' him Blockheads an' wi a skank on down te Madness *he he he*. Yu listen te Pirate Radio Skankdown, I mon Winston here pley yu som' music."

"Dat right DJ, dis time mi choose Mark Foggo's Skasters but 'fore mi pley, let mi tell a lickle 'bout dem."

Mark Foggo is well known on the Ska circuit for not only singing about "weirdos" but for acting like a lunatic too. He was born in Liverpool and moved to London in the mid seventies when he was seventeen. For a time he shared a flat with a Declan Macmanus, later known as Elvis Castello. He'd been playing the guitar since fourteen and when in London played the pub circuit in various Punk / R&B bands – gradually working his way into the music business.

He wrote and recorded his first single, "New Shoes" on his own label Top Hole. The single was recognised by Polydor who offered him a contract for an album which resulted in "Speeding My Life Away", released in '80.

He didn't see eye to eye with English laws so before its release in '79 he moved to Holland. There he stole musicians from several bands which involved a lot of secret meetings. When he'd stolen enough musicians, it was an obvious choice to call it Mark Foggo and the

Secret Meeting. Together, they played a mix of Ska, Two Tone and New Wave.

In '84 they released the album "A State of Mind". The line up was never a stable one and in '87 a new band, Mark Foggo's Skasters, was put together. In '89 they released the 100mph "Ska Pig" on Link Records, and in '90, the live album "Captain Skarlet" on Skank Records.

Winston said, "A lot happen since I an' I start de show, dis track is te remind yu de listeners an' I an' I here at Pirate Radio Skandown weh wi a go. Dis is 'Train to Skaville' from de 'Captain Skarlet' LP." The needle lowered down into the groove and Mark Foggo announced

Let's all get aboard the train to Skaville
Oooh, oooh, oooh, oooh,

Said I can hear the train, to Skaville oooh,
oooh.
Said I can hear the train to Skaville oooh, oooh.
All aboard, all aboard

Said I'm a riding on the train to Skaville
All aboard, all aboard
Said I'm a riding on the train to Skaville
All aboard, all aboard,
And it goes like this.

(instrumental)

Were goin' to rock steady tonight
You and me all right
Thank god you look so cool
And nothing's gonna be so cool
When we get to Skaville
I take you up to Skaville
Come with me to Skaville

I take you up to Skaville
Won't you

I'm a riding on the train to Skaville
All aboard all aboard
I'm a riding on the train to Skaville
All aboard all aboard

Last train to Skaville

DJ, in his element, and lost in the sounds of this last record, came on the air with, "Higgit higgit higgit, pick it up, pick it up, ska, ska, ska. Dat was Mark Foggo's Skasters wid 'Train To Skaville' deh. Tcha mon I an' I on a train, an' I an' I goin' te Skaville."

"Irie DJ wi a skankin' up an' down in de studio deh, wi pley anudder one fe dem latah, firs' I haffe introduce ar nex' two guests."

"Who de nex' two guest?" asked DJ.

Winston told the listeners that because there were and are musical events all over the country that to go from gig to gig or festival to festival you have to travel. Out of this travelling a culture developed. He said he was going to tune into two people – Sticks and Bones – who live their life as one big festival. They would tell the listeners how the culture developed.

Sticks and Bones, still drinking their Callamucho and smoking funny smelling roll ups and not much else, saw the red light come on.

Sticks began to talk:

Travellers had been roaming around Britain for centuries with gypsy families and nomads basically living their own life without particularly bothering anyone. How Travellers in masses came to be living in (double decker) buses, vans, trucks, horse boxes, ambulances and lorries converted into mobile homes during the eighties follows sequences going back to the late sixties and early seventies.

There was a notable event in '70, when an estimated 600,000 people attended the 3rd "Isle of Wight festival" It's line up of 50 artists included The Who, The Doors, Jethro Tull and Jimi Hendrix, who set his guitar on fire. And just like America's '69 "Woodstock", fences were torn down. It became a free festival.

This free festival gave Bill Ubique Dwyer a dream to organise "The People's Free Festival" in Britain which he did together with Sid Rawle and Alexander Graham (Phillip) Russell – better known as Wally Hope. The festival, which attracted 700 visitors, took place in '72 on which was once common land – "Windsor Great Park" (the Queen's back garden). They saw it as claiming it back. Dwyer and Rawle supported squatting and communes which is why the festival was titled "Pay No Rent".

The festival became an annual event, attracting 8,000 visitors in '73. With it came a rally for cannabis, which was was opened by space rock band Hawkwind. '74 was planned to be a 10 day event having at one point a 15,000 crowd. Free LSD was also handed out but on the 6th morning 600 police came in with brute force, breaking it up and causing an outcry.

Some of the festival goers jumped into the back of the truck with the stage that stopped en route at the prehistoric monument Stonehenge in Wiltshire for the night. The next morning a reporter asked if the festival had moved there. At the time it wasn't the intention but someone confirmed that yes, it had.

It was reported in the papers that the "The People's Free Festival" was carrying on at Stonehenge (Wally Hope made a poster and is credited as founder) and people began to make their way to the historic site.

In '75, Bill and Sid were arrested for planning to organise that year's "People's Free Festival" – and just in case things did get out of hand, 300 police turned up to keep an eye on the group of six pic-nickers in one part of the park, seven in another and the two people walking their dog.

Most festival goers then began to gather at the June 21st Solstice festival at Stonehenge. This also continued to grow in numbers yearly.

Matt had closed the toilet door and moved further down the corridor, trying to put the scene out of his mind. He came up to Recipe man's kitchen, thinking there should be another two suspects right behind this door.

He knocked and entered, saying, "Good evening gentlemen. Matt Davis Special Agent. I'm sorry to interrupt at this late hour but I'm going to have to ask you some questions." Then, smelling the delicious odours, he commented, "Why, that sure smells good."

"Well it will be good if I'm allowed to do my work," said Recipe Man. I'm not a five star chef for nothing. Worked my way up from the bottom to the very top, I've had my own TV show and now here I am right down at the bottom on a train cooking for all the outcasts of society."

"Calm down Mr Recipe, I know how you feel."

"Know how I feel? How can you know how I feel? You're not me."

"No, I'm not you, but like yourself I too worked my way up from the bottom, from desk duty, to on the beat, private investigator to F.B.I. Special Agent. Then I fell down the long slippery slide all the way back down to the U-bend. Toilet duties."

Bones carried on where Sticks left off.

In '78, Punks began to move out of squats into vehicles. They weren't following the love peace and cosmic awareness of the Hippies but were certainly showing their dissatisfaction with society. It brought a bigger influence of anarchy into the culture.

On the 3rd of May '79, Britain had a new prime minister which not everybody supported. Peace groups would march singing "Maggie, Maggie, Maggie, out, out, out".

Because of mass unemployment there became more homeless people and at the same time London's boroughs evicted thousands of squatters, many of whom decided to live in a vehicle rather than in a cardboard box. From '80 the number of Travellers began to double at a yearly rate.

From this mass of people coming from all backgrounds, a new culture evolved that was slightly middle-aged, slightly anarchist, and slightly dangerous. Basically, they wanted their English freedom back. They came to be known as New Age Travellers.

In '82 a group of 150 travellers that were camped out at Stonehenge called themselves "The Peace Convoy" and convoyed down to RAF Greenham Common airbase to give some support to the Peace camp set up on September 5th '81 by the Welsh group "Women for Life on Earth", who were protesting against the storage of nuclear weapons.

The police were waiting for the convoy at the front gates and tried directing them onto an old airfield for a bust. The Travellers drove past as if going on to Skegness, then drove round the back and up an old, long forgotten and unused track through the woods coming out behind the police lines and on to Greenham Common. They camped here for the next four months.

Like the peace movement and the striking miners who Thatcherites saw as the enemy, the Travellers – who were mostly groups of young adults that opposed the government – were also seen as a threat. The Travellers had built up a life outside of society, often living in self-contained communities with schools, doctors and mechanics travelling from camp to camp or festival to festival selling crafts, performing arts and taking part in the centuries-old tradition of bantering. In '84, Stonehenge drew a crowd of 65,000 and in '85 action that had been planned months in advance titled "Operation Solstice" was about to be taken against them.

"There's nothing wrong with a U-bend," said Slimey, who added, "I've foraged out some of my best ingredients from the U-bend."

"Slimey, I don't think the special agent is here to hear about your fascination with the sewerage system," remarked Recipe Man.

"On the contrary, Recipe Man. There seems to be a connection between going to the toilet and disappearing," said Matt.

"You don't mean down the toilet," asked Recipe man.

"Well unless you're a contortionist I think that's humanly impossible. But if someone was to chop up a body... with, say, a meat cleaver... and flush it piece by piece down the toilet... I would think that's very possible," said Matt.

"Is this an accusation? Because I don't like the tone of your voice," said Recipe man.

"And I don't like Mr Axe Man's statement about you threatening the aforementioned and Mr Caine with *the only thing you're likely to get is this meat cleaver.*"

"Oh surely you don't think I've got time to chop somebody up and flush them piece by piece down the toilet. I've got to cook for 21 here."

"And what exactly is it you're cooking? Not 7 Belly burgers, I hope."

Slimey, who up till now had been subconciously sticking a finger through the plastic of a tray of herbs and spices jars, looked down and to his horror saw that between every jar was a hole in the plastic. To avoid a scolding from Recipe man, he quickly put a tray of apples on top of it and said, "I like the sound of that I do, sounds bigger than a Big Mac; bigger than a double cheese burger, it sounds like seven burgers, 7... Belly... burgers. Buy one, and feed the whole family."

Bones continued.

A high court injunction was obtained which prevented the gathering for the '85 "Solstice festival" at Stonehenge. An exclusion zone with a four-and-a-half mile radius was set and anyone coming within that radius would be arrested.

On June 1st the police redirected a convoy of about 120 vehicles (seven miles from Stonehenge) into a country lane with the end of the road blocked off. The police then from the front and the back began smashing windscreens with their truncheons, pulling the travellers out through the windscreens and arresting them.

Seeing what was going on, vehicles in the middle turned off the road and drove through hedges and onto a field to escape. There they were trapped for four hours and told if they tried to leave with their vehicles they would be arrested. At 7.10pm the police numbers had grown to 1,600, and with tactics learnt from dealing with the minors they stormed the field in riot gear wearing helmets and shields and armed with batons, fire extinguishers and flints. They broke into the travellers' vehicles, dragging them out and again beating them. Two of the victims were pregnant women.

The Travellers, now fearing for their homes and safety, tried again to escape by driving into the next field – a bean field. This would be the site for what became known as the "Battle of the Bean Field" (though one traveller stated it was not a battle but an ambush). Here, they were again attacked by the police and their vehicles (homes) were smashed. At least one was set on fire and the owner was made to watch.

The whole operation cost taxpayers £800,000. In total, from the bean field and around Stonehenge, 530 travellers were arrested and transported to police stations all over the country where they were charged with unlawful assembly (most charges were later dropped). Eight police and sixteen travellers, one with a fractured skull, were taken to hospital and much of the film footage and photographic evidence of the police brutality disappeared.

From the moment he walked in Matt had observed that everything was in its place and absolutely spotless. It made him think the kitchen would be an ideal place to carry out a murder and dissect the body. Anyone would have enough space, and with worktops, tools and privacy to carry it out, it could make it the perfect crime. Almost the perfect crime if Matt Davis wasn't on the case.

"What a clean kitchen. Why, you can see your own reflection in everything. I would imagine chopping a body up you'd have blood splattered everywhere."

"Well then you obviously wouldn't know the first rule of cooking is cleanliness," replied Recipe man.

Matt who could feel a bit of banter was building between them, and was quite enjoying himself, said, "And how do you get it so aerospace laboratory clean, Mr Recipe man?"

"Nothing but hard work and elbow grease," answered Recipe man.

"And what is it you're cooking in such a meticulously clean kitchen?" asked Matt for the second time.

Looking totally disheartened, the cordon bleu chef took a deep breath and let out a sigh before he said, "I'm cooking the 2.00pm menu for the alternative cast, which is totally beneath me, but obviously not for the dregs of society. Bacon sandwiches."

"Put me down for two," said Matt enthusiastically, before pursuing his investigation.

"Now, after Mr Axe Man left here with Mr Caine, did you at any other time see Mr Caine or Mr 7 Bellies and murder them with the aforementioned meat cleaver? Did you then chop them into pieces and flush these pieces down the toilet? Or fry these pieces and sell them off as 7 Belly burgers?" Then, as another thought came to him, he added, "And Mr Caine oven chips?"

"This is absolutely absurd."

"Please answer the question."

"No!"

Sticks concluded his talk:

With Stonehenge being declared an exclusion zone, the Travellers had their festival in Uffington, Oxfordshire, on a hill above the prehistoric chalk white horse with a smiley temporarily placed in its eye. They then headed for Glastonbury. The farmer, Michael Eavis, who had put on the yearly Glastonbury festival since '70, opened a gate in a top corner field and gave them a place to camp.

For the coming festival, the Travellers built a replica Stonehenge from cars and on the Saturday night of that weekend's festival, thousands of people came and drummed like zombies with all kinds of bits of metal on the replica till the early hours.

The travellers ended up staying there for five years, but by '90 times had changed from the peace loving dope smoking Hippies of the sixties – a lifestyle that the first New Age Travellers had clung on to.

New drugs like ecstacy, smack and easily available cocaine had taken their place. The camp started fighting over drugs and split into two groups. (This split many other camps which had been living for years as self-contained communities. It's also stated that police hit on cannabis users while turning a blind eye to smack dealers knowing its self and community destroying effects).

That same year there was a rivalry between the security and the travellers. Security officers were confiscating drugs and selling them on, so the travellers started throwing petrol bombs at them. This turned into a full scale riot known as the 'Battle of Yeoman's Bridge' and resulted in £50,000 worth of damage including five burnt out Land Rovers.

Farmer Michael Eavis had had enough. After five years of giving them a free place to stay, providing water and toilets, it was time for them to leave. And so the camp disbanded – in the nineties many Travellers left England for France and Spain.

Following state procedure, Matt moved on and asked the next question. "And do you have an alibi?"

Bewildered, Recipe man answered, "Slimey, Slimey can vouch for me. I've been here the whole night."

"Is this true, Slimey?"

"I don't know because I haven't been here all night I take my breaks out in the corridor."

"Thank you Slimey, it's been a pleasure working with you," said Recipe man sarcastically.

Matt, now feeling confident, said, "So Recipe Man, it seems your alibi won't stand up in court. I will have to confiscate this meat cleaver for human or animal DNA tests in my forensic toilet er lavatory er laboratory."

Recipe Man protested. "This is absolutely insane." Looking at Slimey he said, "See what trouble you've got me into? Now I"m accused of murder, and tomorrow we've got steak on the menu. How am I going to chop steak without my meat cleaver?"

After he'd finished blaming Slimey, Matt addressed Recipe Man. He said, "Well actually, you're both suspects. Just as Slimey can't be your alibi because he was out in the corridor, you can't be his because you were here in the kitchen."

"You devious rat," said Slimey.

"This is preposterous," said Recipe Man.

Matt, being totally immune to insults, didn't even hear

them. He asked, "Say, have either of you visited the toilet next door?"

"What?" said Recipe Man and Slimey together.

"Well I wouldn't if I was you. It looks like chemical warfare in there. I think we've got a terrorist on board; it will need a full hose down and defumigating."

"What?" said Recipe Man.

"I will nip back to my cleaning cupboard to pick up my rubber gloves, gas mask and a bottle of –"

"What?" interrupted Recipe Man.

"Erm, I mean I will have to return to HQ for my suitcase of gadgets. Erm, I mean call in for reinforcements."

"What?" said Recipe Man.

"Oh, and I'll have mine well done."

"What?"

"The steak."

Recipe Man was about to refuse to cook him anything at all when Matt said, "Well that'll be all for now, I've got some more statements from Mr Axe Man to check out, some more suspects to interview."

Again Recipe Man wanted to have his say but Matt beat him to it, saying, "Good night day." As he turned and left, Recipe Man and Slimey looking at each other, believing he was insane.

"One good ting 'bout music, when it hit yu feel no pain, Sticks an' Bones deh on Pirate Radio Skankdown de show dat bring yu al de facts an' roots 'bout ar music, movements an' cultures," said DJ.

"Yeah mon an' here dat udder track fe Mark Foggo's Skasters," said Winston as he placed the album "Ska Pig" on the turntable and set the needle on track five of side one – "Two Legs".

Dominique Dubois on keyboards played the introduction followed by George Coenraad on drums with Paul Berding and Ronald Oord on Sax and Trumpet coming in together which was followed by them all playing the same rhythm together. Then the Mad Hatter, Foggo himself, his eyes popping out, started singing:

> *I never give my seat up on a train*
> *And if the lady don't like it, it's a fucking shame*
> *I bet she's got two legs and they're just the*
> *same*
> *And so I never give my seat up on a train*

Matt had closed Recipe Man's door, turned around and came face to face with Bones who asked, "Oi Geezer, got any faags?"

"Err no, I don't smoke," answered Matt, caught off guard.

"Well bog off then and I'll just hav te blag em from someone else innit," said Bones.

"I think I should inform you I'm Matt Davis Special Agent, and will have to ask you some formal questions."

"A fink I should inform you, I'm Bones and I will hav' to tell you to formally... fack off."

Matt, looking down at his passenger list, said, "Excuse me, but what did you say your name was?"

"Bones, git face, and this 'ere's my man Sticks, git face, we're the git face cunts innit."

Sticks, who had been up to now staring out of the window, said, "Why aye man we's noo far away from the toon."

"Excuse me?"

"How man we's far away from Newcastle."

"Oh yes."

Sticks, now facing Matt, looked him up and down.

"Man Matt yuz a Special Agent, a blurk that knaas lurds aboot detecting, soonds canny."

"Leave it out, he's nothing but a trumped up bog brush, innit," commented Bones.

I said the lady's got two, two legs
The lady's got two, two legs
The lady's got two, two legs they're just the
same
I said the lady's got two, two legs
The lady's got two, two legs
The lady's got two, two legs they're just the same

As usual, Matt didn't let the insult get to him. But as usual, he did feel the need to explain. "Well actually, I used to be a Special Agent. I'm now working for Mr Dread, investigating the murders of Mr Caine and 7 Bellies. Do you know the whereabouts of the two men in question?"

Sticks answered, "Why the wuz drinkin' in The Devil's Arms just the other neet."

"I mean since you boarded this train, say within the last 48 hours."

"They're probly just chilling out in one of the compartments, innit," answered Bones.

"Erm you wouldn't happen to know which compartment would you?"

"Not in our compartment geezer," answered Bones.

Matt, suddenly realising there were possibly two new suspects – not that they were on a curfew but they were out after hours – asked, "Say… what you doing wandering the corridors after midnight?"

Sticks had gone back to looking out of the window. While staring outside, he said, "How man Matt jus' tek a look oot the window reet."

Matt joined him and together they stood side by side looking out the window. Sticks continued addressing the window and outside. "Canny or what... the stars... the moon and yuz all tucked up in yuz beds... having a wank."

"Now's the time we can be creative and that. We're working on a new song we're going to sing for the punters at the Skaville festival, innit," added Bones.

I never give my seat up on a train
Even if the lady's got a varacose vein
'Cause she got two legs and they're just the
same
And so I never give my seat up on a train

Matt thought about this but couldn't think of anything else to say. However he'd been in this game a long time and over the years he'd learnt that sometimes, something that at first means nothing could actually mean something. So he decided to go with the conversation until something revealed itself.

"So you're writing a song are you?"

"Why aye and it's a killer, wipe the fuckin' floor with the rest of 'em," said Sticks.

Matt's instincts had paid off. He cautioned, "Now just hold on now, a song like that should be behind bars."

"We gonna murder down Skaville, steal the show, and walk away wiv it, innit," bragged Bones.

"I can't believe my ears, murder and grand theft," said Matt.

"It's about smoking and that innit, it goes, I get up about eight, feed the pigeons –"

"If this is true I will have to ask you to return to your compartment immediately," said Matt, interrupting.

"Fack orf, we still got the chorus to write innit," argued Bones.

I said the lady's got two, two legs
The lady's got two, two legs
The lady's got two, two legs they're just the
same
I said the lady's got two, two legs
The lady's got two, two legs
The lady's got two, two legs they're just the
same

Matt insisted they returned to their compartment and insisted he would escort them. He didn't say, but he wanted to search it for any clues of anyone else chilling out in there.

Bones led the way, walking through the next carriage. Matt was subconsciously thinking if Mad Axe Man's report was accurate this would be the carriage GBH and Sparrow were occupying, Matt made a mental note to call in here on the way back.

Bones picked up the pace while Sticks made small talk, holding Matt's attention. Bones was now some four metres in front and entered their compartment first. As Matt and Sticks, some two seconds behind, entered she was sitting on the bench, her legs stretched out with her feet crossed on the tie-dyed travel bag. To Matt's observation it was obvious she was or had hidden something – but what, and where had she hidden it?

Matt let his eyes wander around the compartment. Apart from empty wine and cola bottles, joss sticks and a candle burning on the table, plus a lot of torn up Rizla packets, there was nothing to see that would suggest a murder had taken place. Matt observed that under the bench was a pan of water which he thought strange. But, he thought, it must be another Traveller's thing and didn't comment. He casually walked over to the wardrobe and said, "And what have we in here then?" as he opened it.

I never give my seat up on a train
If the lady don't like it, it's a fucking shame
I never give my seat up on a train
Even if the lady's got a varacose vein
I never give my seat up on the train
'Cause shes got two legs and they're just the same
I never give my seat up on the train
No I never give my seat up

'Cause the lady got two, two legs
The lady's got two, two legs
The lady's got two, two legs they're just the
same
I said the lady's got two, two legs
The lady's got two, two legs
The lady's got two, two legs they're just the
same

The wardrobe was empty.

Bones had had enough and and let it be known. "Oi geezer, this is an invasion of our privacy innit."

"I'm sorry to intrude, I'm merely –"

"Merley snooping around innit," interrupted Bones.

Matt had found no convicting evidence of a mis-adventure and still having to follow up on the rest of Axe Man's statement closed the interview. He said, "I believe I'm finished here if you will excuse me. It's time –"

"Yeah it's bog off time innit," interrupted Bones again.

"Had away and shite," said Sticks, who was sitting back making himself a roll up.

Matt turned and walked out into the corridor. As he was closing the door behind him, Bones called out, "Oi geezer, that's a nice trilby hat… where ye nick it?"

Matt didn't hear the question, though. He was deep in thought, weighing up this new found information... a killer song eh? This sure adds another twist to this thriller of a show.

It was true. What had started out as the Train to Skaville show going out live as they went, was now the Murder on the Train to Skaville show as Winston played another track by The Jam. It was the B-side from "That's Entertainment", and The Modfather announced, "We're going to take you –

"Down in the tube station at midnight!"
The distant echo –
Of far-away voices boarding far-away trains
To take them home to
The ones that they love and who love them
forever
The gazed, dirty steps – repeat my own and
reflect my thoughts
Cold and uninviting – partially naked
Except for toffee wrapers and this morning's
papers
Mr Jones got run down
Headlines of death and sorrow – they tell of
tomorrow
Madmen on the rampage
And I'm down in the tube station at midnight

Matt walked back up the train still trying to put all the facts together. But no matter how he arranged and rearranged all the pieces, he couldn't get them to fit the puzzle. Maybe he was still missing a few. Who's next on my list? Erm, the Mods – GBH and Sparrow – maybe they can fill in a few blanks. Matt knocked and entered, saying, "Good evening, gentlemen."

Sparrow and GBH were sat back drinking a beer, smoking a cigarette and playing a game of cards. Leaving the study of his hand, GBH looked up from his cards and said, "It might be good evening where you're coming from Guv, but from this side it's an annoying disturbance of recognisable faces coming barging in one after another."

Matt cleared his throat and introduced himself. "Matt Davis, Special Agent. So you're not denying Mr Caine and Axe Man called in earlier this evening?"

"Oh, you hear that Grievous? He's a Special Agent," said Sparrow, who seemed to go unheard.

I fumble for change and pull out the Queen
Smiling – beguiling
I put in the money and pull out a plum
Behind me
Whispers in the shadows –gruff blazing voices
Haiting, waiting
"Hey boy" they shout, "have you got any money"
And I said –"I've a little money and a takeaway
curry,
I'm on my way home to my wife.
She'll be lining up the cuttlery,
You know she's expecting me
Polishing the glasses and pulling out the cork
And I'm down in the tube station at midnight

"Do what John how's your father called in. They came barging in, telling me Axe Man is accused of murder, asking for a beer, asking for a lavvy. I told 'em, hop it or I would murder them myself," said Grievous, getting red in the face and finishing out of breath.

"That's exactly what's written in this statement, Mr Grievous."

"Do what John, leave it out, yer mean them dirty pair of snitches went and grassed me to the filth?"

"They're not a pair anymore; Mr Axe Man gave this statement regarding the disappearance of Mr Caine."

"Oh you 'ear that Grievous? The Special Agent says Axe Man's murdered Coke," said Sparrow.

"I did not say he murdered him. He is however under suspicion, as you are yourself, Mr Grievous."

"You what, you what, you what you what you what –" said GBH.

"Did you did you not just state you threatened to murder the pair of them? So I put it to you Mr Grievous, did you murder Mr Caine?"

I first felt a fist, and then a kick
I could now smell their breath
They smelt of pubs and Wormwood Scrubs
And too many right wing meetings
My life swam around me
It took a look and drowned me in its own
exsistence
The smell of brown leather
It blended in with the weather
It filled my eyes, ears, nose and mouth
It blocked all my senses
Couldn't see, hear, speak any longer
And I'm down in the tube station at midnight
I said I was down in the tube station at
midnight

GBH took a long draw on his cigarette before blowing it out in Matt's face and saying, "Leave it out Guv, coming in here accusing me of murder."

"I'm not accusing you. I'm merely following up the aforementioned statements."

GBH denied murdering Coke and told Matt that he must be bleedin' mad if he thought so. He went on to explain that they all sat in a card school and drank together at The Devils Arm's, and that you couldn't take them seriously because they were always telling wild stories. They were all just big kids that had never grown up. Then he said, "Sparrow, nip down the bookies – I'll put a pony on. This is all just a huge joke they've concocted between themselves."

"Well I don't think the disappearance of two passengers on this train is a huge joke and I object to a dead pool. Mr Sparrow, can you account for Mr Grievous's statement that he has not murdered Mr Caine?"

"Oh yeah, he's as honest as the day is long," answered Sparrow.

"It's after midnight," Matt pointed out. Then he said, "Thank you for your time, gentlemen. It just leaves me to say that if you hear some cigarettes singing it's eight o' clock in the morning and the pigeons are getting up. Block your ears, apparently they're killers."

The last thing that I saw
As I lay there on the floor
Was "Jesus Saves"painted by an atheist nutter
And a British Rail poster read "Have an away
day, a cheap holiday –
Do it today!"
I glanced back on my life
And thought about my wife
'Cause they took the keys and she'll think it's me
And I'm down in the tube station at midnight
The wine will be flat and the curry's gone cold
I'm down in the tube station at midnight
Don't want to go down in a tube station at
midnight
Don't want to go down in a tube station at
midnight

Having left Grievous and Sparrow, Matt had returned to headquarters for back up and was about to mount an attack on the terrorist's toilet when he heard what sounded like someone being strangled.

Help help. Hold on, what's that? he thought to himself. Help help – he heard it again and it was getting closer. He thought someone was in trouble and went running in to the next carriage where he ran in to Sir Johnny O.B.E. Flannel, who was in shock, reacting in total panic, shaking all over and couldn't get a word out.

"It's me, Matt Davis," said Matt, taking off his gas mask and rubber gloves in an attempt to calm him. He then asked "Are you being chased by the murderer?"

"I've seen just scared the most, I'm a ghost"

"Johnny, calm down. You're making no sense at all. Now, it looks like you could use a drop of this – it's pure alcohol, I use it for removing graffiti from the toilet walls," said Matt, taking a bottle from his inside pocket and offering it to Johnny.

Johnny took the bottle. Holding it in his shaking hands he slowly put it to his trembling lips and started pouring it down his throat, drinking heavily. *Gulp gulp gulp.*

"Hold on just a drop Johnny, this is one hundred percent."

On hearing one hundred percent, Johnny tried to drink some more before Matt had to physically tear it from his hands.

"Now, Johnny, take a deep breath and in your own time tell me what's troubling you."

Johnny's eyes went 360 degrees, disappearing to the back of his head before coming back round again. Then, standing on the spot, swaying backwards and forwards, he slowly focused on Matt and began to feel his normal self.

"I'm scared the most – I've just seen a ghost."

"A ghost... are you sure? What makes you think it was a ghost?"

"He looked like someone from the past, like he used to be one of the cast. He looked familiar, yet he looked dissimilar – yes as if he was – and no, as if he wasn't"

"Mr Flannel, you're contradicting yourself. Can you describe him?"

"Maybe if I had another drink of that one hundred percent."

"I'm sorry Mr Flannel I will have to say no, you've already drunk half a bottle and you are intoxicated"

Johnny argued "If I've only drunk half a bottle, then I'm only half intoxicated"

Matt desperately wanting to get his statement, against his better judgement agreed -

"Okay, you have had a bit of a shock. But just a nip, Mr Flannel."

Johnny grabbed the bottle and started drinking as much as he could, as fast as he could, before Matt had to fight it from him again.

"Now do you feel you can describe this ghost?"

Johnny, more sober than he'd ever been in his life, as if he'd had elocution lessons, pronounced, "Sombrero, poncho, appeared to have no cash. Cowboy boots, sun tan, beard and a moustache."

"Erm, that sounds like the description of a shadow I thought I saw when we pulled out of the tunnel in Madrid. I wonder if he boarded? If so we've got a stowaway on board. Did he say anything to you?"

Johnny repeated in fluent Spanish:

'Hola señor Johnny Flannell, si' acabu de comer paella, un plato de pescado. Es cierto que Sen'or Dread sabe organizar cosas. No podi'a creer cuando reibi'una post al de e'l que dijo que tuve que estur en la estaccio'n de Madrid a medianocte e'sta noche. Vamos a Skaville.

Pregunta Si Coke y 7 Bellies esta'n en el tren, van a asustarse cuando me ven, adios amigo."

"And what does this mean?"

Johnny's soberness was short lived. The 100 percent alcohol was taking it's affect making Johnny's head feel as if it was a washing machine on fast spin, he saw four Matt Davis's before him, picked one out and answered "Gibberish doesn't speak Spanish a load of Johnny. Another little had if but of maybe I drink.

Matt himself didn't speak alcoholic, but being surrounded by a train full of them, was quickly picking up the language and disiphoned. A load of gibberish, Johnny doesn't speak Spanish. But maybe if I had another little drink of –

"No more little drinks for you Mr Flannel. Let's look at this like mending a cistern. We take it all apart and study the pieces, identify what's broken, fix or replace it and put it back together. Now this ghost, you said it spoke gibberish and you don't speak Spanish. Of course we've just passed through Madrid; my Spanish is a bit rusty but let's see if I can translate.

'Looking at my notes I see we've got some keywords: Señor Johnny Flannel, Señor Dread organizar, Madrid, Skaville, Coke, 7 Bellies, adios amigo and you said *'You look like someone from the past, you must be a ghost'*.

"You know what Johnny? I think you're right. Only the Skankdown cast know about this train. You said he looked familiar … like a Spanish version of Mr Caine and 7 Bellies, who he also mentioned. I wonder if when you die your spirit takes on the nationality of the country you die in… which all makes perfect sense. Mr Caine and 7 Bellies must have been murdered in Spain; their spirits went to heaven and came back in the form of a ghost waiting in the tunnel in Madrid."

Matt's brain, working faster than he could think, continued.

"They boarded the train again in order to make the trip to Skaville, their final destination and resting place… or… to make contact with us and tell us where their murdered bodies lie and most importantly of all… who murdered them. If only my Spanish was better I could have this case solved and bagged up by the morning."

Then, summing up his report, Matt said, "Okay we've now got Mad Axe Man, a meat cleaver wielding chef cook and skulking assistant, a very angry Mr Grievous, a terrorist, a ghost, you yourself and a killer song on the loose."

"Mine's a double."

"I suggest you go back to your compartment and lock the door Johnny, I have to report all this to Mr Dread and Winston." Then, as an afterthought, he added, "Oh, and look out for a clock that's smoking eight singing pigeons."

"Make that a triple"

Chapter Eleven

DESTINATION SKAVILLE

"If everyting is not wrong den everyting is alright, yu listen te Pirate Radio Skankdown, Winston wha' yu goin' tell de listener?" asked DJ.

"Mi seh hearlier as de secon' wave Ska finish de t'ird wave areddy begin," said Winston.

He then reeled off a list of years, places, bands formed and a few facts.

'82, Hot Knives from Horsham, Sussex, released '89 the classic "Hotknives Live and Skanking" album.

'82, Skaos from Germany whose '88 debut album was "Beware".

'83 Potatoe 5 (a.k.a The Spuds) from London, with a brilliant '87 debut album "Floyd Lloyd & The Potato Five meet Laurel Aitken" (included the original "Sally Brown"), released on Gaz's Rockin' Records LP, Gaz 001.

'83, The Deltones – ten women and a man on drums (put together by Penny Leyton and Sarah Jane Owen from The Body Snatchers) – released their '89 debut album "Nana na Choc Choc in Paris".

'83, Bim Skala Bim from Boston, Massachusetts, were voted best US Ska band '83 by The New Musical Express. They have been personally thanked by Sir Coxanne Dodd for pushing Ska music and keeping it going.

'84, Napoleon Solo from Denmark playing Ska and Soul. "How to Steal the World" was their mini debut album released '88.

'84, The Braces from Germany featured on the '88 compilation album "Licensed to Ska" on the skank label.

'85, Skin Deep from Doncaster who went on to form 100 Men in '89.

'85 / '86 Capone and the Bullets from Glasgow, Scotland. Opened the 1st London International Ska Festival.

'86, The Trojans led by Gaz Mayal playing a blend of Irish, Folk, Ska, Blues and Reggae. Has played a big part in spreading Ska with his Gaz's Rockin' Records label putting out other bands and his Gaz's Rockin' Blues Club putting on shows. Has contacts in the Ska circle around the world – The Trojans are big in Japan.

'87, The Loafers, Newbury, also on "Licensed to Ska" with "Julie Julie".

All these bands were to come together at The First International Ska Festival in Decemeber '88. The festival was organised by Sean Flowerdew, the keyboard player from The Loafers and took place in London at two venues. The first night was held on the 20th at the Sir George Robey, Finsbury Park, and turned out to be an historical evening when Prince Buster himself walked through the crowd and took the stage with headlining band The Trojans.

The second night took place at The Fridge, Brixton Hill, where another Ska legend "The Godfather of Ska" Laurel Aitken (the first artist on Blue Beat) played alongside newcomers and the band that outlasted the Two Tone movement, Bad Manners, who headlined the evening.

Winston then said that at the time, Buster Bloodvessel was buying the rights to the Blue Beat label but had some legal problems with the release of their latest album, "Eat the Beat", meaning he coudn't sell it in the shops.

"Dat right Winston an' if I remember right, him sell copies at de festival fe jus' one dollar," said DJ.

"No mon yu don' remember right 'cause it was one pound," reminded Winston.

Just then Matt knocked and entered their compartment.

"Great great, tell I yu fin' Coke an' 7 Bellies alive an' well," said DJ.

"Erm, not exactly," answered Matt.

"Don' tell I, yu fin' dem murdered an' ded."

"Erm, not exactly."

"Den wha' exactly did yu fin'?"

"Well to be exact I will have to refer to my notes where I've logged a detailed account of my investigation." Matt flicked through the pages of his book and said, "Ah, here we are," and began to read forth.

"Number one, disinfect toilet handle

Number two disinfect toilet seat

Number three clean under rim. Oh excuse me, gentlemen, this seems to be my toilet duty check list."

Flicking through some more pages he looked up at DJ and Winston, saying, "As I stated I would start where Mr Axe Man saw Mr Caine for the last time, being the toilet next to Recipe Man's kitchen. On entering I was overcome by the scene and stench left hanging there – I've been in this game a long time but there are some things you just never get used to. The smell of...."

Matt stopped mid sentence and stood there looking as if he was reminiscing over some horrible scene as his face contorted this way and that. He kept swallowing as if he was trying to keep himself from being sick and shook his head slowly as if he still hadn't come to terms with what he'd seen.

DJ couldn't stand the suspense anymore. Believing the worst, he finished Matt's sentence off – "De smell of a ded body, I an' I knew it, murdah," as another murder remix went off in his head.

"Murder, I say murder
Don't wanna be cremated or buried in a grave
Just shove me in a plastic bag and leave me on
the pavement
My Friend Jack, My Friend Jack stab him in the
back, murder
He was drunk and disorderly and now he's
dead"

"The smell of what we in the business call a wipe out," continued Matt. "I code-named the offender Picasso Splash Arso. The job was too big for me alone, I needed to go back to headquarters and call for back up. What I needed was to put WC Duck into action... but there was no time."

DJ started waving his hands about. He said, "Time out, time out, who dis Picasso Splash Arso?"

Matt explained. "Gentlemen, when we have an offender and we don't know who it is we give him a name linking him to the crime being investigated. In this case, Picasso Splash Arso."

"Yu seh Picasso Splash Arso murdah Coke and 7 Bellies?" queried DJ.

"Absolutely not."

Winston asked, "Isn't Picasso a famous artist?"

"Exactly. And this artist painted the insides of the toilet bowl with his arse. In fact, 'he painted it' is an understatement. It was more like he pebbledashed it from top to bottom – not only managing to reach under the toilet seat but even decorating under the rim, too."

Winston, looking puzzled, asked, "Who dis WC Duck, him not a Skankdown character."

"Tcha mon, I tought yu werk alone," said DJ.

"WC Duck is a cleaning detergent named so because of its unique duck-shaped neck, which allows the user to reach under the rim," Matt said.

DJ, finally getting a grasp of what Matt was telling him, and with veins sticking out of his neck, exploded. "Yu seh som' raasclaat mess up one a yu toilet' an' yu use som' fancy cleaner on it?"

"Exactly... well that was the plan but as I stated there was no time. But I'm glad you're following me so far."

DJ was furious and burst out "Wha' haffe dit te do wid de murdahs fe Coke an' 7 Bellies?"

"Mr Dread, please calm down. I'm giving you an exact account of my investigation."

"Yu no haffe te be so exact mi waan nor."

Matt cut him off. This was his moment, it was his report and he was giving it his way. He went on to say that an investigator, just like a toilet janitor, has to totally scrutinise everything – everything – and leave no toilet seat unturned because EVERYTHING can be evidence.

For example, by knowing the human digestive system has about a 24 hour cycle an investigator could deduce that Picasso Splash Arso had a curry for breakfast. And judging by the extremity of it, it was a vindaloo. And if he was to investigate further and enquire as to who ordered a vindaloo yesterday he would have a list of names, and he could then start to question to who used the toilet.

DJ flipped a lid, pulled his dreads out, had a benny, got his knickers in a twist and went bananas all at the same time, and screamed, "DON' TELL I YU SPEN' DE LAS' TWELVE HOUR' INVESTIGATIN' WHO SHIT IN YU TOILET."

Winston, calm and collected, said, "Axe Man use dat toilet, him seh himself dat weh him see Coke fe de last time, so Axe Man is Picasso Splash Arso."

Matt himself seeing the light and trying not to look surprised said, "Erm yes, well of course I knew that, I was merely using that scene as an example. For the trained eye every little detail can be a clue which can lead to something else."

DJ in a sarcastic tone asked, "An' wha' someting else did de toilet dat Picaxe mon Splash Pebble Dash Arso lead yu te?"

Matt then stalled and asked, "Before I go on, may I first request my backing track?"

DJ pleaded, "Is it really necessary, cyaan' yu jus' tell I wha' yu fin'?"

Matt protested. "Well yes I think it is necessary, in all the other Skankdown productions I always have my backing track and I don't see why this one should be any different".

DJ, now losing his patience, ordered. "Winston, hit him wid de backing track."

Winston duly picked up a compact disc and hit Matt over the head with it.

"Ouch, don't you know it's a federal offence to assault a Special Agent?"

DJ scolded Winston. "Mi don' mean hit him literally, mi mean pley him backing track."

"Oh sorry Matt," apologised Winston, who realised it was a CD from the US third wave Ska scene

Winston said the US third wave Ska scene – inspired by the Two Tone movement – started pretty much around the same time as England's. He stated that in the US there are three states with the biggest scenes, with many of the bands mixing Punk with Ska and playing it much faster than Two Tone. Many bands are short lived or drop the

Ska beat along the way. Then, just as he had with the UK scene, he reeled a list of dates bands formed and important facts to the development of the scene.

California, '79. Fishbone formed after hearing The Selecter and being blown away.

'81 Uptones, Berkeley, California, came from punk. The whole band were 15/16 year olds and went on to play sold out shows around San Francisco Bay for seven years. It is stated they inspired most of the bands that followed and were way ahead of their time. If they had still been around in the nineties they would have been massive.

'81, The Untouchables, from West Coast Hollywood, played a mix of Ska R&B.The members were Mods having a love of Soul and Funk. They released their first single "Twist and Shake" on their own label Dance Beat in '82. By '84 they had built up a big following and were known for their high energy shows and attracting black and whites from different cities and counties joining the Ska Mod revival. In '85 they released their first album "Wild Child" on Stiff Records which was produced by Jerry Dammers and reached number 51 in the UK charts.

'86 Let's Go Bowling, Fresno, California played traditional sixties Ska, and recorded the album "Music to Bowl by" in '89.

'87 Operation Ivy are credited with being the first to mix punk with ska and although they split in '89 they were a huge influence to following bands. Six months after the split everything they'd recorded was released on their one and only album "*Energy*". With 22 tracks, it's one to check out.

Two of its former members Tim Armstrong and Matt Freeman formed another band in '89 – Dance Hall Crashers. The same two then went on to form high energy third wave Punk band Rancid in '91.

'88, Sublime from Long Beach California who played Ska Punk and released on Skunk Records their debut album named after the malt liquor bottle (40 Oz.) to Freedom in '92.

Boston

Boston was renowned for having the largest number of colleges providing an almost ready made following, with the huge amount of stages and halls full of young adults to play to.

The Mighty Mighty Bosstones formed in '83 and were credited as the first to play ska-core mixing ska with hardcore punk with a touch of rock and metal, creating a very powerful, energetic and original sound. They debuted with the song "The Cave" on the Ska compilation "Mash It Up".

New York

'83, The Toasters coming from Batman city Gotham, the lower part of Manhattan, must be credited for doing so much for the Ska scene.

The band was started by Robert "Bucket" Hingley, an Englishman who had lived in Kenya, before moving back to England. Having some African roots he was drawn to the sixties Skinhead Reggae scene which prompted him to go out and buy "My Boy Lollipop" which was number two in the charts 1964, and which he still proudly owns to this day.

In '81 he moved to New York to manage a comic store. When he learnt he was going to be there for more than the six months first discussed, he put a band together for something to do.

After going round all the big labels who believed Ska would never be popular and showed him the door every time, Bucket saw it as his mission to put Ska on the American map, so started his own label calling it Moon

Ska. Moon Ska put out many other Ska bands and went on to be the biggest Ska independent label in the world. The Toasters released their first single "Beat up" in '84 and the Recriminations EP in '85.

Winston was still holding the CD he'd hit Matt over the head with. It had sentimental value as it was the first CD Winston had bought. CDs came out on the music market on Oct '82, but while Winston prefered vinyl, The Toasters' "Naked City" was only available on CD at the 2nd International Ska Festival on the '89 May bank holiday weekend. Bucket has since told him that the CD is a pirate copy brought out by some Mark ? on Unicorn Records, Matt's backing track was lifted from a live Toasters album titled "Skaboom" which was brought out on record and tape in '87 with only 300 copies being pressed. So this version is a pirate copy of which Bucket himself has given permission to Pirate Radio Skankdown to play. Bucket has also told that one day The Toasters were rehearsing a song that they didn't have a name for, when a friend walked in. That friend was called Matt Davis.

Matt, still standing there with his report in his hand, had been listening to Winston's commentary. He beamed proudly and said, "I didn't know you knew The Toasters."

"Tcha Mon I an' I 'nor de Toasters," said DJ, then added, "Winston hit him wid him backing track mi waan hear him report."

Winston, understanding, DJ this time, put the CD in the player and skipped to track 10.

Dem listen te a big bwoy now
Biggest bad bwoy wid a plan
As you can see on him skin
Him code name
It's because him hear dem Babylon sound
Me ask for de second time

You have to come up wid a code name
Special Espionage
Matt Davis Special Agent

As Matts backing track, the almost instrumental "**Matt Davis Special Agent**" played in the background. DJ sarcastically said, "Happy noh?"

Matt thanked him and proceeded to come forth with the statements. "I followed Mr Axe Man's statement to the letter. On exiting the toilet I entered the kitchen of Mr Recipe man and Slimey, and on interviewing them I got this statement. Mr Recipe admitted making the threat *"I'll see you off with this meat cleaver"* but denied killing Mr Caine. I took the liberty of bagging the cleaver for forensic evidence and tested it for human blood deposits. What I found was totally irregular for a kitchen utensil used for chopping up meats."

"Yu fin' 7 Bellies blood?" asked DJ.

"Exactly the opposite."

"Yu fin' Coke's blood?"

"Nope."

"Dan wha'yu fin'?"

I found no human or animal blood deposits whatsoever. Mr Recipe's utensils are cleaner than a surgeon's instruments. I really must get a sample of his elbow grease to try out on my toilets...."

Here Matt went into a dream, leaving DJ and Winston waiting for him to get to the point. Finally he continued with,"Imagine a toilet so clean you could shave yourself in the bowl."

DJ, who was not a violent man, grabbed Matt by the lapels of his rain coat and shook him. "Matt, ge' back te de report an' tell I wha' yu fin'."

"With no evidence of blood, I crossed Mr Recipe Man off the suspects list... and then got to thinking."

"Wha' yu ge' te t'inking?" asked DJ curiously

"I got to thinking that if his kitchen was so clean he must have been trying to cover something up... so I put him back on the suspects list."

"Fe havin' a clean kitchen" queried DJ.

Matt explained, "Slimey is partial to taking his breaks in the corridor so having no alibi I kept him on the list."

Matt's eyes lit up, and like a smart alec, a quirk came over his face as he said, "Then I saw it...." He left the sentence open with Winston and DJ again having to ask:

"Wha' yu see?"

"Something that's being staring us in the face the whole time."

Not waiting for the long pause DJ jumped in "Wha'?"

"An oversight."

DJ again jumped straight in. "Wha' oversight?"

Winston, who did not sound surprised at all, said, "Oh, an oversight," and waited for Matt to continue

DJ was however frantic with anticipation to know the outcome and asked again. "Wha oversight?"

Matt continued, "Who says we're looking for one killer? What if they're working together? What if Slimey wasn't taking his breaks in the corridor, but was keeping lookout so Recipe could dismember the body? So I put them both on the list again."

Seeing the looks on DJ and Winston's faces Matt knew he had them eating out of his hand but this time he was in his stride and didn't give them time to query. He finished his sentence in one continuous flow. "I know what you're going to say – that means they're both on the list twice. But that's the answer."

DJ looking puzzled asked "Wha' de question?"

Matt told DJ and Winston that what he had to say might not be easy to take so they had better brace themselves before saying. "Who killed Mr Caine and 7 Bellies? The answer being Mr Recipe Man and Slimey."

He then left another pause giving DJ and Winston time for this new information to sink in before continuing. In a loud and commanding voice, he said, "Double killers."

DJ nearly fainted, and hung on to Winston as Matt explained.

"They killed Mr 7 Bellies, got away with it and now they've killed Mr Caine too."

DJ shaking his head in disbelief, almost crying, said, "Recipe an' Slimey mi cyaan believe it."

Matt continued, "Of course this is all theory and speculation I don't as yet have any proof, so for now they're just another two of my suspects."

"Yu seh yu got more?" asked Winston.

"For sure I got more I've got a whole note book full of suspects."

Matt's backing track was coming to an end and Winston realised they had been broadcasting since Matt's entrance and didn't think Matt's report was prime time listening for the rudies tuned in from all over the world. He told the listeners about Ska Parade Radio, from Southern California, a show that first premierd on Nov,15, 1989 during KUCI's 20th anniversary week. That show by Tazzy Philips and his brother was the most listened show in the stations broadcasting history. On the success of that show they started a weekly Ska Parade Radio on Jan 7th 1990 which has played a big part in the third wave of Ska. As well as playing Ska records on the show, just like the (John) Peel sessions in the UK, it featured bands, and went on to help promote such names as No Doubt, Let's go Bowling, Reel Big Fish and Sublime.

Tazzy has also met many of the originals from the first wave and been told, "*They don't want their music to become fossilised, but want today's musicians to grow with it.*"

Winston then selected another third wave Ska track from The Potato 5's debut album and announced "Dis ones fe all yu rudies out deh." The needle lowered on to track 5 of side one.

A steam train blew its whistle, followed by the sound of steam blowing out the funnel faster and faster as the instrumental "*Western Special*" skanked its way across the air waves with the brass section taking you back through time to the wild west. Gun shots fire from all directions making you believe you could be in the middle of a Clint Eastwood Spaghetti Western.

Hardly daring to speak, DJ asked, "Who else is a suspect?"

Matt explained. "On exiting Recipe Man's kitchen I bumped into the git face cunts, errm, Miss Bones and Mr Sticks. I enquired if theyd seen the whereabouts of Mr Caine and 7 Bellies. The reply they gave was not what I expected.

"Wha' dem seh?" said DJ and Winston together.

Matt explained. "Without the batter of an eye lid, they openly stated – and at first I couldn't believe what I was hearing –"

"Wha' dem seh?"

Matt himself couldn't believe what he had heard so had to stand and think again if he really had heard it and read from his own notes in his own hand writing to justify that he indeed had heard it.

"Wha' dem seh?"

"They're dead and laid out in an ice room."

With the look of horror on DJ's face and disbelief on Winston's he continued. "They wouldn't say which compartment though"

"Dem seh dat? asked DJ.

"Well the exact words were … if I may refer to my notes, Miss Bones stated "*they're probably just chilling out in one of the compartments, innit*"

Then Matt added "But I knew what they meant"

DJ felt the tension flowing out of him and smiled as he said, "Dat no mean dem a ded, dem a jus relaxin', dem a takin' it eeeasy."

Matt was not taking it easy. Matt was taking it very seriously and countered with, "I don't know how anyone could take it easy with those two around. They're like Myra Hindley and Ian Brady and what they said next only confirms it."

"Wha' dem seh nex'?" aked Winston.

"They said *'They're writing a killer song, they're going to murder down Skaville, steal the show and walk away wiv it, innit'.* Now if that's not conspiracy to murder and grand theft I'm not a car sales man."

"Nah yu a bloodclaat, tell him why Winston."

"A killer song mean it goin' te be a hit, a song dat everybody like, an' goin' te murder down Skaville an' steal de show mean everybody tink dem haffe de best performance fe all de udder bands."

"Well if everybody would stop speaking in double entendres it would make my job a lot easier."

"Yu suppose te be a professional," retaliated DJ.

"I am a professional, a professional from the United States of America, where black is black and white is white."

"I an I a Rastafarian weh everyting is red, gold an green. *He he he*," said DJ, enjoying his little joke.

Matt, having no time for humour, defended himself. "Don't you know a professional investigator follows up all his leads, even when it looks like he's solved the crime and caught the offender? Where there's one crime, there's always another. Take this case for instance – we've already got a pirate radio station, a hijacked train, sneaking over borders in the middle of the night, graffiti, a toilet having to be taken out of service...."

Before he could finish reeling off his list he was

interrupted by DJ who said, "Tcha mon wha' 'bout de murdah' fe Coke an' 7 Bellies?"

A horse breys twice before the whistle blows again, as the brass section brings the journey of The Potato 5's "*Western Special*" to an end.

Winston bent down to the mike and told the listeners about S. H. A. R. P – Skinheads Against Racial Prejudice – which was started in '87 in New York by Marcus Pacheco. In '89, Roddy Moreno of Welsh Oi band The Oppressed visited New York and met some members of the organisation. He designed some logos based on the Trojan label and brought them back to the UK where he made flyers and handed them out at concerts and other Skinhead gatherings. This then spread out to Germany and other European countries before spreading across the continents.

S.H.A.R.P. is a very loose and non-political organisation, however it does have one policy: the opposition of neo-Nazis. The aim behind S. H. A. R. P. is to build public awareness that not all Skinheads are racists; it is in fact only a small minority who are.

Winston felt it was time to spin another record, he told the listeners of the German band Skaos from the Bavarian town Krumbach who since forming in 1982 has been led by his good friend Mad Wolley. Skaos won third place in a talent competition with their song "South African Struggle" which led to their first EP "Inside" released in 1987. The following year they released their debut album "Beware". Of which Winston had selected, he then lovingly lowered the needle on the 3rd track of side one and said "*Destination Skaville*" as the conductor blew his whistle and the train chugged out of the station. As the train picked up speed and blew its own whistle, the guitar came in playing a skank, and was joined by the drum and brass. Mad Wolley sung:

There's a place where I want to be
Where everyone's feeling high
It's a city called Skaville yes indeed
Where people are dancing in the street

"Tank yu Winston," said DJ, who was too engrossed in the outcome of Matt's report to be able to conduct the show.

Matt continued.

"After searching Git Face Cu... erm... Mr Sticks and Miss Bones' compartment and finding no evidence of foul play, I moved on and interviewed Mr Sparrow and G.B.H. The latter, like Mr Recipe Man, admitted threatening Mr Caine but denied murdering him...."

Again Matt left his sentence open. DJ was just starting to think Sparrow and G.B.H. were off the hook when Matt continued. "However, they were both each other's alibi, so I put them down as suspects."

Surprised, DJ burst out with, "Yu put dem down as suspects 'cause dem each udder alibi, why?"

"Because they might have murderd Mr Caine together and are now simply covering for each other. Believe me, I know how criminals work."

"Tcha mon, ye unbelieveable, tcha mon. Winston an' I ar' each uddah' alibi."

"Good point," said Matt. "I will put you two down along with the other suspects."

"Wha' dis goin' noweh, ye like a merrygo roun'," complained DJ.

"Excuse me?" asked Matt.

"Ye going roun' an' roun' in a circle."

"Not so fast, Mr Dread. Because this is where a spanner gets thrown in the works and this merry go round comes to a grinding halt."

Only one train can take you there
A very special train
It's the train to Skaville iye iye iye
So get right in and don't lose time

"On leaving Mr Sparrow and G.B.H, I called for back up with the intention of making an attack on Picasso Spash Arso's assault on the toilet. As I was on my way back to the toilet I ran in to, or rather he ran in to me..."

"Who?" asked DJ and Winston together.

"Sir Johnny O.B.E. Flannel. He was absolutely petrified. I took off my gas mask and rubber gloves and assured him it was me Matt Davis and there was nothing to be afraid of."

Winston asked "Why yu wear a gas mask an rubber gloves, was yu in disguise or sumting?"

"Really gentlemen, I do wish you'd pay more attention. I told you I had been back to HQ for back up to clean Picasso Splash Arso's assault on the toilet. Matt flicked forwards through his note book and said. "To cut a long story short...."

"Wha?" said Winston and DJ together in disbelief that Matt was finally going to get to the point and reveal the murderer.

"Oh sorry, you're absolutely right. Let's do this by the book," said Matt as he flicked backwards through his notebook and continued. "Mr Flannel gave me this statement." He then read forth

"I'm scared the most – I've just seen a ghost."

"A duppy," said DJ.

"Him probably drunk again," said Winston.

"What it came down to," explained Matt, "is he described a man whose silhouette I thought I saw myself standing in the shadows when we pulled out of the tunnel in Madrid. Johnny described him as a Spanish version of Mr Caine and 7 Bellies."

Guitar (instrumental) solo

"*He he he,*" laughed Winston.

Matt, looking at DJ who looked as surprised as himself, then looked back at Winston and asked, "You know something we don't."

"*He he he,* him a surprise," laughed Winston again.

"What, a ghost?" asked Matt.

"Him no a duppy, him a special gues' fe de show," answered Winston.

"And could your special guest be a murderer?" asked Matt.

"No mon, him a cool, him a bruddah."

"Well he sure scared the hell out of Sir Johnny O.B.E. Flannel."

"Trus' I, him a cool."

Matt said he'd been calculating and recalculating and that something had not added up.There were 20 passengers on the train and Recipe Man was told to cater for 21. When everybody slept he had sat puzzling this out and thought there was something wrong with his maths. Every time he counted and checked the passenger list he always came up with 20. He then confronted Winston, "So you knew all the time? Why wasn't I told another passenger would be boarding?"

"Mi seh him a surprise fe de show, him no a surprise if mi tell everyone?"

"Respect," said DJ, trusting Winston.

Winston added, "Besides Coke and 7 Bellies were murdered in France afore wi reach Madrid. So if de surprise guest no de murdah'ah an' mi cyaan believe someone fe de skankdown cas', den who?"

"I must admit I had my doubts too. When I discovered a foreign body, everything started to fall into place."

Steaming through valleys, steaming through
towns
The train that never rests
Hey it's got one aim one destination
Which it's going to reach today

"Wha' yu talk 'bout?" asked DJ.

"Wha' foriegn body?" asked Winston.

"What I'm talking about is apart from your surprise guest, I believe we've another life form on board. And I think it's responsible for the disappearances of Mr Caine and 7 Bellies."

DJ and Winston looked at each other and without saying a word to each other they were telepathically communicating, "Here we go again, this should be good." DJ was the one who asked, "And wha' evidence haffe te support dees assumptions?"

"These," said Matt, as he slapped down on Winston's sound unit a hand full of Polaroids and said, "which clearly show some kind of tentacle prints."

DJ and Winston looked through the Poloroids and saw a toilet with smudges on the toilet seat, on the sink, on the floor and also some kind of prints in a carpet, probably taken in a passageway.

"Wha' dit?" asked DJ, seeing the photos but not knowing what to make of them.

"Alien," said Matt.

"Wha' mek yu tink it an alien an' no' a animal?" asked Winston.

"And how many three legged animals do you know?" asked Matt, who then added, "Besides, the prints are clear enough to see they're not feet, paw, hoof or any other animal prints I've ever seen. I believe they're suction pads and that gentlemen, is extra-terrestrial."

Winston and DJ took a closer look at the Polaroids and indeed in every photo there were only three prints, each undistinguishable from an animal's.

Train to skaville that's the train
The whistle blowing again
Hey train to skaville that's the train
Train to skaville riding again

Matt said how he'd found the first prints while on a routine check of the toilets three quarters down the train and that he'd followed them up and down the corridor before he lost track of them and thought he'd better come back and report all his findings. He then read from his list of suspects. "So we've got Mad Axe Man, Animal, Semi Concious, G.B.H, Sparrow, Sir Johnny O.B.E Flannel, Recipe man, Slimey, a ghost, a terrorist, Sticks and Bones, eight smoking pigeons singing a song about a clock, and yourselves, Mr Dread and Mr Winston. And an alien."

"An' hoh yu nor yuself no murdah Coke an 7 Bellies?" Asked DJ.

Matt stood motionless, looking at first terrified as if he had been found out about something he didn't want anyone finding out about. You could see the concentration on his face as if he was trying to think of a way out, trying to think of a reason which would exempt him from the crime. Then he seemed to cotton on that DJ was pulling his leg. As a smile spread across his face, he said, "Oh I know I didn't do it, Mr Dread."

"Den yu bettah stick wid dis alien t'eory, it de only evidence yu haf."

DJ, obviously wanting to get back to the show, put his hand on Matt's shoulder and led him to the door saying, "Mi waan yu go tell Axe Man him innocent, den track down dis alien, catch him, interrogate him, an fin' wha' him done wid Coke an 7 Bellies."

Matt was now standing in the corridor suddenly faced with the reality of single-handedly going to go catch an alien. He was umming and ahhing about it. "Err... well... I might need –" As DJ closed the door on him.

Destination Skaville
Destination Skaville
Destination Skaville
Destination Skaville
Destination Skaville
Destination Skaville
Destination Skaville
Destination Skaville
Destination Skaville
Destination Skaville
Destination Skaville
Destination Skaville

Chapter Twelve

DIAL M FOR MURDER

"Love is Jah an' Jah is Light, Yu listen te Pirate Radio Skankdown de hottest show in tohn, seh Winston wha' I an'I tell de listener' noh," asked DJ.

"Wi tell dem 'bout Rock 'N' Roll, Ska, Rocksteady, Mods, Skinhead Reggae, Reggae, Punk, New Age Travellers but I an' I no tell 'bout Rastafarianism an' mi tink yu can tell dat bettah," answered Winston.

Pirate Radio Skankdown was DJ's show but he didn't see himself as being anyone special. As long as the message of "One Love" got out, which DJ had taken upon himself as his mission, he was happy. And he used music as his weapon to get that message out, preferring to stay in the background and let Winston do most of the talking. Being a Natty Dread himself, Rastafarianism was something he liked to talk about. So he sat up, and with a smile on his face and with a proud voice, talked about it.

Marcus Mosiah Garvey was born 1887 in St Ann's Bay, Jamaica. In 1927 he took from the bible, Psalms 68 "Princes shall come out of Egypt, Ethiopia shall soon stretch out her hands unto God," and prophesised, "Look to Africa for the crowning of a black king, he shall be the redeemer."

On the 23rd of July 1892 in the Harare province Ethiopia a boy named Tafari Makonnen was born. In1910 at 12 years old he was made govenar of Harare and on September 27 1916. He was given the reign name Ras meaning Head, equivalent to Duke, and often translated as Prince. He was baptised Haile Salassie meaning "Power to the Trinity".

On the 2nd of Nov 1930, three years after Garvey"s prophecy in the capital of Addis Ababa at the cathedral of St George, Haile Salassie – the 225th descendant in a direct unbroken line from King Soloman and Queen of Sheba – was crowned Emperor of Ethiopia.

He was given 38 titles taken from the bible, of which some would be used in his office title of His Imperial Majesty Haile Salassie I. "King of Kings", "Lord of Lords", "Conquering Lion of the Tribe of Judah", and "Elect of God". At that time Salassie was the only black leader accepted among the Kings and Queens of Europe.

Many followers of Marcus Garvey's prophecies and ideals were known as Garveyites.

Now they had a black head figure to worship and in the Christian culture of Jamaica a new religious movement was spawned. Ras Tafari became Rastafari, and a member of this movement would be a Rastafarian. Rastafarians (Rastas a.k.a. Natty Dreads) worship Haile Salassie.

Some Rastas believe God was incarnated on the earth as Jesus Christ to give his teachings to humanity. Haile Salassie is seen to Rastas as Jesus Christ in the second coming, He is also named Jah (Jahovah), with Jah Rastafari meaning God. He is literally seen as an incarnation of the Christian God who had made Man as himself.

Rastas believe only one God exists and is called Jah. Jah is God and God is Jah in the form of The Holy Trinity being God the Father, God the Son and the Holy Spirit. Rastafarians believe the form of the Holy Spirit lives within them, which is why they refer to themselves as I and I. We is also refered to as I and I to emphasise the equality between people.We all have holy spirit in us: we are all the same.

Rastafarians believe Haile Salassie will lead the righteous way into a righteous world called Zion. Africa is Zion, the original birthplace of mankind, and Zion means ultimate paradise – a utopian place of unity, peace and freedom. Ethiopia will be the capital of Zion, the New Jerusalem.

Matt knocked and entered.

"Err about this alien… I mean if it's completely eaten Mr Caine and 7 Bellies without leaving a trace, then it must be quite big. I mean, what if it resists arrest?"

DJ looked Matt straight in the face and told him, "Matt in dis life yu mus' learn te tek no shit fe no one, no if him a teacher, a big shot government minister or a mister policeman, mi don' care who de guy is, dem all bald heads, dem not God an dis is mi life." DJ went on to say, "Jus' remembah de biggest man yu evah did see was once a baby."

Matt stood for a full minute, deciphering all this before he replied. "Erm, a bald headed baby, well that certainly makes sense. But erm, hold on. If this alien is just a baby, I hope it's mother's not on board too."

"Ar' yu tryin' te seh dis job te big fe yu Matt?"

Matt was shifting his weight from foot to foot, looking at the ceiling trying to avoid the question. He knew he'd lost face and been caught out; he spoke with a quiet voice now. "Well we don't know exactly how big this alien is, it could be monstrous."

DJ, taking control of the situation, said, "It seem' like total destruction de only solution, dem raasclats mess up I show. Winston put anuddah track on fe de listener', someting positive, wi gi Matt here som' back up an' mi don' waan' nun a dis gas mask rubber glove stuff righ'. Come, wi begin fe de front a de train an' wi work ar wey te de back, till wi fin' dis monster."

Winston reached out without looking and grabbed the first record that his fingers touched. He said, "All dese records ar' positive". He looked at it and then went on to say that this one was a traditional Gospel song first recorded in 1936 by Sistor Roseta Thorpe which was titled "This Train". It also became a Blues standard when Willie Dixon rewrote it for Little Walter in '55 retitling it "My Babe". It has been covered by many artists including The Wailers but this one is the '1967 version from The Ethiopians. Winston announced "Train to Glory" as the needle found the groove and sent its message out to the Pirate Radio Skankdown listeners.

This train is bound for glory
This train is bound for glory

The three of them left the studio. The carriage was shaking and rattling as they walked to the next and entered the compartment.

"Hello deh wi go' som–" DJ stopped mid sentence and changed his words to, "Hey Pot Belly weh Mad Axe Man?"

Pot Belly was sitting in a corner with a bag of sweets looking all worried. With a mouth full of toffee sticking his teeth together he said, "He'sgonetolookforCokeandmy7B elly'sbruvverman, toclearhisname hesaid, butIfinkhe'sgo neoutlookingforsomeoneelsetomurder."

"How long ago was this?" asked Matt, his police training automatically coming into action.

"Oh a don't know I cant tell the time, I wanted to come and tell you but Winston said we had to go back to our compartment and give DJ some space."

"Good boy Pot Belly," said Winston, "It 'bout som'ting fe space, dat wi com' te tell Axe Man 'bout."

227

"Tcha mon" said DJ. "Matt here believe it som'ting fe outta space dat responsible fe de murdah fe Coke an' yu 7 Belly' bruddah man."

"What you mean like E.T? I like E.T; E.T wouldn't hurt anyone would he?"

Matt answered, "I think if it can consume a human, then it is not at all like E.T. It's more like a... a... a three-legged man eating alien."

"You mean it's only got three legs?" asked Pot Belly.

"Only? How many legs do you want it to have?" asked Matt.

"Com'" said DJ, "wi go tell Mad Axe Man him innocent, maybe him nex' door."

Pot Belly looked alarmed at being left alone with a three-legged man eating alien on board and pleaded, "Can I come, cana cana?"

Get on board
You don't need no money
Get on board you don't need no money
This train is bound for glory, glory
Get on board
You don't need, no baggage

"In ya pyjama'," asked DJ.

"I'll get dressed," said Pot Belly.

"No time, Mr Axe Man maybe in danger himself, move out," said Matt taking back the command. Now that he had a small troop behind him his bravado was growing. He left the compartment taking long confident strides up the corridor with DJ and Winston following.

"I'll put my dressing gown on, and bring my secret weapon," said Pot Belly, running behind them in his slippers. Matt suddenly stopped, and like a clown's act everyone ran into the one in front of them. They piled up behind Matt who said, "We'd better be cautious from here on."

With his nose pressed up against the back of Matt's trilby, DJ replied, "Tcha mon if yu tell us wat de plan is, maybe wi can be cautious fe here on."

This train is bound for glory
This train is bound for glory
Get on board
You don't need, no baggage
Get on board
You don't need, no baggage

"The plan is to check in on the Punks Animal and Semi Concious," said Matt.

As they entered the next carriage, knocked on the door and entered.

"Where dem a go?" asked DJ on seeing an empty compartment.

"Erm it's 4.00am, they should be here," answered Matt as he observed the compartment, his trained eye taking in the scene. The floor was litterd with crushed McEwens lager cans, two ash trays were upturned and scattered among them. The compartment was completely trashed, the curtains were torn down, the beds were ripped from the wall and the wardrobe lay in splinters.

"They might have been giving it a bit of anarchy in Espana," said Winston hopefully.

DJ wasn't so hopeful. All the positiveness from the last record left him – he felt in his heart that he'd lost another two of the cast and in his head he heard:

– Scotland Yard were baffled – Dial M for
murder
De same t'ing happen inna Birmingham
De same t'ing happen inna Brixton
Haffe yu turn ya back
An' yu start te yorn

An' wehn yu turn dan back
Ya video gone
Dial M for murder
Dial M for murder

Matt, still studying the room, the floor, the door and the corridor said, "Look here, the same three footprints I found in the toilet further down the train. I'm afraid it got here before we did; it appears they put up quite a fight before it ate them."

"Ate them," said Pot Belly.

"Yes," answered Matt. "It completely consumes and devours its victims whole; as you can see there's no trace of our friends here whatsoever. Come on, we've got no time to lose."

Pot Belly, thinking of his brother, bit his lip and said, "I've got my secret weapon" as they all raced out and up the corridor.

"Let's try Zoot's bargain train to Skaville carriage," suggested Matt, who was leading the way. Then he warned, "And keep your wallets buttoned down. This guy can squeeze a dime out of the I R S."

"No' tedey," said DJ on seeing the shop was empty.

"Maybe him gone out te mek a deal," said Winston.

"I think the alien made him a deal he just couldn't refuse. Look – more prints by the door," said Matt.

DJ's heart sank even deeper as he heard this, and this wasn't all he heard. Like a shot out the dark –

The Potato 5's **Dial M for murder sung by the Godfather of Ska himself Laurel Aitken** fired off in his head again.

De same t'ing happen inna Brixton
De same t'ing happen inna Birmingham
Haffe yu turn yu back
An' yu start te yorn

An wehn yu turn dan back
Ya carpet gone
Dial M for murder
Dial M for murder

"We'd better move on," said Matt, the pace now slowing down as he was taking more caution. He led them all from one carriage in to the next with DJ and Winston close behind and Pot Belly still following up the rear saying, "I've got my secret weapon."

Matt had been studying the floor, looking for more prints from the alien. He found them again right outside the next door. He held his hand up as a signal for everyone to stop, then with his back pressed on the corridor wall he reached out at arm's length and slowly opened the door. He cautiously peered inside, with DJ, Winston and Pot Belly's heads all under his.

He was saying, "I'm sorry gentlemen it's as I suspected," when they all heard a noise.

All four heads shot back into the corridor. They all stood in a row, their backs pressed to the wall with their hearts beating ten to the dozen.

"Wha' dat nise?" said DJ, eyes white with fright.

"It com' fe de wardrobe," said Winston.

"I think we might have caught our alien," said Matt.

"Wha' de plan?" asked DJ.

"I an' I seh wi rush him, an' stick de boot in," said Winston.

"Let's hope it's unarmed then," said Matt.

"Wha' him haffe tree legs, an yu tink him haffe no arms," remarked DJ.

"I hope it hasn't got any lasers, because we've only got my service revolver between the four of us," answered Matt.

"I've got my secret weapon," said Pot Belly.

"Jus' wha' exac'ly is yu secre' weapon, Pot Belly?" asked DJ.

"This," said Pot Belly as he took out a cylinder shaped object from under his dressing gown.

"Mild green fairy liquid" read DJ from the bottle.

"And what's in it, a concentrated mix of sulphuric acid?" asked Matt.

"This," said Pot Belly, squeezing the bottle and emitting a spurt of green liquid.

"Well let's hope the alien is allergic to washing up then," said Matt.

"Mi still tink wi mus' rush him, an' gi him a good kickin'," said Winston.

"OK this is the plan," said Matt, then whispered, "DJ you go in first – don't worry we'll all be right behind you. On the count of three take hold of the wardrobe door handle, pull it open and step aside and out the line of fire."

"OK,... seh why wi whisperin'?" whispered DJ.

"So it doesn't hear the plan," whispered Matt.

He then whispered for Pot Belly to change places with Winston who was to be their back up and said as soon as DJ opened the door they were to open fire, emptying their weapons into the alien. Once they were empty, and if they had failed to immobilise it, Winston was to jump in and give it a good kicking.

They all nodded and crept in behind DJ who was calm and wanting to see this alien dead. Meanwhile, Matt and Pot Belly behind him were both shaking like leaves. Winston behind them was rolling his sleeves up, ready for a rumble.

Everyone was in position in front of the wardrobe. Matt held a closed fist out then opened fingers counting out one, two, three. DJ pulled the door open and stepped aside so fast that Matt and Pot Belly were both shocked by his speed and agility and nearly let their weapons fall, when from out the wardrobe they heard, "Oh what a surprise, is it a party?"

"Take this," said Pot Belly, squeezing Fairy liquid in to the wardrobe.

"Hold your fire!" said Matt.

"What you all doing here? It's not my birthday" asked Jerry.

"Wha' yu doin in de wardrobe mon?" asked DJ.

"And this, and this," said Pot Belly.

"Cease fire, cease fire. Pot Belly I said to hold your fire, why are you covering him in washing up liquid?"

"You said on three to fire," answered Pot Belly.

"Yes, when I thought it was an alien," said Matt.

Matt assisted Jerry out of the wardrobe, trying to wipe him down with a handkerchief which didn't seem to have any effect at all. In fact it only made it worse, spreading it out through Jerry's shirt and shorts. Jerry didn't mind at all, and was enjoying the action untill Matt realised he was thrusting his groin out and stopped.

"An alien from outer space, ooh I wonder how many balls it's got," said Jerry.

"I believe you mean testicles, erm, tentacles," said Matt.

"No, I mean balls," confirmed Jerry.

Matt, almost thrown off his train of thought, recovered and questioned Jerry. "Mr Juggler, why were you hiding in the wardrobe?"

"I heard someone shuffling around outside my door and thought it was the murderer."

"Good thinking, that probably saved your life. It's eaten Mr Caine, 7 Bellies, Animal, Semi conscious and Mr Zoot Sharp already. Wait a minute, that's five people in less than 24 hours. That means it needs to eat about every... erm... five people, 24 hours –"

"Four hours," answered Winston.

"Wha," said DJ in shock. "A dis rate deh will be no one lef' by de time wi reach Skaville."

Matt pulled them all in, telling them to keep calm, that they could beat this thing, but that the only way to do it was to stick together. They had to work as a team, be smarter than it (DJ was looking at Matt, Pot Belly and Jerry as Matt was saying this). They could outwit this alien, together they were a force.

"A farce," said DJ.

"Wehn de goin' get tough, de tough get goin'," said Winston.

"When you're pointing the gun of life, you better make sure it's loaded," said Matt.

"Jugglers do it with their hands," said Jerry.

"If yu ar' a big tree, we ar' de small axe," said DJ, thinking positively.

"When you're up shit creek... then you hav'nt got... a paddle," said Pot Belly, not thinking at all.

The Hawkwind rattled on and so did time.

"There's no time to delay. Look, the prints lead into the next carriage," said Matt. They followed them to Sir Johnny O.B.E. Flannel's door. "Expect the worst, gentlemen. Ready Pot Belly?"

Pot Belly nodded. This time Matt had a change of tactics and from the corridor wall opposite Johnny's door Matt took a one step run and kicked the door down. Or at least that was his intention.

What he actually did was kick the door, sprain his ankle and hop about on his other foot looking for words of comfort, Winston reminded him of the words he used when Mad Axe Man put his foot on his turntable, saying they always worked for him, and that the technique was to say them as fast as you could. Matt thanked him and made a note of them, saying he would give them some consideration.

DJ turned the handle and opened the door. They all entered an empty room.

"I'll check the wardrobe," whispered Pot Belly. As he nervously approached, taking smaller and smaller steps, he found himself uncontrollably shaking from head to foot. DJ tapped him on the shoulder; he let out a yell giving everybody a near-fatal heart attack. After all their hearts started beating again, DJ silently gestured that he would again open the door which he did the same way he had previously.

He opened it, to everyone's surprise, not to an alien, nor Johnny himself. Instead, they were confronted by an avalanche of empty Jack Daniels bottles which poured out, and like a giant oil slick, spread over the floor. Everybody stood motionless with their mouths open watching the endless stream, thinking there were more bottles flowing out than was physically possible to fit in. Still they kept coming. The slick crept to the door and out into the corridor before the last bottle rolled out with a final clink, leaving silence.

"Well him no' in deh," said DJ.

"I'll check the bed," said Jerry.

"Anything?" asked Matt.

"It's nice and soft," said Jerry.

Hang up ya bomber jacket
Yu pick mi pocket
Yu nor it was a racket
Dial M for murder

De same t'ing happen inna Birmingham
De same t'ing happen inna Brixton
Haffe yu turn ya back
An' yu start te yorn
An' wehn yu turn dan back
Ya false teeth gone
Dial m for murder

"Mi keep hearin' Dial M fe Murdah. Mi tink a hit mon fe a rival station affa I," said DJ fearing the worst. He went on to say, "It got him an it goin' te get all of us, Winston mi waan pley I funeral music noh wihl deh still som' fe us te pley it."

Winston switched on his cordless microphone, allowing him to speak live on the air. "Hello everybody, Rude Boy Winston here. Wi gathered here te pey I an' I respects te de late great err early err late, well him still great and him not yet late 'cause him right here, Leroy, Higgs bettah known te him friends an' de Babylon as DJ Dread. Winston instinctively new which track to play, he had it already set up, it was DJ's and his home town band Little Chief. They'd seen them support Desmond Dekker, Bad Manners, tour as Laurel Aitken's backing band and in their own right play on the '89 Third London International Ska Festival. This was from the demo they had given DJ the night before they left England of which he'd promised to play on Pirate Radio Skankdown. Winston pressed another button on a remote control connected to the studio.

Lead singer Lorry Dowling opened Little Chiefs own version of Train to Skaville with a Pukamine vocal percussion of -

Shhkk ttkk ttkk ttkk, shhkk ttkk ttkk ttshh
Shhkk ttkk ttkk ttkk, shhkk ttkk ttkk ttshh
Hup
Haba ba ba habba ba ba bam
Ska ska ska ska ska ska ska
Baa ba ba ba ba ba ba
Haba dabaabaa habadahbababab
Shkk ttkk ttkk ttkk, shkk ttkk ttkk ttshh
Shkk ttkk ttkk ttkk,

"Very moving. Now come on gentlemen, we've got a tram to catch ourselves. Erm, I mean a bus, a train, no... errm... an alien, or a hit man," said Matt, interrupting DJ's funeral sevice.

"Oh isn't it exciting?" said Jerry.

"Which way Mr Toilet Duties?" asked Pot Belly.

"Why this way of course. We're covering the train from one end to the other, searching every compartment."

"Wardrobe," interrupted Pot Belly.

"Bed," interrupted Jerry.

"... As we go. Now this is the toilet where –" Matt stopped mid-sentence. Something had either startled him or caught his attention. DJ, Winston, Jerry and Pot were all looking at him, and then looking in the direction he was looking, but they couldn't see anything out of place.

"Wha'?" asked DJ.

"This wasn't here earlier," answered Matt.

"Wha'?" queried DJ, Winston, Jerry and Pot Belly together.

"Graffiti," answered Matt as he read forth.

"Life is like a pubic hair on a toilet seat. Sooner or later, tha gets pissed off."

"This graffiti wasn't here when I last passed this way. I'm certain of it because I combed this toilet top to bottom," he added.

"You combed a toilet," said Pot Belly.

"Bottom, whose bottom have you combed?" asked Jerry.

Matt ignored their comments – he was too deep in thought, still studying the graffiti. Something was staring him in the face and he couldn't see it.

This is your train...train to Skaville
This is...train to Skaville
Get your seat
This is...train to Skaville

Get your seat
This is
This is your train, train to Skaville
This is your train, train to Skaville
Come on, come on
Trains waiting at the station
Rock It to your destination oh
Trains waiting at the station
Rock It to your destination
This is your train
This Is your train
This is your train
This Is your skin up train

After two minutes of study and silence, Winston enlightened him. He said, "It written in red ink in Axe Man' handwriting."

Matt, feeling like a failure, but trying not to show it, didn't react to Winston's observation as though that was obvious. He said, "So we know Mr Axe Man has made it this far without encountering the alien and look – there's more tracks going this way. So saddle up posse, we're hot on its tail."

"High roll," said Winston.

"Who him call a pussy?" asked DJ.

"Ooh we're hot on its tail," said Jerry.

"Has it got a tail Mr Toilet Duties?" asked Pot Belly.

"Ooh how big is it?" asked Jerry.

They all followed Matt who limped up the corridor. His ankle was swelling by the minute and becoming more painful by the second. They entered the next carriage and formed a group outside G.B.H and Sparrow's door.

Matt instructed DJ to open the door. He and pot Belly would stand there ready to fire. DJ turned the handle and pushed the door in.

"De room emptee, wi te late again," said DJ.

"But only just," said Matt.

"How do you know we're only just too late?" asked Pot Belly.

"Observe the cabin. What do you see?" said Matt.

"De ash trey' ar full," said Winston.

"De crate'fe Holston Pils a' emptee," said DJ.

"The wardrobe is empty," said Pot Belly.

"And so are their beds," said Jerry, sounding disappointed.

"Yes, these are all facts, but you miss one small detail which gives us so much information," said Matt.

"Wha't?"said DJ, Winston, Pot and Jerry together.

Matt explained the observation. If they were to look closely at the ash trays, they would see a smouldering cigarette stub. He then went on to explain that if you leave a whole cigarette to burn itself out, it would take ten minutes to burn down to the filter. However the cigarette they were observing had been smoked down to the last centimetre and then stubbed out, but not completely stubbed out. Matt estimated no more than a minute ago.

Then throwing all caution out of the window Matt set off running, calling over his shoulder "Follow my lead." Two steps futher his ankle gave way, forcing him to hop. He remembered Winston's words of comfort and used them between gritted teeth to some success, hopping and skipping along.

DJ, Winston, Pot Belly and Jerry all hopped and skipped behind him singing, "Shit, bugger, bastard, fuck, tit, wank, shit, bugger, bastard, fuck, tit, wank."

Shkk ttkk ttkk ttkk, shkk ttkk ttkk ttshh
Shkk ttkk ttkk ttkk, shkk ttkk ttkk ttshh
Get on board, get on board this train
Get on board, get on board this train
Don't need a ticket to get on board
You just get on board this train right now

Don't need a ticket to get on board
Get on board this train right now
Taking you away for a year and a day to the land
of milk and honey flow
Taking you away for a year and a day to the land
of milk and honey milk and honey flow
Milk and honey flow, milk and honey flow, milk
and honey flow

Halfway down the corridor Matt stopped, his troop behind him did likewise. He was studying the floor saying, "OK, what do we have here then?"

"Carpet," answered DJ.

"Cigerette ash. Now this is interesting,"said Matt.

"Wha' interestin' 'bout cigerrette ash?" asked DJ.

Matt explained that the ash was running down both sides of the corridor at intervals and hadn't been trodden in the carpet – instead laid on top of the pile. Yet there were human foot prints right next to them with the three legged alien prints in the middle. When people smoke they flick the cigarette at the side of the body so as not to get it on themselves, therefore it's very probable that the persons smoking these cigarettes were the last ones to pass this way, otherwise it would be likely that someone would have trodden them in. "Are you following me?" he asked. "Tcha mon, ge' te de poin'," answered DJ.

"It no' rocket science," said Winston.

"I don't understand Mr Toilet Duties," said Pot Belly.

"I wonder how many balls it's got," said Jerry.

Matt explained further. Judging by the amount of cigarette stubs in Mr Grievous and Sparrow's ashtrays they're both chain smokers.The position of the ashtrays opposite each other indicates that if they were sitting opposite each other at the table then one of them is left handed. This explains how the ash has fallen on both sides of the corridor.

"Gentlemen I believe our theory of the alien needing to eat every four hours is confirmed. I believe it ate Mr Flannel no more than a half hour ago and I believe it's taken Mr Grievous and Sparrow captive to eat later."

"Maybe it's having a party," interrupted Jerry.

"Which is good news," said Matt, finishing his sentence.

"Good news, yu seh him tek dem captive fe a party an' dat good news?" said DJ.

"It means they're still alive," explained Matt.

He then ordered everyone to follow him. His ankle was by now swollen to twice its normal size and he could barely put any weight on it at all as he limped along. Expecting to come face to face with the alien at any moment, he wasn't in such a hurry now anyway. Holding his revolver out in front of him, he ordered Pot Belly to cover him as he inched his way into the next carriage saying, "Approach with extreme caution gentlemen. This may be our encounter with the third kind."

"Who was de firs'?" asked DJ.

"Who was de secon'?" asked Winston.

"Who was the fourth?" said Pot Belly, thinking he was being smart.

"Ooh it's putting the willies up me," said Jerry.

"Or the smoking pigeons," said Matt, as another thought entered his head.

DJ and Winston glanced at each other with a look that said how did we get here?

Nevertheless, here they were. In the next carriage, Matt was studying the floor. Winston studied the floor himself this time. Matt said, "The same tracks, human footprints and cigarette ash down the sides with the alien tracks still in the middle."

"An alien wid two lef' feet," said Winston.

Everyone looked at Winston then began to study the floor, turning their heads this way and that. Matt got down on his knees and took out a magnifying glass. After some time studying, DJ helped him as he struggled trying to stand up with one leg. He confirmed it:

"Winston, I believe you're right."

"Not righ', lef'," said Winston.

"A tree-legged alien wid two lef' feet," said DJ.

"You can't deny evidence. Do you have a better theory?" said Matt.

"Mi still believe it a hit man," said DJ.

"A hit man with three legs," countered Matt cynically.

"Maybe him haf an accomplish who haf a bad righ'ankle an' him hop nex' te him," replied DJ.

"Hugh," gruntled Matt. "Well let's find out shall we? Because they lead to this door which is Recipe Man's kichen."

haba habada ba ba
Ska ska ska ska ska ska
Skubuddy bib skibiddy bib........ yeahhhh
Shhkk ttkk ttkk ttkk, Shkk ttkk ttkk
ttshh
Shhkk ttkk ttkk ttkk

Matt told them they were nearly at the end of the train now and that there was every chance the alien would be behind this door. He also told them that even if they were too late they still might have some luck.

When DJ questioned how they could be too late and still have luck, Matt explained that Recipe man is meticulous as to how his kichen is laid out.

"Me, me-tict, meticyer... who's he going to tickle?" asked Pot Belly.

"Ooh he can lay me out and tickle me any time," said Jerry.

Matt explained that he was meticulous in the sense that he's very precise about where all his utensils are hung; that everything has its own place; that nothing is allowed to be out of place and everything is spotless –

"Ooh well, if his utensils are well hung and kept clean he seems like my kind of guy," interrupted Jerry.

Ignoring Jerry's entendre, Matt continued. "So if there's been any foul play, a disturbance in Mr Recipe man's work, then possibly there will be clues left as to how his kitchen appears."

Matt then said, 'I must stress it is vital to this investigation that nobody touches anything... agreed?'

"Do you think Mr Recipe Man will have some lemon curd sandwhiches? I like lemon curd sandwiches," said Pot Belly.

"We won't know until we enter, so let's waste no time. Gentlemen, on the count of three, we charge. Three!" said Matt.

DJ had only time to say, "Wha' –" before he and the rest were bulldozed in, with Matt charging at the rear. They had only just entered when seemingly from nowhere a chopping board from the left flew like a frisby across to the right. At the same time, a carving knife gyrated like a helicopter's rotor blade and came towards Winston at eye level. Pot Belly and Jerry, with their heads down, had already ran under it. Winston ducked and it went straight through Matt's trilby hat, taking it off his head.

They were then showered by a whole set of pans, which came down on them from the left followed by another chopping board, skewer, soup ladle, forks and other utensils coming from the right. The chopping board hit Jerry full in the face, knocking him off his feet and sending him swimming backwards through the air.

DJ was already in mid-air on his back, his legs kicking out in all directions. He could only see the ceiling and a surreal scene of one of his hands waving a spatula like a flag (where it came from and how it got there he didn't know). Suddenly from above he was attacked and sprayed with a green gooey substance which filled and stung his eyes, sending him into blindness.

Everyone and everything was also being covered in a white, foul-smelling liquid. Pot Belly with his arms raised was for some reason running on the spot, when a sauce pan that was going round and round in the air came down on his head and floored him. He was laid out, spread eagled on the floor, when a skewer came down between his legs and missed his family jewels by a whisker. Then all the wind was knocked out of him and he blacked out.

They had all been totally taken by surprise; they never had a chance. They had been under attack from all sides and outnumbered from the start. As quickly as it had started, it was all over. They found themselves immobilised, and like captives, were all stacked up on top of each other. Then like a classic "Crash Bang Wallop", a pan lid that was spinning on its axis lost its speed and came down lower and lower to a jazz drummer's cymbal crash.

One more time
Hup hup hup hup,
Hep hep hep hep
Ska ska ska ska ska ska ska ska ska
Ska ska ska ska ska ska ska
Skibbiddy bib skibiddy bib skibiddy bib
Shkk ttkk ttkk ttkk, shkk ttkk ttkk ttshh
Shkk ttkk ttkk ttkk

Chapter Thirteen

END OF THE RAILS

Seamus was tired, having worked all night. His face was black with soot and grime, he looked at Michael and said, "Oh this is the life son, how I've missed this.The Hawkwind has got a heart and soul. She drinks water and breathes fire, she belches steam and farts smoke.

"I be telling you these trains were individually made by hand with love and care. They're all unique and have a character of their own. Be Jezus, they can be tempremental at times, but all women can be – they just need looking after. Give them enough love and attention and they won't let you down.

"Not like the Diesel Electrics that came in to service in the early seventies and put these girls out of commission. They're just assembled on production line, they're all the same with a different number. If something is stuck it's just put in a new part.

"These girls never broke down and would have run forever. Take The Hawkwind here – she's a hundred years old and still giving 100%. OK the electrics are cleaner and faster now and you don't need to stop for refuelling and cleaning out the boilers, but that was half the fun of working with these girls. You worked on them and they ran their heart out for you."

Michael, just as black as his father, bent over and pushed another sleeper into the furnace. His biceps were nearly bursting through his sweated overalls. He stood up, straightening his back, and opened a can of Guinness. Then he saw the red light come on.

Seamus saw it too and began to tell the Pirate Radio Skankdown listeners

Thomas William Hicks – Tommy Steele, took his name from his grandfather Thomas Stil Hicks. Stil was pronounced Steel, so Tommy added an E. Steele was Britain's first teen idol Rock and Roll star. He had started out playing skiffle (jazz, blues, folk, country, and roots music improvised on washboards, combs, paper etc, originally from the US in the early 1900s and revived in Britain early fifties) on guitar and banjo, aged 18. He'd been on a ship, and when it docked in Virginia, he heard Buddy Holly. He was immediately taken by Rock and Roll and formed a band: The Steelmen.Their first single in '56 was "Rock The Caveman", which reached number 13 in the UK charts.

It was custom to pick US hits, record and release them before the US version reached the UK.

In '57, Steele copied "Singing the Blues" by Guy Michell whose version had already arrived in the UK and was at number one on January 4th. A week later, on January 11th, Tommy Steele's version took the number one spot.

Whilst playing with The Steelmen, nine out of 11 singles reached the top 20 including "Knee Deep In Blues" at number 15, "Butterfingers" at number eight, "Shiralee" number 11 and "Water Water" at number five – all in 1957 – while in '58 "Nairobi" hit number three.

Seamus added that '58 was the peak of British R&R. In '59 Cliff Richard and the Shadows were to follow. Then in the sixties, The Beatles and The Rolling Stones came along and R&R was old news.

As Seamus finished, Michael said, "It won't be long before it's daylight."

"That be another one of the perks working the night shift son, seeing the sun coming up over the horizon while everyone else sleeps in their beds."

But not everyone else was asleep in their beds. DJ Dread, Winston, Pot Belly, Jerry Juggler and Matt Davis Special Agent were all piled up on top of each other inside Recipe Man and Slimey's kichen.

Pot Belly came round, groaning. "Oow, get off me."

To which DJ said, "Fe Winston ge' fe I an I ge' fe ya."

To which Winston replied, "An' fe Matt ge' fe I, Winston could ge' fe ya."

To which Matt said, "Well if Jerry would stop wriggling about in ecstasy on top of all of us, we could all get off each other."

"Oh I don't know what... came over me," said Jerry, climbing off.

"I don't know what came over all of us," said Matt as he climbed off the pile observing himself the others and the kichen. All was covered in white and green matter.

"Who's got the alien?" asked Matt.

"No one haffe de alien," answered Winston, climbing off DJ.

"But I saw DJ jump six feet in the air, attacking the alien with a spatula, followed by a big daddy slam," said Matt.

"No, that was me," groaned Pot Belly.

DJ rolled himself off Pot Belly and wiped his eyes clean of the green stinging substance. He was relieved that he could see again. He asked, "Wha'ppen?"

"We were attacked by the alien," answered Matt.

"Did anyone see an alien?" asked DJ.

"It must be invisible like Predator. That's why we havent seen it, it must have been hiding and living in one of the tunnels we parked in during the day. Then, it entered the train and started killing us off one by one," concluded Matt.

"Den weh him noh , an' why is de attack stop?" asked DJ.

"Deh is no alien an' no one attack us," said Winston. "De whole ting go wrong fe de start wehn ya sen' everyone in a panic wid yu count te tree."

"Yeah yu bluurdclat, weh one an' two," asked DJ.

"Ah… well… you see… that's an old F.B.I trick. If the enemy is listening on the other side and you miss out one and two, you can still take them by surprise."

"Yu raasclat tek I an I by surprise," said DJ.

"If no one attacked us then how do you account for all this?" said Matt looking around at all the missiles that had been thrown at them. He removed the carving knife from his trilby.

Winston, with an earphone, heard that the engineers were finished telling the story of Rock and Roll. He pressed a button on his remote going live and said, "Tank yu Michael an'Seamus an' fe all yu Pirate Radio Skankdown listeners here wha' jus' happen in Recipe's kitchin."

He then explained how Matt's count of three and charge of the light brigade from behind pushed everyone forwards in a panic and off guard. DJ, at the front of the line, went flying through the door off balance, running in head first. He reached out to the left to try and take a hold of something to steady himself but instead of grabbing the work top, he grabbed a chopping board protruding an inch over the edge which in his grasp came off the work top, doing nothing whatsoever to stop his forward momentum.

He was now falling forwards and released the chopping board, throwing it spinning across the kichen to the right in order to put his hands out in front of him. On the chopping board was a carving knife – the spin of the board sent it gyrating skywards.

Pot Belly ran in, secret weapon a blazing, but because he was crushed between DJ and Jerry he couldn't raise it, so instead squirted green Fairy liquid down on to the floor.

Jerry, also off balance, put his arms out to try and steady himself, and in doing so knocked a set of pans stacked up on top of each other from the work top on the left which all came down on top of us.The chopping board ricocheted off the utensil rack, dislodging ladels, spatulas, cooking forks and a skewer, which all fell and bounced off another work top in our direction.

Meanwhile DJ, still falling forwards, slipped backwards on Pot Belly's Fairy liquid and armed with a spatula he'd some how caught, went flying through the air – his arms and legs flaying in all directions like a Wing Chun fighter.

Pot Belly slipped behind DJ, who raised his arms in an effort to regain his balance. He was still squeezing his secret weapon, squirting Fairy liquid in the air (blinding DJ in the process) while his feet were running backwards on the spot.

Jerry, not one step behind him, slipped and went swimming backstroke through the air. He reached out for anything to save him from falling – unfortunately a saucepan handle on the cooker top came into his grip. His hand still swimming backwards went like a Pete Townsend windmill, splattering everyone and everything in a French cheese sauce.

Winston, with Matt bent over, and hands on his shoulders for support behind him, came running and limping in at top speed, like a theatrical cow out of costume. Winston saw the carving knife at eye level and ducked, his movement luckily enough causing Matt to duck with him as the carving knife took his trilby hat off.

DJ and Jerry were both in the air. Pot Belly's running backwards on the spot had turned into a Fred Astair tap dance. Meanwhile, Jerry's Pete Townsend windmill came round for one last time bringing the saucepan down with so much force on Pot Belly's head, it put an end to his Fred Astair impression and floored him. Which was just in time to break DJ's fall, who landed on top of him. Winston and Matt tried to put the brakes on and slid into them like school boys on ice, piling up on Pot Belly and DJ. While Jerry somersaulted backwards, not like someone out of the Matrix, and came unceremoniously down on top of the pile.

"Well any evidence the alien may have left is now either disturbed, covered in cheese sauce or Fairy liquid," said Matt.

"Oow Pot Belly you've shot your load all over the floor," said Jerry.

Pot Belly, with the saucepan stuck on his head, almost cried. He complained, "Ooh my secret weapon, it's all flat and empty."

DJ took it from him and threw it in the bin saying, "Dat can only be a blessing fe Jah, noh it safer fe everyone."

Standing on the other side of the kitchen with his back to the rest of them, Jerry's arm was going up and down like a fiddler's elbow.

"Mr Juggler, what are you doing?" asked Matt.

"Tossing," answered Jerry, looking over his shoulder.

"Tossing," repeated Matt.

"The salad," said Jerry, turning around with a sieve full of lettuce in his hand. "I'm good at tossing, they used to call me tosser at school you know," said Jerry.

"Yeah mon wi can all believe dat" said DJ.

Matt's brain working overtime said, "This is a clue, but what does it mean?"

DJ answered saying, "It mean Recipe Mon, him mek a

salad an' Jerry," (DJ now giving a long pause himself) "…
him a tosser."

Matt picked up the lead again, saying, "Obviously we
were too late to save Mr Recipe Man and Slimey. We had
better cut our losses and move on."

They all left the kichen, Pot Belly being the last coming
from behind the sink.

Out in the corridor, Matt said, "We must be getting
closer. I can almost smell it."

"All I can smell is shit," said Winston.

"Phoar," said Pot Belly, catching them all up.

"Mon dat stink," said DJ.

"I think I'm going to be sick," said Jerry.

"Gentlemen this is the toilet in which Picasso Splash
Arso made his famous painting," Matt told them.

"Ooh, what famous painting, can I see it? Can a can a
–" said Pot Belly.

"A painting that took the enamel off the porcelain. I've
never seen anything like it in all my professional services
to the constabulary."

"Wha'?" said DJ.

'Oh that sounds important. Can I see it? Can a, can a?'
asked Pot Belly.

"I must strongly advise you not to enter Pot Belly.
You're unarmed and not wearing any breathing apparatus,"
warned Matt.

"I've got my new secret weapon," said Pot Belly.

He was ignored by all as Matt said, "Look, the tracks
go this way." He set off following them, but now his
right ankle was twice the size of his left and the pain was
excrutiating. He tried taking a big step with his left foot as
quickly as he could so as not to put pressure on his right,
followed by a small step with the right foot. But this took
so much effort and was bringing him out in a sweat.

"This is going to take too long," he said. "I need some
assistance – I need to climb up on someone's back."

"Ya no climb up on I back, I no donkey," said DJ.

Winston, checking his crisply ironed Ben Sherman shirt, spotlessly clean Levi jeans and gleaming polished Dr Marten boots nodded his head. He said, "No mon."

Jerry stepped up front, bent over and said, "Ooh, you can jump on my back."

"Er, no thank you Jerry."

"AAAAGGHHH" came from behind them and they all jumped turning quickly round to see Pot Belly come screaming out the toilet panting and gibbering. "Err! It's horrible, it's horrible!"

He was red in the face, his eyes were smarting and his stomach was wrenching. Between gasps he said, "I can't breathe, I can't breathe –"

Pulling out some smelling salts from his pocket, Matt held them under Pot Belly's nose and said, "Calm down Pot Belly. Relax and try to breathe slowly. You've had a shock; you have witnessed something no one should have to witness."

Pot Belly stood trembling like a little boy. He gibbered, "It was horrible Mr Toilet Duties."

"I did warn you not go in," reminded Matt. "Now, I need you to be brave for me. Can you do that for me?"

Pot Belly, with his bottom lip sticking out, a saucepan stuck on his head, standing there in his pyjamas and slippers still sobbing, nodded a yes.

"Because you're so big and strong I've chosen you for a special duty."

Pot Belly stopped sobbing and grew in height, standing tall and proud with his shoulders back and his chest out.

DJ, Winston and Jerry curiously looked at Matt, but didn't say anything.

"Now, I want you to give me a piggyback into the next carriage. Do you think you can carry me?"

"Oh a don't know, a fink so," answered Pot Belly.

They left the stench and Mad Axe Man's work of art behind them and entered the next carriage, now coming to the compartment of the New Age Travellers Sticks and Bones. "Time for a new plan," said Matt.

"I've got my new secret weapon," said Pot Belly.

"I suggest we administer the W plan. Everybody ready? One, two –"

"No mon, everybody no ready, wha' de fuk de W plan?" interrupted DJ.

"Oh sorry I was forgetting I'm working with ordinary citizens." He looked at DJ who was one minute a petrified schizophrenic Rastafarian, and the next a take-no-shit-from-no-one. He looked at Jerry, this clown juggler with suspected homosexual tendancies. He looked at Pot Belly, a kid in an adult's body. And he looked at Winston. Winston, well Winston was just cool, he carried on.

"Did I really just say ordinary citizens? Sorry, I meant to say untrained recruits. The W plan is the code name for the wardrobe plan, meaning as before. You, DJ, open the door and step to the side. Pot Belly and me will take the front line –"

"I've got my new secret weapon," interrupted Pot Belly, still going unheard.

"With Winston ready to give it another good kicking."

"And what do you want me to do Mr Davis?" asked Jerry.

"You can give support at the... rear." Matt heard himself say it and began to cringe, but before any one could comment he said, "No time to waste gentlemen. Let's put the W plan into action. DJ, if you would be so kind."

Pot Belly looking straight a head standing with his feet apart and both arms holding the legs of Matt made him look like a gun slinger about to draw both his pistols as DJ opened the door and stepped to the side

As they stood there facing another empty compartment, Matt held up his arm, holding his revolver and giving everyone the sign to stay behind him while he examined the room. Nobody spoke, and nobody moved – except for Pot Belly as Matt pointed out directions for him to piggyback him across the floor, to the bed, back across the floor, to the table, back to the bed then again back to the table. After a full two minutes of study and silence Matt said, "Pot Belly you can put me down."

Pot Belly turned around and squatted to lower Matt on to the bench.

"Now what have we got here?" asked Matt.

"Another emptee room," said DJ.

"Another empty wardrobe," said Pot Belly.

"Another empty bed," said Jerry.

"An emptee Rizla packet," said Winston.

Sitting down on the bench, Matt told everyone it was a good job he was there otherwise they would have all been clueless as to what was going on. He then told them his observation of three-legged footprints not only on the floor but on the bed and the table too. "And what's this?" he said, picking up a sheet of paper from the table.

"With any luck they had time to leave us a note before they were abducted... or eaten," he said as an afterthought. He read the words which looked hurriedly scribbled down on the sheet of paper.

"Parkdrive
Oi Geezer got any faags... parkdrive
I get up about eight and feed the pigeons...
parkdrive
I feel fucking great, innit

Startled, he let the sheet fall to the floor and held his arms out again as a sign to keep the rest away from the note.

"This must be the killer song about the eight smoking pigeons," he said.

Pot Belly and Jerry took two steps back from the lyric sheet.

DJ and Winston looked at each other with a look that said remember when we first came to England and on a Saturday morning, instead of doing our own thing, we had to go shopping with Mum at the Co-Op? Out of boredom we swapped all the price stickers from one product to another. Mum caught us and threw a wobbler.

Matt, who was weighing up the evidence – the footprints over the floor, bed, table and the killer song – said, "We have to think this through rationally. What does it all mean, where is it leading us to, where is it going to end, how is it going to end?"

It was then he saw something protruding from Pot Belly's pyjamas. "What's that you're concealing there?" he asked, pointing to the bulge.

"Oow's a big boy," said Jerry.

"It's my new secret weapon," answered Pot Belly.

"Mi taught mi trow dat ting awey," said DJ.

"That was my old secret weapon; this is my new one," said Pot Belly.

"Ok, wha' ya new secret weapon, Pot Belly?" asked DJ.

Pot Belly proudly pulled out of his pyjamas a bottle of Jif, showing it to the rest of them.

"Where did you get that from?" demanded Matt.

"Recipe Man's kitchen," replied Pot Belly in all honesty.

"What?" said Matt (but he didn't say "what" as in the curious "what" one might use when one would ask "what" time is it please. It was more the "what the fuck" one would say if one was all dressed up for one's wedding and walking up to the church entrance and had just stepped in a deposit left by a huge Doberman).

He then went into a rage, saying "The liar, the cheat, the trickster, the lying cheating false devious bastard, I tell you, I hope the alien has eaten him because if I ever catch up with him I will rip his head off. Of all the low down –"

"Matt, Matt, cool it mon. Irie mon, wha' de problem?" asked DJ, interupting him.

"Recipe Man's the problem, he told me he kept his kitchen so spotlessly clean with nothing but elbow grease, while all the time he's been using Jif behind our backs, the lying, cheating –"

"Matt dat no big deal mon, everybody use som' kin' a cleanin' ma-terial, tek yuself, yu haf ye WC Duck."

Matt, calming down, said, "Boy this case is really starting to get to me."

"It gettin' te all of us Matt," said DJ.

"I don't think I can go on from here. I'm broken, you'll probably be better off without me anyhow, I'm just slowing you down. I've been a failure fom the beginning. Look at me, from a Special Agent to a toilet cleaner. That not only takes the biscuit, it eats it, digests it, and shoves it back out the other end."

Pot Belly, who was looking all concerned, asked, "How did you come to be Mr Toilet Duties?"

"Oh," said Matt, "you don't want to hear about my troubles. You go on ahead without me."

"Course I an' I do Matt yu one fe de cas'. Remember wehn I an' I firs' met in de Devil's Arms and yu was drinkin' yu sorrow awey an' need a ear te tell yu story' te, I an' I was dat ear. I an' I tek yu in an' let yu tell yu story' te all de listener', 'cause dem reality story' Matt, no film script, no theatre pley, real life reality story' dat happen te yu Matt. So go on, tell how yu com' te be Matt Davis Toilet Duties."

DJ then turned to Winston and whispered, "Haffe go' yu mike on, I an' I cyaan mis dis." Winston's mike was still on and they were still broadcasting live across the airwaves.

Matt, sitting comfortably, began. "Well you all know the Weasel, Hubba Bubba and Singing in the Rain stories."

They all nodded yes.

"After those three incidents and three demotions in three months, the station's psychiatrist said I needed to take a three month break. He said the work was too much for me and I was having a burn out, but what did he know?

"I was orderd to take a vacation and sent to Europe. I chose France because I occasionally liked a bottle of Merlot. After my plane landed I checked in to a chateau then went out to get some supplies and that's where it went wrong from the start."

"What happened Mr Toilet Duties?" asked Pot Belly.

"You see I couldn't just take a vacation, a detective can't just switch on and off. Your life depends on your being alert at all times. It's not just a job, it's your life. I had given up everything to be a detective, my friends, my clubs, my hobbies – it even cost me my marriage, you're a detective 24-7 and on the look-out 25 hours a day, 8 days a week."

"Yeah Matt, Wha'ppen?" asked DJ.

It was 9am Monday morning time to go to work. Today's job was to stake out the local Intermarche, a French supermarket. I put my 10 francs in the shopping trolley. It released the locking mechanism. To the public I was just another Monday morning shopper, but underneath my trilby, my raincoat and my badge, I was Matt Davis Special Agent. To look like an ordinary shopper I pushed the trolley in front, and I walked behind. This job was going to be easy. I tried to push the trolley through the turnstyle. It wouldn't go, a woman behind pointed me to put the trolley through the gate at the side. And there was just me supposed to go through the turnstyle. Maybe this wasn't going to be so easy after all.

The first thing I saw was onions. Nine francs for five kilos. Not a bad price. I made a note of it.

Next were mushrooms. Only now they were called champignons – something I would have to check out back at the chateau.

Something caught my eye. I stopped at the fruit and veg counter, and removed a price bargain placard from my iris.

Carrying on as I casually browsed in the meat display, I noticed bacon, 200 grams, at 12 francs. Just next to it was another 200 grams at seven francs. Something was starting to smell fishy. It was a display of mackerel layed out on crushed ice. I checked their pulses. They were all dead.

What had started out as an S22 routine stake out, had turned into a Tee ripple M for Murder

I had to stay cool; maybe the murderer was still in the store.

I filled my trilby and pockets with ice, then made my way down the next aisle. There, I saw the murderer disguised as an old lady pretending to choose between a tin of Chappy or Winalot.

Now was my chance. I looked on the shelf for a projectile. Tin of Casserole, eight francs or two for 14.

I took the two and trajected my missiles at the murderer.

She went down like a sack of spuds. 20 kilos for 20 francs, a bargain. I searched the murderer for identification, and found an old aged pensioner's card. It read Madame A Christie. I helped her on her feet and dusted her down. She looked a bit disillusioned and staggered off towards the whisky shelf.

I was quickly back on the case, going down the breakfast cereal aisle. I observed Weetabix 16 francs; I'd seen them in a store not ten blocks away for 14. Somebody somewhere was making profit. The case was getting bigger all the time

First murder, now extortion.

I went straight down alcohol lane, thinking it would be a good place to check out. A suspicious character was lingering about at the other end. He was my man. I moved in and karate chopped him in the back of the neck, only to discover he was Monsieur Hercule Poirot – a Belgian detective.

It was time to get out before I blew my cover.

I thought quickly I must buy something. Kronenburg 4.7%, 10 bottles at 18 francs. Or Strasburg 4.5%, 17 francs.

No time to think I took them both. I can't just buy beer I thought. So I grabbed the next four items. Washing line, Sellotape, rubber gloves, and Vaseline. I got a funny look at the counter, but I stayed calm waiting for my change like an everyday shopper. The ice was now melting and raining down from under my trilby. And I had pockets dripping in to puddles of water around my feet. I took my change and slushed out the door –

Where I was arrested by the Gendarmes and handed over to International Security and deported back to the US where I was demoted to Matt Davis Toilet Duties.

"Shit happens," said DJ.

"Then you die," said Pot Belly.

"Demoralised I quit and moved to England to make a fresh start as a private investigator. The night I arrived was the night I met Mr Dread in the Devils Arm's who has now invited me on this trip to Skaville to give a live on stage reading of one of my stories.

"Tcha mon, so wha' yu seh, ar yu a quitter?"

Matt having shared his story with his fellow compatriates suddenly felt a huge load off his shoulders. He now felt revived, a born again, positive new man and with an abundance of energy he said, "Come on. We got an eight smoking singing murdering alien hit pigeon man to catch." Then he added, "That doesn't sound right but come on anyway."

He stood up and fell down, rolling about on the floor in agony while screaming, "Shit, bugger, bastard, fuck, tit, wank, shit, bugger, bastard, fuck, tit, wank," a few times before the pain of his ankle eased off enough to be able to sit up.

Catching his breath back he said, "Okay, let's start again. Pot Belly will you piggyback me into the last carriage we've got to catch something?"

With Matt on his back, Pot Belly led the way. DJ and Winston took the side ranks and Jerry covered the rear. Together, they silently inched their way forwards up to the end of the carriage. The last carriage had no compartments; when in service it would have been the post carriage. There was a door between them and what ever secrets the last carriage held.

Matt saw the door lock was broken and whispered, "The door has been forced open. Probably by something with a lot of weight behind it." They all took another step forward.

Matt, still on Pot Belly's back, suddenly froze with fear. It was felt and followed by the rest as they all heard some unhuman sound.

"Sounds like a wild animal," whispered Jerry from the back.

"A beast," whispered Winston.

"It's a monster," said Pot Belly.

"Gentlemen that is our human eating alien," confirmed Matt.

"Soun' like a set a pigs," said DJ.

Standing at the door, Matt said, "Gentlemen this is it. The last stand. We've searched the whole train front to back and this is the last carriage and the last door. Behind this door hides a chain smoking trained hired killer disguised as an alien who can metaphorse itself into a pigeon. Gentlemen, I understand if you want to turn back – there will be no hard feelings. I can not do this – it's my job, but you can save yourselves. Gentlemen, with or without you I'm going in.

DJ said, 'Dat raasclat haffe eat de res' fe de cas', de show is mi life, widout de cas' I haffe no show. I bring dem characters on dis train, it I fault dem a ded I owe dem dis las' stan' I seh I an' I kill de bùmbaclat.'

Winston looked down at his feet and said, "Dr Marten boots, do ya stuff."

Pot Belly armed with his Jif said, "For my 7 Bellies bruvver man."

"Before we go in I have to do one last thing," said Jerry as he put his hands in his pockets and started to rummage around.

"Wha' ya got dere?" asked DJ.

"My balls," answered Jerry.

"Do you have to?" asked Matt.

"Tcha mon" said DJ.

As Jerry produced 9 wire balls from his pockets, he then proceeded to throw them in the air consecutively, one after the other, until he was juggling a perfect cascade – catching them all and saying, "I've got more balls than all of you."

"Very impressive," complimented Matt.

"Wha' dem tings in de middle Jerry?" asked DJ.

"Wicks, these are my fire balls," answered Jerry.

Winston, now ready for action, said "Time te rumble. Matt wha'de plan?"

This was not the reaction Matt had anticipated. With all his past failures flashing before him he had rather hoped they would have all turned back. He would have waited a couple of minutes then gone back himself, saying he hadn't found anything, but now they were all hyped up and ready for the kill.

Remembering his combat training and strategy, the objective of the operation, element of surprise and the need for swiftness in and out, he pulled himself together and made a plan. Matt beckoned them to form a circle like basketball players discussing team tactics, and told them the plan.

"OK Jerry, you're the ace up our sleeve you follow me and Pot Belly in juggling fire, all animals are scared of fire it's the last thing it will expect, DJ what weapon do you have?"

"Jah"

"Erm...."

Winston with his Dr Martens at the ready and all psyched up, said, "We will go out as heroes. It will be just like the end of that film Butch Cassidy and the Sundance Kid as we run in to a hail of bullets.

Matt, believing Winston had seen too many films, wanted to say something else. "Gentlemen we don't know what's on the other side of that door. Are you sure you all want to do this?" But he didn't get the chance. Jerry was lighting his fire balls as DJ said, "Let finish de game." Then, DJ, with a voice of authority, took the lead. He shouted, "On I count... JAH... RASTA... FARI."

They all charged forward like warriors of Gengis Khaan, Matt's bravado having failed him gave the last word "All for one... then run like fuck".

Pot Belly, wearing his Superman dressing gown and pyjamas with enormous Sugar Puffs Honey Monster slippers, ran unevenly as he charged forwards. He was still giving Matt a piggyback, and Matt was now riding the equivalent to a bucking bronco, swinging side to side hanging on with one arm for his dear life. His other arm was stretched out holding his revolver over Pot Belly's shoulder aiming every which way but forwards.

The train carriage was now illuminated by a ring of fire as Jerry, like a human running inferno, juggled a perfect nine fire ball cascade behind them. Winston was at the rear, boots and braces at the ready with DJ and his Jah next to him singing, "We're goin chase dem crazy bald heads outta de train."

Pot Belly ducked his saucepan head down with the intention of ramming the door open with his shoulder. But because Matt on his back was higher than Pot Belly, it was with Matt's head that nearly took the door off its hinges. They all stormed through the last door and were blasted with the ear splitting sound of:

Magically bored
On a quiet street corner
Free frustration
In our minds and our toes
Quit storm water
My generation
Uppers and downers
Either way blood flows

Inside outside, leave me alone
Inside outside, nowhere is home
Inside outside, where have I been
Out of my brain on the five-fifteen
Out of my brain on the train
Out of my brain on the train

Who said Pot Belly. Matt dazed and confused had a sore head and slid down off his back on to one knee, taking a police combat position, pointing his revolver saying "Who ?"

The carriage had been used to store a complete bar and all the wines, beers, brandies and whisky etc for the festival. Like all Scots, junkies and drunks, wherever they are, be it abroad, at a festival, in a strange pub, they always manage to find one another and the Pirate Radio Skankdown cast were no exception.

Underneath the deafening sound, except for Zoot who was sitting in the shadows at the end of the bar and for Mad Axe Man who was laid out on his Harley Davidson, they were all there. 7 Bellies, Coke, Animal and Semi, Sir Johnny O.B.E. Flannel, Recipe Man and Slimey, GBH and Sparrow, Sticks and Bones. (And called so because he's always two or three sentences behind) another hippy, the surprise guest, the old member of the cast – Speed all crashed out on the carriage floor which was covered in empty bottles.

7 Bellies who had pissed his trousers came around. Sitting up, he held his glass out to DJ slurring "Whallo gisatopup." Then he fell back into a coma.

Pot Belly told Matt, Winston, DJ and the listeners that it was "5.15" a rock track from the "Quadrophenia" album by The Who, and that Coke and 7 Bellies always played them on The Devil's Arms juke box.

He then went on to say that The Who, being Pete Townsend, Roger Daltry, John Entwistle, and Keith Moon, formed in late '62 and early '63 playing under the name The Detours with Roger, John and Pete. In Dec '63 they opened for the Rolling Stones. Townsend was a Mod and suggested to look different from The Stones by cutting their hair and dressing in US Ivy League college clothes.

In Feb '64 they changed their name to The Who with Moon joining in April and somewhere round here they changed their name again, this time to The High Numbers. They released a single aimed at the Mods titled "Zoot Suit" bw "I'm The Face", both written by Mod Peter Meadow their then manager. The single flopped (however they both later featured in the film soundtrack Quadrophenia). In October '64 they changed back to The Who.

In 1965 they released their second single, "I Can't Explain", reaching number eight followed by "Anyway, Anyhow, Anywhere" a song about a Punk kid. It was their own composition which they promoted 2nd July on the TV show "Ready Steady Go," with Moon wearing his RAF roundel T-shirt in a studio full of Mods. The song featured distortion feedback which was played for the first time on television. The song reached number 10.

Still in '65 (and on a train incidentally) Townsend wrote "My Generation" which was released 5th Nov and reached number two in the charts. It was a song speaking for the Mod youth of the day with all the fire and energy of Punk which followed eleven years later. Some say the lyric *"hope I die before I get old"* made it the first Punk song.

Townsend is credited with using the term "power chords" and setting trends with his guitar jump kicks, sticking guitars in amplifiers and smashing them up. This happened one night in the summer of '64 whilst playing in the Railway Tavern, Harrow, Wealdstone, London. The tavern had a small stage with a low ceiling and when Townsend over enthusiastically jumped up and purely by accident shoved the head of his guitar through the ceiling, the crowd mocked and jeered him.

Townsend's recollections are that he then smashed it up on the floor and jumped all over it. Luckily he had a spare 12-string which he picked up and carried on playing as if it was part of the show.

A week later when they played there again it appeared the audience was only waiting for Townsend to smash his guitar and when he didn't, they were disappointed. Moon, annoyed at the lack of public enthusiasm for their performance, took his anger out on his drum kit, smashing them in.

This smashing up of instruments then became a ritual, and so they made Rock and Roll history and set the way for generations to follow.

Moon a.k.a. Moon the Loon, known for his mad antics such as dressing up as Hitler and undressing in airports and interviews, took this instrument destruction one step further. He had a fascination for blowing up hotel toilets with cherry bomb fireworks and in '67 on The Smothers Brothers Comedy Hour (live TV) thought he would surprise everybody by rigging his drum kit to go off at the end of "My Generation". He loaded it with so many cherry bombs that it blew him and his drum kit three feet back and gave Townsend a perforated ear drum.

On 14 Aug '67 the pirate radio stations operating out at sea were declared illegal. As a tribute during the winter, The Who released the album titled "Sell Out" which between tracks contained jingles from these stations. In '69, The Who wrote the first ever rock opera – "Tommy" – a double album that was filmed in '75. An outstanding feature was Sir Elton John standing on top of a pair of 54-inch high Dr Marten boots during the performance of the classic "Pinball Wizard". Also in '69 they played the legendary Woodstock festival on August 15th,16th and 17th.

In '73 The Who recorded Quadrophenia, a double concept album quoted as the most influential rock album of all time, which was portrayed on film in '79 becoming a cult classic and provoking a Mod revival. The film was set in '64, the peak of the mods versus Rockers fights, and was named The Battle of Hastings Two.

In '76 they played a concert in Charlton Athletic football club so loud it earned them a place in the Guinness Book of Records as the loudest rock band, a feat they held for more than a decade.

In '90 they were placed in the Rock and Roll Hall of Fame with the quotation "In the minds of many they are the world's greatest rock band." They are also quoted next to The Beatles and The Rolling Stones as making up the holy trinity.

They have inspired Cream, The Jimi Hendrix Experience, Led Zeppelin, Rush, The Jam, Sex Pistols, Clash, Ramones and many more.

"Interesting," said Winston, giving Pot Belly a pat on the back to compliment him for his knowledge.

"What I'm interested in," said Matt, still on one knee and holding his revolver out, looking at everyone on the floor who were now waking up with a hangover, "is the fact we've just spent the last 72 hours searching the train from top to bottom looking for an alien, a ghost, a hit man and killer pigeons smoking After Eights, believing you had all been murdered."

"Shite," said Mad Axe Man.

"You what, you what, you what you what you what? You're a fackin' nattah," said GBH.

"Howay, we wuz droonin in alcohol, divven't go an bring it all doon," said Sticks.

"Oh wow maan have you been taking acid? That's some mother trip you're having," said Speed.

"Oi Geezers got any faags?" said Bones.

"See you Jerry, what's with the circus and that?" said Semi, looking at Jerry and his fire balls.

DJ was still coming to terms that everyone was still alive. But Matt was detecting and wanted some answers. Looking at Coke, he asked, "Mr Caine, what do you have to say for yourself?"

Coke anwered by singing along. *Sniff.*

A raft in the quarry
Slowly sinking
On the back of a lorry holy hitching
Dreadfully sorry

Apple scrumping
Born in the war
Birthday punching

Jerry stopped juggling his fire balls which had now gone out. Winston, smiling to himself, was looking at everyone rubbing sleep from their eyes, stretching and slowly getting up off the floor on to their feet. DJ was still taking the scene in, counting the heads and reassuring himself that everyone was still alive. He was also realising that except for a bottle of Pina Colada standing on the bar the whole alcohol stock for the festival had been consumed.

Pot Belly was repeatedly drawing his Jif bottle from his pyjama pocket holster, pointing it at everyone then palming his hand along the length, pretending to fire off six shots as one before re-holstering it.

"If tha squirts t'shite on thee, thee'll shove t'jif bottle up tha's arse," said Mad Axe Man.

Matt was just about to confront Mad Axe Man when Speed, a mountain of a man, still wearing his poncho, sombrero and acoustic guitar stood up in front of him.

"So this is our mystery surprise stowaway guest is it? Mr Speed I believe, and what's your major contribution to this show?" asked Matt.

Speed stared through Matt, not only looking like he'd had one drink too many, but like he'd lived two or three lives too many as well. And this one had already passed its expiry date.

Matt couldn't tell if Speed had heard him and was trying to think of an answer or was spaced out somewhere else, when Sir Johnny O.B.E. Flannel, who was staggering around as if he was made of rubber, bumped into him.

Johnny also looked like he'd seen better days, although whenever they were would have been a long time ago – probably before he reached the age of 10. Matt could see he was painfully hungover but tried to interview him anyway, asking, "Mr Flannel, how did you come to be here?"

Johnny went into an automatic routine of being able to talk without thinking and answered, "We're on a train. What was the question again?"

Matt not only felt like he'd lost all authority but that he'd never had any to begin with. Still he tried again by asking in general, "Can't anyone give me a straight answer?" When Speed who was back from planet far away suddenly pointed a finger at Matt and said "I let the music speak for me."

He man drag
In the glittering ballroom
Greyly outrages
In my high heeled shoes
Tightly undone
Know what they're showing
Sadly ecstatic
That their heroes are news

Now that they were nearly all standing up, they formed a crowd and loomed over Matt who was still in his combat position on one knee. He struggled to stand up and tucked his revolver under his raincoat behind his back. He searched through their faces looking for an answer and came eye to eye with Slimey. Matt confronted him, "A bit far from the kitchen aren't you?"

"I was following Recipe Man," answered Slimey.

Matt addressed Recipe Man. "I'm surprised to see a man of your standards mixing with a rabble like this."

Recipe man retaliated. "I was surprised when a man of your standards came interrupting my work, confiscating my cleaver and accusing me of adding 7 Belly burgers to the menu. I took a break and wondered down the train where I met the alive and well, living life to the full, man himself. He greeted me with an open heart and offered me a drink, and then another drink and after that I can't remember but I've learnt he and his friends are a damn sight more sane and respectable than you, Mr Good Night Day."

DJ was quite now enjoying the tit for tat between Matt and the rest of the cast and had made sure Winston's microphone was still on, sending it out live across the air waves.

Matt, feeling ticked off, turned to 7 Bellies who was now back in the land of the living belching, farting and scavaging through empty bottles looking for something to drink.

"This whole escapade is your fault. What's your story, Mr 7 Bellies?"

7 Bellies answered. "Well adunno, I set of walking with Axe Man yeah, looking for some Thunderbirds and beer that I'd stashed, and then it went dark. I lost Axe Man and just kept walking in the dark till a fell through a door maan, and I was surounded with all this beer and drinks maan. At first I thought I'd died and gone to heaven but then it turned to Hell cause there was nothing to eat. I haven't had anything to eat for days maan; I've had to live off alcohol, it's been 'orrible."

Inside outside, leave me alone
Inside outside, nowhere is home
Inside outside, where have I been
Out of my brain on the five fifteen
Out of my brain on the train
Out of my brain on the train on the train
Wow I'm out of my brain
Whooh, out of my brain on the train
Here it comes
Whooh out of my brain on the train on the train
Out of my brain on the train

Matt was still looking for someone to blame, someone to find guilty and came back to Mad Axe Man. "You" he said, "Mr Picasso Splash Arso, graffiti extraordinaire."

Mad Axe Man, who was still laid out on his Harley, said, "Whats all bloody panic like, nobody's been murdered, there's no aliens, hit men or killer pigeons. Thee's just had a bit of a little party like and we were all crashed out sleeping a hangover off when tha comes barging in nearly knocking door of its bloody hinges. Which in process like swung into stereo knocking play button on, tha nearly give thee a bloody heart attack."

"That still doesn't explain how you came to be here Mr Axe Man. Please answer the question."

"Well like thee went fer a ramble like looking fer 7 Bellies and Coke, like thee knew thee 'adn't murdered 'em so thee thought thee must be somewhere like. And when thee found 'em, it wore like finding thee long lost brothers like, thee felt an enormous sense of relief and it called fer a celebration like. We had t' beer and that till it ran out like," he said, sounding upset, then picked up again with, "luckily there were wine and brandies, otherwise thee don't know what we'd ev had to do."

Matt still had a lot of unanswered questions but couldn't remember any of them. So instead, he said to anyone who was listening, "And it didn't occur to any of you to come and tell any of us you had found them? Where were you educated?"

Sniff. "Woodstock, maan," answered Coke.

"Yeah we've been havin' our own little festival an dat innitt," said Bones.

DJ, still following the investigation, looked at Bones, seeing her wearing dreadlocks with a Rasta coloured hair band. She had on her black leather jacket with Global Skank sprayed on in silver paint, a tie-dyed skirt with beads and tiny bells at the bottom, a pair of unlaced Dr Marten boots, and there at her feet was....

DJ started laughing. It wasn't a little chuckle you might give to something slightly amusing, it was more the big hearty laugh you would give when you had been convinced by an incompetent ex Special Agent that your cast had been murdered by a three-legged alien with suction pads and seeing there was a perfect natural explanation.

"Deh is ye tree legged alien wid two left feet *he he he*," said DJ, pointing next to Bones' feet. Startled and drawing his revolver, Matt looked down at Bones' feet and saw a three-legged dog wearing child-sized Dr Martens.

Matt, feeling fooled, took the offensive side and began with the rule: "No dogs allowed, how did that get on board?" Then he answered himself as all the clues started to fall in to place. He said to himself, "That's why the pan of water was under your bench. That's why you raced back to the compartment – you hid it in your tie-dye travell bag and put your feet on it to disguise the movements, the same bag that appeared to be alive at Selby station. That's why all the prints were all over the table bed and floor in your compartment.

"So why were prints all up and down the length of the train?"

"Howay, yeez divven't think a dog canna ga oot," said Stick.

"Yeah he has to piss and shit innit," said Bones.

"Why yeez dunna hav te worry, heez hoos trained reet," added Stick.

"That's why prints were all over the toilet and sink. Hey why's it wearing child-sized Dr Marten boots?"

"Why? Coz heez a travellers dog yeez knaa," said Sticks.

"Yeah he's our little Skank. He's like a kid to us innit," said Bones.

"And why has it only got three legs?" asked Matt.

"Why aye, coz eez seen plenty action, man," answered Sticks.

"Yee haw" said Mad Axe Man, kicking his Harley into life. He pulled a wheelie and shot off down the train singing –

Why should I care
Why should I care

Perhaps Mad Axe Man should have cared more. A ball of fire rose up over the horizon, casting a red light which crawled across the wasteland turning everything that came in its path red.

DJ was looking out the window seeing rocks, sand and cactuses turn red as it reached out, racing towards The Hawkwind. He pointed at the red light as it went through the carriage and carried on spreading a red shadow the other side. It was as if God was the lighting technician at a subtle moment in a concert. He said, "It's a phenomenon."

7 Bellies, holding up half a glass of a get-pissed-quick mixture of a collection of wines, brandies, whiskies and the last drops from all the empty bottles, said, "DJ's a messiah, he just phen, phenome, fucking turned my white wine red."

Sniff. "It's psychadelic maan," said Coke.

"Like Jimmy Hendrix and Pink Floyd," said Pot Belly, going unheard.

As DJ followed the sun's path towards the mountains, a huge black shadow was cast next to the train line. Pointing to it, he said, "Check dis out mon."

"Cor blimey," said Sparrow, standing next to him.

"Biggest bleedin' bird I've ever seen" said GBH.

"Mus' be a condor a som'ting," said DJ.

"Nope, it's a chopper," said Matt.

Everybody got sprayed with pina colada as Jerry rushed to the window saying, "Where's the biggest chopper you ever did see?"

"It gone noh," said DJ, who couldn't see it anymore.

"See yu Mr DJ, it's gettife light oot there," said Semi.

"Ne kiddin, should we be no pullin' inte a tunnel, by the way," said Animal.

"No mon, I an' I one hour fe Skaville, tedeh wi ride on," said DJ.

"Far out maan," said Speed, referring to 7 Bellies' red wine phenomenon.

With all eyes on him and all tongues hanging out, the lot of them licking their lips like dogs at the dinner table, Matt sipped from his bottle of 100% graffiti removing pure alcohol.

"Wha' dis?" asked DJ, confronting him.

"If you can't beat 'em, join 'em," answered Matt and took another sip.

DJ slapped him hard on the back, saying, "Dat de spirit."

Matt swallowed a huge mouth full and started choking as the pure alcohol burnt his lungs. Everybody else was laughing at Matt doubled up, coughing and spluttering and gasping for air.

"*He he he*, it time fe celebration," said DJ.

"Wid wha' DJ everyt'ing is finis' 'cept fe Jerry's pina colada," said Winston.

"Jah wil provide," said DJ.

Just then, Zoot, with the ninja skills he'd learnt from years trading on the streets (being able to blend in with the background whenever there was trouble or sign of the police) stepped out from the shadow at the end of the bar. He said, "Yo bro, welcome to Zoot's bargain mobile accessories. If you got the cash, I got the stash. If you want to make a deal, I'll give you it at a steal."

As he opened up his suitcase which transformed into a small shop, he presented on the front shelf a £50 bottle of champagne.

"Dis train is mine," DJ said, looking at all the empty bottles discarded on the floor. "All dis drink mine fe de Skaville festival, I no pey fe wha' mine in de firs' place an' I no mek no deal wid a bruddah, gi I de champagne."

"Such is life, life is such. This time I'm out of luck – I didn't even make a buck."

Zoot handed over the champagne. Recipe Man and Slimey behind the bar had set up a pyramid of champagne glasses. DJ popped the cork and poured in the top glass a fountain of champagne. Everybody took a glass, clinking each other's and saying cheers. Jerry said "Bottoms up" and someone else called out "SPEECH". Everyone looked at DJ who said, "Long live Pirate Radio Skankdown, an' all dem dat skank wid us."

Just then The Hawkwind went round a bend causing the half open door to swing fully open into the stereo. It started to play:

Everybody's doing the brand new beat now
Come on baby, do the locomotion.

"This song has been number one twice in the US charts and once number three by three different artists in three different decades. This is the '74 version by hard rock group The Grand Funk Railroad," said Pot Belly.

Still drunk with hangovers, drunk with happiness, high on emotions and high on other things, the whole cast formed a chain behind Pot Belly who led them down the train singing, **"Come on baby do the locomotion,"** and back again, in fits of laughter, with hugs, shaking hands and patting each other on the back. DJ was beaming with a big smile. This was the "One Love" message he was trying to get out through Pirate Radio Skankdown. Mods and Rockers, Punks and Hippies, Skinheads, Rastas and all walks of life getting on down together.

Winston had told how Blues had led to Rock and Roll which led to the record industry which led from the Sound Systems to Ska, Rocksteady and Reggae, with Motown, Soul, Mods, Skinheads and Reggae coming in between. During the sixties, he'd told how experimental periods of Psychadelic Rock had gone on to disco in early seventies, alongside Glam Rock, plus Heavy Rock which through bordom and oppression led to independent labels and Punk Rock followed by second waves of Punk and Mods and Two Tone Ska and third waves to the present.

Meanwhile Sir Johnny O.B.E Flannel was with a box of records at the stereo. He'd plugged in a microphone and set the first record on the turntable. After the glass of champagne he was all fired up and ready to go; he was about to show them there was still life in the old dog DJ yet.

"Hair of the dog, my alcoholic top ten, it's number 10 from their "Live 'N' Skankin" album released in '89 on Skank Records... it's them Hot Knives with "Holsten Boys".

"Saturday morning, you think you've learnt your lesson
There's a knock at the door are you ready for more
Time for another session
We're the Holsten boys"

GBH and Sparrow nooded approvingly, Holsten Pils being their favourite tipple, as Johhnny took to the mike. "Happy hour and It's number nine, originally done in '54 by Jay Riggins Jr better known as Floyd Dixon or "Mr Magnificent," from Marshall Texas, it's also been covered by "The Godfather of Ska" Laurel Aitken, but this version's taken from their debut album, "A Briefcase full Of Blues", released in '78 that went double platinum and became the best selling blues album of all time. It's John Belushi and Dan Akroyd playing as Joliet Jake and Elwood Blues – The Blues Brothers with "Hey Bartender"!"

Well we was having so much fun
I didn't know it was half past one
I turned around to have one more I looked at
the clock and it was half past four
I said hey bartender
Hey man look here
A draw one, draw two, draw three, four glasses
of beer

DJ topped everyone's glass up. The party was swinging.

Johnny announced "Drinks are on the house, it's the nine and only Bad Manners at number eight, live in '83 with an introduction from the fat man himself.

"Are there any alcoholics in the audience? This is for you, Special Brew"

Everyone looked at each other, some saying, "I could stop tomorrow if I wanted."

Need some more to restore all the feeling that I
get from you
I want more give me more all I want is a barrel
of you

I love you yes I do 'cause I know that you love
me too
I love you yes I do gonna spend all my money
on you
I don't care the way they stare that I'm always
with you
We're a pair its not fair when they say we're a
Special Brew

"I think I've had one not enough, down to number seven and I'm in heaven with the magnificent seven, it's them North London boys Madness with "The Young and the Old.""

Staggering home everybody sings
All the old songs the cockney routines

GBH and Sparrow jumped in and started doing some nutty dancing, miming to the lyrics.

Knock back the drinks hitch up your skirt
Fall over backwards undo your shirt

With DJ and Winston joining in skanking up and down the carriage.

Have a quick short forget about work
Have a couple more then you go berserk

By now everyone was getting on down, having a good old-fashioned knees up and singing the chorus together:

Old man in the morning
Young man at night
Breakfast full of wisdom
Until you hit the lights

Followed by another round of champagne and another speech by DJ "Dis Train is boun' fe Skaville." Just then, however, The Hawkwind gave two blows on its whistle and the brakes started screeching. Everyone shot forwards, thrown to the floor.

Empty bottles and glasses fell from the bar, smashing around them and still the train was braking. Pot Belly slid under a bench, Johnny fell through the door out into the corridor, Speed was behind the bar with his legs up in the air, Recipe Man and Slimey banged their heads on the window and slid down to the floor, DJ and Winston fell over, 7 Bellies came to rest in the door way, the rest were scattered throughout the carriage as The Hawkwind came to a halt.

Picking himself up and rubbing himself down, DJ was the first up. He asked, "Is everybody alright?" Just about everyone gave some sort of confirmation as to being alright even though they had fallen in to all sorts of unnatural positions. As hardened drinkers, all of them were still holding their glasses upright and hadn't spilt a drop. Coke, who had fallen in a half backwards roll with his legs over his head, was stuck under a bench still holding half a glass of champagne. He looked up between his legs and said something in a muffled voice.

"Wha' dat?" asked DJ, looking around to see where the noise came from.

"Whoah don't listen to him" said 7 Bellies getting up "He's talking out his arse"

"How lads, who's thaat blurk ridin this train I'mz gonna –" said Sticks.

"Irie," said DJ interrupting him. "Deh mus' be cows on de line or somet'ing."

Matt looking out the window could see The Hawkwind on a long bend further up and announced, "The cows have got blue flashing lights on their heads."

"Deh mus' haf been an accident," said DJ.

"Help Mr DJ Dread. Help, I'm stuck down here," said Pot Belly still under the bench.

Then they heard the sound of helicopters overhead. which flew down on both sides of the train. Over the tanoy came, "THIS IS THE INTERNATIONAL POLICE, DJ DREAD AND YOUR PARTY ARE UNDER ARREST. REMAIN ON THE TRAIN, DO NOT TRY TO ESCAPE, YOU ARE SURROUNDED."

"Raasclat Babylon, who invited dem?" said DJ.

They all heard a roar as Mad Axe Man raced in on his Harley saying, "Ey up lads, there's coppers all over the place, we're surrounded."

"Gentlemen."

Everybody looked at Matt who said, "We're busted."

"Look at it dis way, ye cyaan get lower dan cleaning de toilets."

"Gentlemen, this is serious," said Matt. He went on to name a list of crimes they'd committed.

1   Hijacking a train

2   Kidnapping engineers

3   Crossing state borders without permits

4   Trafficking alcohol

5   Drinking after hours without a permit

6   Broadcasting without a permit

7   And I wouldn't be surprised if all the kitchen and food and drink supplies had fallen off the back of a lorry

"No mon, me use a fork lift," said Zoot.

Matt continued:

8   Assisting to extradite a wanted man for armed robbery

9   Destroying gardeners' sheds, pulling up trees, fences and stealing railway sleepers, yes don't think I havent smelt burning wood for the last 3,000 miles

"Ten", said DJ, having had enough of being lectured to. "Exporting fire arms across borders."

"You're right," said Matt. "What am I going to do?"

"Yu could always flush it down de toilet."

Matt thought about it and said, "No it would block up the U-bend."

"THIS IS THE INTERNATIONAL POLICE."

"Ya ya ya," said DJ, not caring to listen. "Every time I an' I begin a station, Sheriff John Brown, him cut I down."

"What does it mean?" asked Pot Belly.

"I an' I goin' te do time," answered DJ.

Mad Axe Man, feeling ravished, said, "Well thee hope's prison kitchen's open, 'cause thee could murder a curry."

Matt clicked his pen, and made a note of it.

THE END

EPILOGUE

After being caught, they were exported back to England where they were trialled and sentenced as follows.

Seamus and Michael are released. They were forced to participate against their will although this was not strictly true. Once they knew their destination, no one said otherwise.

Matt was released for co-operating. He handed in all his notebooks showing a detailed account of events.

Coke, 7 Bellies, Pot Belly and Mad Axe Man were sentenced to five years for kidnapping and hijacking a train.

DJ was sentenced to ten years for putting out Skankdown without a licence exporting alcohol across state lines, encouraging an allotment to be dismantled and burnt, along with masterminding the whole operation.

Winston was jailed for two years for pirate radio offences.

The rest of the cast were jailed for two years for wilfully participating in the plot.

LAST WORDS

You're probably wondering why I named the train **The Hawkwind** and not something in keeping with the Ska/ Reggae theme of the book. I could've called it Engine 54, Skinhead Train or Ivor, for instance. Well for One I think The Hawkwind is a bloody good name for a train. Two, they're a bloody good band formed by Dave Brooks and Robert Calvert. They've played for more than 30 years, doing free gigs at festivals, supporting various causes living a completely unpublished anarchist lifestyle and have stayed true to their ideals. Three...

Three, the book was not written just for skins. Music is for everyone – not punk for punks or ska for rudies. As we've seen, all music cultures lead or inspire in one way or another to the next. It's progression. Hawkwind came from rock to form their own style of space rock but if you're still wandering, here's the connection: John Lydon used to go see **Hawkwind** and play their records. Hawkwind – Lydon – Rotten – Pistols –punk – 2nd wave punk – 2nd wave Ska....

Which all inspired me to write this book. And anyway, it's my book.

If you want to know why I left out other musical genres, such as New Wave, Gothic, New Romantics, Thrash Metal, Techno etc etc, well it's because they haven't made any influence on me. In my view, these genres weren't progressive or influenced by the music styles in the book mentioned. So if you want to read a book on any of the music styles I haven't mentioned, then why not like me write your own? Seriously, why not? All it takes is patience, dedication and passion.

I would like to thank Don and Diane who ran the Co-Op Youth club Ashby, Scunthorpe which put on a discotheek Friday nights during the seventies and early eighties where I witnessed the music scenes change from Disco, to Rock, Northern Soul, Mod, Punk, Two Tone Ska and Reggae which with the opening line from The Specials "Do The Dog" gave the basis for this book.

Acknowledgements and Bibliography

The author would like to acknowledge the following for reference or inspiration.

Magazines/music papers: Zoot Skazine by George Marshall, S.T.P 1988/89. Skinhead Times by George Marshall S.T.P 1989/91, Press cuttings from Smash Hits, NME, Melody Maker and Sounds 1980/83. Madness fan club mail, The Specials fan club mail, Bad Manners fan club mail, The Beat fan club mail, UB40 fan club mail, Viz Comics.

Books: The Two Tone Story by George Marshall, S.T.P 1990. Total Madness by George Marshall, S.T.P 1993. Bad Manners by George Marshall, S.T.P 1993. Your Wandering Now, A History of The Specials by Paul Williams, S.T.P 1995. Sent from Coventry, The Chequered Past of Two Tone by Richard Eddington, Imp Books 2004. Ska'd For Life by Horace Panter, Pan Books 2008. Bob Marley, Soul Survivor by Maureen Sheridan, Seven Oaks 1999. Bob Marley, Reggae King of the World by Malika Whitney/ Dermott Hussey, Kingston Publishers Ltd 1984. Bob Marley, Songs of Freedom by Hal Leonard Publishing corporation 1992. Marley Legend by James Henke, Simon & Schuster UK Ltd 2006. Bob Marley, Music in Review By Dave Thompson Edgehill Publishing Ltd 2005. Reggae The Story of Jamaican Music by Lloyd Bradley, BBC Worldwide Ltd 2002. History of Jamaica by Clinton v. Black, Longman Caribbean 1980. Understanding Jamaican Patois by L. Emilie Adams, Kingston Publishers Ltd 1994. Dr Martens Air Wair Ltd 1999. Interviews with the Blues Legends & Stars by Dan Aykroyd and Ben Manilla, Backbeat Books 2004.The Secret Life of A Teenage Punk Rocker, The Andy Blade chronicles, Cherry

Red Books Ltd 2005. Rotten by John Lydon with Keith and Kent Zimmerman, Hodder & Stoughton 1993. Gimme Danger The Story of Iggy Pop by Joe Ambrose, Omnibus Press 2007. A Riot Of Our Own with The Clash by Johnny Green & Garry Barker, Orion 2003. AC/DC Maximum Rock & Roll by Murry Engleheart and Arnaud Durieux Harper, Collins Publishers 2006. Hell's Angel Ralph "Sony" Barger with Keith and Kent Zimmerman Perennial 2001.

CD liner notes: Bob Marley, Songs of Freedom, Bob Partridge, Timothy White, Chris Salewicz Island Records Ltd 1992. Bob Marley and The Wailers, At Studio One, Leroy Jodie Pierson & Roger Steffens, heart beat 1991. Bob Marley Soul Almighty the formative years, Roger Steffens, JAD records 1996. Bob Marley and the Wailers, Trenchtown Rock The Anthology 1969-78, Laurance Cane-Honeysett, Trojan Records 2002. Bob Marley & The Wailers, Roots of a Legend, Michael de Koningh, Trojan Records 2004. The Complete Wailers 1967-1972, Bruno Blum, Roger Steffens and Leroy Jodie Pierson, Jad Records.The Skatalites, Foundation Ska, Chris Wilson, Brian Keyo, heart beat 1997.Ska after Ska after Ska, Chris Wilson, Brian Keyo, heart beat 1998.Specials, Stereo- Typical 2 Tone, Adrian Thrills 2000. The Jam, In The City, Polydor, Pat Gilbert 1997.

DVD documentaries: Bob Marley, Spiritual Journey 2004. Bob Marley, Time will Tell 2003. Bob Marley Rebel Music 2001. Bob Marley Catch A Fire 1997. Heartland Reggae 2001.Reggae In A Babylon by Wolgang Buld. Punk in London by Wolgang Buld. Punk In England by Wolfgang Buld. Don Letts The Punk Rock Movie 2006. The Great Rock 'N' Roll Swindle. The Filth and the Fury 2007. Punk Icons The Sex Pistols 2005. Punk Icons The Clash 2005. The Clash Revolution Rock 2008. The Quadrophenia Story 2005, Glastonbury The Mud The Music The Madness 2006.

Wikipedia: King Tubby, U-Roy, Dennis Alcapone, Mystery Train, Elvis Presley, Junior Parker, Rock and Roll, Rock and Roll History, Rock and Roll Hall of Fame, Alan Freed, Blues, Bill Haley, The Who, Quadrophenia, Ethiopians, Chuck Berry, Desmond Dekker, Little Richard, Quotes, Pat Boone, Rocksteady, Alton Ellis, Hopeton Lewis, Lyn Taitt, Gladstone Anderson, Punk Rock, Reggae, Derick Morgan, Bunny Lee, Teddy boys, Bob Marley, Mod (subculture), Motown, Stax, Booker T and the MG's, Rod Stewart, The Faces, Soloman Burke, Ramsey Lewis Trio, Smokey Robinson and The Miracles, The Capitals, Gerry Spencer Group, The Temptations,

Four tops, Skinhead, Symarip, The Jam, Purple Hearts, Secret Affair, The Lamberettas, 6.5 Special, Oh Boy, Boy Meets Girl, Madness, New Age Travellers, Windsor Free Festival, Stonehenge Free Festivals (72-85 An illustrated History), Bill Ubique Dwyer, Phil Russell, Sid Rawle, Isle of White Festival, Battle of the Beanfield, Third Wave Ska, Ska Parade Radio, S.H.A.R.P (Skinheads Against Racial Prejudice), Marcus Garvey, Haile Salassie I, Tommy Steele.

Websites: Harley Davidson USA, Chuck Berry official site, Ska, A Brief history of Ska, The history of Ska, Ska Music 101, The History of Ska Music by Ian Van Hoof, History of Ska-The Genuine Guide. Suite 101.com, The Dark Sighed The Ska Music Site, National Graphic Evolution-Ska roots revolution, This is Ska The roots of Ska, WWW.PUNK77.CO.UK, The Specials history, Origins of the Travellers scene, The Here now of Ska The Definitive story of the Third Wave of Ska-Albino Brown-Tazzy Philips, BBC-h2g2 history of US Third Wave Ska, Urban Dictionary – Third Wave Ska, Amazon.com Learn about Third Wave Ska.

Allmusic: The Specials, The Ethiopians biography. You Tube: Ska Rocksteady History, World of Skinhead, SKINHEADS SHARP, Haile Salassie I films and documentary's – Lion of Judah etc. Radio One: Don't watch that-watch this. Google Maps: Leeds Chapeltown. York National Railway Museum.

Every effort has been made to fully and correctly credit and source all information researched for this book. Pirate Radio Skankdown Publishing would be grateful if any errors were brought to attention.

COPYRIGHTS

Pirate Radio Skankdown presents:
CD PRS1 Murder on the train to Skaville

Track Listing

Bedsit Dub (Live)	Little Chief
Train To Skaville -12"	The Selecter
Gobbin' On Life	Alberto Y Lost Trios Paranoias
Murder	The Selecter
Matt Davis Special Agent (Live)	The Toasters
Tube Disaster	Flux Of Pink Indians
Train To Skaville (Live)	Mark Foggo's Skasters
Two Legs (Live)	Mark Foggo's Skasters
The Murder Of Liddle Towers	The Angelic Upstarts
(Live at the London Polytechnic)	
6.5 Special	Don Long
Destinatoin Skaville	Skaos
Dial For Murder	The Potatoe Five/
	Laurel Aitken
Train To Skaville (Live)	Little Chief